PRAISE FOR SARAH ECHAVARRE

Three More Months

"This is a heart-wrenching novel about family and love, with a wide range of well-developed characters. Readers who enjoy novels by Jessica Strawser or Barbara O'Neal will need a box of tissues for this one."

—*Booklist* (starred review)

"Readers will laugh and cry . . ."

—*Library Journal*

"Sarah Echavarre's debut women's fiction is a moving story about second chances and the precious time we have with loved ones. This was a page-turner, immersive, and all-consuming, and the perfect book to pick up this holiday season. *Three More Months* is a must-read."

—Tif Marcelo, *USA Today* bestselling author of *In a Book Club Far Away*

WHAT

WE

REMEMBER

OTHER BOOKS BY
SARAH ECHAVARRE

Three More Months

WHAT WE REMEMBER

A NOVEL

SARAH ECHAVARRE

LAKE UNION
PUBLISHING

Published by Lake Union Publishing, Seattle

www.apub.com

Amazon, the Amazon logo, and Lake Union Publishing are trademarks of Amazon.com, Inc., or its affiliates.

ISBN-13: 9781542032650
ISBN-10: 1542032652

Cover design by Amanda Kain

Printed in the United States of America

For Chuck, Josh, and Beth. Love you guys.

Chapter One

I shouldn't be here.

Parking my car in this lot, working at this hospital, wearing this name tag that says, ISABEL MYLES, INTERFAITH CHAPLAIN. It's all wrong, and not just because I'm hungover.

When I step out of my car, a wave of nausea hits, and I fall back into my seat. With my head against the steering wheel, I deep-breathe for a few seconds, then try standing again. I don't fall or vomit. Yay.

Then I walk through the parking lot and cross the street to the entrance of the hospital. Despite the headache that's waging war on my skull like a tiny, out-of-control orchestra, I nod politely to the always-smiling elderly greeter who stands just inside the all-glass entrance of this twenty-story medical center. I pump a dollop of hand sanitizer in my hands as I pass by reception; then I stop by the water fountain and fill up my bottle.

When I don't spew chunks on the white-tile floor, I silently applaud myself. What was I thinking?

You thought a bit of liquid courage would give you the strength to do something you haven't done in more than two years.

Shame blankets me like a slow-moving cloud. Bingo.

Two years and two months. That's how long it's been since I've gone to a social gathering. But last night, I honestly thought I'd give it a go. Because Keely Kingston asked me to.

Keely.

Just the thought of her name makes my skin burn with regret. She was such a good friend—my best friend. And last night, she sent me a string of text messages. It was her birthday. I totally forgot. I guess that's not unexpected, given she and I haven't spoken, seen each other, or exchanged texts in more than two years. So when her name popped up on my phone, I froze.

Even through my pounding headache, I recall each of her messages.

Remember how you'd always call me on the morning of my birthday every year and sing "Happy Birthday" to me totally off-key?

It was my favorite part of the day.

I know you won't text me back. And that's okay.

I just wanted to say that I miss you.

Okay, there's one more thing . . .

If by some miracle you want to come out tonight and see me, I'll be at the Grey Plume with some people from work. You're welcome to come. I hope you do.

As I stood in my kitchen reading her string of texts, emotions landed square in the middle of my chest. It was weird. She wasn't the only one I'd been ignoring for more than two years. By now, friends don't really reach out anymore. I think they realized when I stopped going out and stopped answering their calls and texts, it was a quiet sign that I wasn't interested in socializing anymore. So last night when my phone dinged with text message after text message from Keely, I was jolted. Because I could feel the tenderness in her typed words. And the pain. The pleading.

After all this time, after what I did, she still cared about me and wanted to see me.

And so I made the decision to do something I never, ever thought I'd do again: socialize with a group of people.

It was a daunting-as-hell prospect after spending so many evenings after work alone in my house. So I opted for some liquid courage. I thought it would be easy enough—have a few drinks to loosen me up, take a rideshare to the Grey Plume, say hi to Keely, then go home.

But I'm not much of a drinker. I never was. Why didn't I remember that?

After downing almost an entire bottle of wine, I passed out on the couch. And then I woke up, my stomach in fiery knots, my head pounding. I could barely open my eyes when I started retching. After vomiting the contents of my stomach into my hallway bathroom, I checked the time. It was just past 4:00 a.m. I'd missed Keely's party.

A heavy sigh rockets from me when I make it to the elevator bank in the middle of the first floor of the hospital. That invisible blanket of shame wraps so tightly around me that every inch of my skin is on fire.

I am a horrible, horrible person.

I should explain.

Two years and two months ago, reality became a nightmare. When the memory of That Day resurfaces, it starts as a crushing feeling at the top of my chest that seeps slowly down my torso. Then my vision turns blurry. Then my hearing goes fuzzy. My head throbs. So hard. Harder than it's throbbing right now in my hungover state. It's so bad, I fully expect my eyes will pop out of their sockets.

After That Day, everyone rallied around me. Keely, my family, the rest of my friends, my coworkers. And it was too much. I know they all meant well, but everything was a reminder of what happened. Every "I'm so sorry, Isabel." Every "how are you holding up?" Every pitying glance, every hug, every hand squeeze, every time someone dropped by my house unannounced with yet another casserole dish "just to make sure you weren't wasting away." I'd end up a sobbing mound on the floor, unable to function. That was the state in which I existed in the months following That Day. And I just couldn't handle it anymore.

So I stopped answering everyone's calls and texts. I quit spending time with friends. I quit socializing altogether. I told my boss and my family that I never, ever wanted them to mention what happened That Day ever again. It was interfering too much with how I wanted to live my life.

People slowly got the picture. They eventually stopped reaching out and stopped checking up on me. If anyone gets curious as to how I'm faring, I assume they get updates from my parents, whom I see only when they make me. The only person I can stand is my little sister, Chantel. We've been close our whole lives—we even live together now.

Is what I'm doing healthy? No. But it's what I can manage.

The elevator at the far end dings, jerking me out of my thoughts. When those shiny stainless-steel doors glide open, I step inside, then hit the button for the tenth floor. I press my eyes shut and shove my palm against the wall to keep from toppling over. Even the smooth movement upward aggravates my headache.

At the fifth floor, the elevator shudders to a halt, my stomach seizes, and I nearly dry heave. Why did I think riding the elevator while hungover was a good idea? I should have taken the stairs.

Just then, the doors open to reveal a tall guy around my age—early thirties—with a short-trimmed beard the color of wheat. His mess of equally golden hair is pulled back in a bun. He doesn't look up as he walks into the elevator and takes the corner opposite me. He's too fixated on his phone.

When he doesn't move to hit a button on the panel, I take a breath and force myself to go into professional mode.

"What floor?" I ask in that pleasant, polite work register—the one where I sound faintly like a grown-up Disney princess working as an empathetic high school counselor.

I wait a few seconds, my finger hovering over the buttons, but he doesn't answer. Whatever staring contest he's waging with his phone screen must be riveting. He doesn't even seem to notice that the elevator doors are still wide open.

"What floor?" I repeat. My head is so heavy, I'm worried it'll topple right off my shoulders.

The stranger just stands, still staring at his phone like he's trying to melt the screen with his unwavering, unblinking eye contact.

Like a reflex, I shake my head, which causes the pounding to intensify. I press my eyes shut, annoyed with myself that I pulled that move. I should know better. I cradle my temple with the palm of my right hand and punch the button for my floor with my left. I dig in my purse for tablets of aspirin that I hope are still there. After a few seconds, I come up empty-handed and mutter a curse.

"Can you please be quiet?"

His low, raspy voice hits my ears. It lands like hot black coffee poured over gravel. I turn my head and look at the stranger, who's still gawking at his phone. He doesn't even have the nerve to look at me when he scolds me.

"Jerk," I whisper to myself, certain the stranger isn't paying one ounce of attention to me.

But then I hear that coffee-gravel voice once more.

"What did you say?"

This time when I look at him, his attention is one hundred percent focused on me. His hard gaze unnerves me for a brief second.

"Did you just call me a jerk?"

"Yeah. I did."

"What the hell for?" The question punches from his tongue, dripping in irritation.

My stomach lurches so hard, I have to press my forearm against the front of my body in an attempt to stave off the urge to hurl.

I grit my teeth and swallow before speaking. "Because I politely asked you twice what floor you needed, and you ignored me, then scolded me, all the while looking at your phone. It was pretty damn rude."

He clenches his jaw and lets out a huff of air through his nose, like he's channeling a bull. And then he looks away, his gaze landing on the elevator doors in front of us. "That's rich," he mumbles as he shakes his head. "Never mind."

And then, against every expectation I have about how this interaction is going to end, he looks up at me. And then he laughs. A full-on boisterous boom from his belly. It throws me so off-kilter, I can't even react properly. All I do for a handful of seconds is stand there with my mouth hanging open.

The elevator shudders to a halt once more, and the doors slide open. It seems to jolt him out of whatever bizarre mood he's in because a beat later, his expression is serious again. The soft lines that flank his smile remain, though. Even under his short-trimmed beard, I can see them. Their smooth shape reminds me of parentheses. Like someone drew a curve on either side of his mouth, then erased them. Only the faintest etch remains. Something about them reads mysterious, like he knows something I don't. It's unnerving and mesmerizing all at once.

But then he clears his throat. It's so loud, my shoulders jump slightly. Then he stomps out of the elevator.

For a second, all I do is stand there, mystified as to what the hell just happened. And then my stomach loses all patience with me. Hot bile shoots up my throat. I stumble to the trash can sitting just outside the elevator and puke my guts out.

"Thank god I made it," I mutter to myself as I wipe my mouth with the back of my hand. And then I immediately scold myself. I've got no business thanking god; I don't believe in anything anymore.

Chapter Two

The elevator doors glide shut behind me as I straighten up and catch my breath. I wobble slightly and turn around to palm the nearby wall. I shift my weight to my left foot, then to my right until I'm steady once more. When I catch my reflection in the shiny stainless steel, I freeze. It's the small stark-white rectangle pinned to the top left pocket of my blouse that catches my eye. It always does. It's why I try to avoid mirrors or any reflective surface if I can, because just the sight of my name tag can be so jolting, so unnerving—a visual reminder of just how much I don't belong here.

Isabel Myles, interfaith chaplain.

What it should actually read? *Isabel Myles, fraud who believes in absolutely nothing.*

I know what you're thinking. I lost my faith, but I'm an interfaith chaplain. How does that even work?

In my experience, being a hospital chaplain has a lot less to do with religion than people assume. That surprised even me when I attended chaplaincy school and started working here. It has more to do with being a good listener and empathizing with people when they're facing a terminal diagnosis, or have just lost a loved one, or are struggling through a health crisis, or are just stressed. So often, people simply want to talk and know that the person they're speaking to truly hears them and supports them.

And that's what I do. I listen. I empathize. I connect them with counselors and therapists when they need professional help. I put them in touch with religious officials if they want specific services performed. I sometimes help them navigate the daunting task of funeral arrangements too.

If you had asked me before That Day if I was religious, I would have said no. Even though I was the obedient little daughter who would happily attend Mass with my family every Sunday, as I grew up, I realized that religion wasn't what I believed in. Spirituality was what I ascribed to.

My whole life, I always believed that something higher, something more powerful existed outside of us and our control. Something that navigated the universe in a way we couldn't understand. Something that put order to the world, something we could look to when we needed guidance. I was never concerned with being loyal to a single religion or church. It was just the belief of something *more* that I found comfort in. That's why I became a chaplain. That's why I attended church with my family.

But That Day shattered everything. I realized there was nothing to believe in anymore. I had said a million prayers on That Day and so many days after. They all went unanswered. There was nothing to save us.

How weak my faith was. It all came apart so quickly.

So why do I stay?

Because when I'm in this hospital, I'm helping people. I'm someone who patients and their families can rely on for guidance and support. They don't know the broken parts of me. They just see me as someone who can help them in their time of need.

I know it's wrong that I'm still here, working as a chaplain when I no longer believe. But I'm selfish. This job still means something to me, and I'm not ready to give it up.

When I walk into the office, I see my boss, supervising chaplain Martha Hale, sitting at her computer.

She turns to me with her trademark grin, but it fades the moment she looks at me.

"Are you all right? You look pale."

I nod and force a smile, which I'm certain looks more like I'm wincing in pain. "Oh, yeah. Fine. Just allergies and a bad night's sleep. Heck of a combo."

I quickly shuffle to the other side of the narrow office space to take the only other desk chair in the room, hoping she believes me. It's not the most professional thing in the world to come in to work hungover.

I down half the water in my bottle, noticing how much better my stomach feels after that second violent purging of its contents. It's the biggest relief that no one happened to be near the elevator then or walking by. I would have been mortified. And I'd hate to have that juicy bit of gossip about me floating around the hospital.

Thankfully, instead of prying, Martha nods her understanding, then turns back to her computer, hitting her knee on the desk.

"You okay?"

She chuckles while rubbing her leg. "I think I'll live."

Cozy is the way Martha describes our communal chaplain office. There's an L-shaped desk that runs along the length of two office walls with room for two people to sit at once. If one person is willing to take the guest chair along the other wall, then three could fit. But the entire half-dozen-strong chaplain staff wouldn't be able to occupy this space comfortably all at once, even if we were just standing.

"Looks like it's a slow start to the morning," Martha says as she begins to gather her purse and lunch bag.

"Nothing exciting happened during the overnight shift?"

"Unless you count the water fountain down the hall stalling."

Dual sets of crow's-feet fan at the outer edges of her blue eyes. They're like underscores for every facial expression she makes. When she smiles, they make her look sweeter and more jovial. When she winces or frowns, they make her appear more sincere.

She pulls her shoulder-length gray-and-blonde hair into a low ponytail like she always does at the end of an overnight shift, right before she leaves to go home.

When she stands, she smooths a hand over the front of her cobalt-blue cardigan. Her ankle-length paisley skirt sways with the movement. "Oh, and just a heads-up: Dr. Walder and Dr. Inuie are getting a divorce."

"Oh, wow. Really?"

Martha nods, her expression sympathetic. "Arlene told me a few hours ago. Apparently, they've been ranting to the nursing staff about each other, which of course is making everyone uncomfortable. It's quite unprofessional."

Martha *tsks* while shaking her head and slipping on her jacket. "One of the techs recommended they chat with one of us instead of venting to the staff. Maybe check in with them today or tomorrow?"

"Absolutely."

"I think you're all set to go, kiddo."

I smile at the nickname she's called me ever since I started working here a handful of years ago. With a single nod and a smile, she heads for the door.

Martha is an angel. She's a walking hug, exuding calm and comfort in every action. She's the best boss I could ask for—and one of the reasons why I choose to keep my crisis of faith to myself so I can stay at this job. I've never had such a supportive and kind boss before, and if I leave—or lose—this job, I'm certain I'll never work for someone as caring and bighearted as she is.

If she finds out that I no longer believe in anything, she'd have every right to fire me. Yes, she's kind and sweet and understanding, but there's a line. What self-respecting chaplain supervisor would allow me to remain on staff if they found out the truth?

After she leaves, I brew a fresh pot of coffee. While sipping from my mug, I dive into my morning to-do list of checking emails and voice mails. I'm halfway through my second cup when the door opens.

When I turn and see my little sister, Chantel, decked out in her green scrubs pulling a funny face at me, I'm all smiles. I jump up and give her a hug, inhaling her floral body spray. It's been almost a month since I've seen her. She's the other reason I want to be here. Being able to see and visit with her when she's home from her travel nursing gigs and picking up extra shifts at the hospital makes work a million times more enjoyable.

"Good morning, Tel."

"Good morning, Bel."

The fact that I'm thirty and she's twenty-seven and we still use our childhood nicknames for each other is ridiculous, and that's why I love it.

I settle back down into my chair. "How was Santa Fe?"

"Hot. And dry. Glad to be back in Omaha where at least there's moisture in the air." She parks herself on the edge of the desk. "I've never seen so many firework-related emergency-room visits. Good lord, that city must be populated by pyromaniacs."

"It's not even the end of May, and people there are messing with fireworks?"

She shrugs. "You don't even want to know."

"I didn't know you were working today."

"Someone called in sick from Labor and Delivery, so I'm covering."

Chantel is an emergency-room travel nurse but spent her first few years after graduating college working in Labor and Delivery.

I shake my head as I turn back to my computer screen. "You work too much. I don't see you enough."

"Hey. Even when I'm not here, I'm here, remember?" She raises an eyebrow and points to the messy bun in her hair. I glance down and see that I have no fewer than three long strands of her jet-black hair on my blouse.

I swipe them away. "Ha. I guess your hair that's clogging the shower drain is an interesting way to leave your mark while you're gone. And the pile of your shoes at the front door that you never seem to get around to putting away. And the scent of your body spray permeating my house. You know that even when I deep clean, that floral smell lingers? And I always, always find your hair. Everywhere."

"Come on, you love it. They're like charming little mementos of me."

I let out a laugh as she yawns and reaches her arms up to stretch. "I mean it, Tel. You gotta lay off the extra shifts. Rest is important, too, especially given how much you travel."

She dismisses my big-sister concerns with a wave of her hand. "I have a plan, remember? The sooner I pay off these student loans, the sooner I'll be able to save for a place of my own. Then you won't have to put up with your little sister forever."

"You're welcome to live with me as long as you want. I've told you that a million times."

"You should be charging me more rent, though."

"Hey. None of that talk."

She gives a playful roll of her eyes as she shakes her head at me. "You're a terrible landlord, you know that? Like, what landlord would ever say no to more money?"

"I'm not a landlord. I'm your big sister. And what you pay is enough. I've got the rest covered."

"I pay two hundred dollars a month."

"I'm aware."

She huffs out a breath. "I can afford to pay you more."

"I don't need it. I've told you that a million times."

"I know, I know."

"How's your saving-for-a-house fund shaping up with all these extra shifts you're taking?"

When she doesn't answer me right away, I look up to find her narrowed gaze on me, like she's studying my face.

"Yikes. You look like a sleep-deprived, disheveled Kardashian."

"I don't even know how to take that," I mutter as I focus back on the computer screen. "And isn't that insulting to you in a way? You're my carbon copy."

Siblings sharing a resemblance isn't unique. Many share just a few features, while others look like they're clones of each other. Chantel and I fall into that second camp. We've looked so much alike for most of our lives that we've often been mistaken for twins. It doesn't matter that our hairstyles are different—she keeps her jet-black hair long, to the middle of her back, while I prefer a short, blunt, angled bob—or that she's two inches shorter than I am. Almost everyone assumes we're twins the first time they see us. Probably because everything, from our wide-set eyes to our small noses to the high angle of our cheekbones to the light smattering of golden freckles on the bridges of our noses, is the exact same. We both even have a dimple that appears in our right cheek every time we smile.

"Ha. Carbon copy." Chantel's messy topknot shakes as she laughs. "I don't know what you're talking about. Clearly I look so much younger than you."

I crumple up a Post-it note and chuck it at her. She laughs as it bounces off her arm.

"But seriously, you look like crap," she says. "What happened? You're not getting sick, are you?"

"No, not sick." Already I can feel my face reddening at the thought of confessing what I did. "I, um, had a bit too much wine last night."

"Oh, really? Miss 'the only beverage I need is water' got wine drunk last night?"

I glare at her.

"Okay, okay. Sorry." Her expression softens. "It's just out of character for you to do that."

13

"I'm aware." I take a long sip of coffee, which thankfully is starting to dull my headache.

"So what was the occasion?"

I let out a heavy sigh, knowing full well I'm going to get an earful after I explain what happened.

"Keely texted me last night. It was her birthday, and she invited me out."

Chantel's brow raises. "Oh."

"Yeah." I tug a hand through my hair. "She was really sweet in her message. Like, I could tell that it took a lot to work up the nerve to text me after all this time."

"I'm sure."

"And I . . . well, something about her message kind of got to me. I thought it would be nice to see her. But I was nervous. It's been a while, you know? And she mentioned she was out with a group, and you know how that freaks me out."

Chantel nods.

"So I thought a little alcohol would help. But then I forgot what a lightweight I am. I never made it out of the house."

She pats a hand on my forearm. "Sorry, Bel."

"It's my own fault. I guess I wasn't ready."

She opens her mouth to say something but seems to second-guess herself and quickly clamps it shut.

I focus on the computer while Chantel pours herself a mug of coffee and sits on my desk. I wonder what she was going to say. She's never given me a hard time about my self-imposed solitude. She's always seemed to understand why I did it. But I know deep down she wishes I could go back to who I once was: Someone who saw my friends and family on a regular basis. Someone who was normal and happy.

"Hey, Bel."

I take a moment before turning to look at her. "Yeah?"

"I think it's great that you tried. Going out last night, I mean."

A small smile tugs at my lips. "Thanks."

I wait for her to say more, but she doesn't.

Instead, she twists to look at the clock on the wall, then hops off my desk and steps toward the office door. "My break's over soon. I should head back. You're headed home to rest after work, right?"

"Where else would I be?"

What's meant to be a joking comment hits differently when I say it out loud.

It's not a joke if it's the sad truth.

"Ha. Right." Her mouth twitches slightly before a forced smile appears on her face. A second later, it's gone, replaced by pursed lips and a concerned frown.

I expect her to turn and leave, but then she leans down and pulls me into another hug. I close my eyes, relishing just how tightly she squeezes me. No one hugs like my little sister.

The office phone rings, and we break apart. She leaves me with a smile and a wave before walking out the door.

I answer the phone.

"Isabel. Hi." Charge nurse Arlene's breathy voice hits my ears, making me wonder if she sprinted before she called me. She always sounds like she's rushing whenever I talk to her on the phone. "Can you run to room 1020 when you get the chance? It's a bit of a situation, and we could use your help."

"Of course. What's going on?"

"Elderly patient with dementia. Her name's Opal. She's in good spirits. I mean, she doesn't understand the situation, of course, but her mood is happy. Her grandson seems to be taking it hard, though. Maybe you could stop by and offer some support? You're so good with elderly dementia and Alzheimer's patients, what with your background."

In high school and college, I worked at a memory care facility for elderly folks with dementia and Alzheimer's. I was one of the few people there my age who lasted more than a handful of months. I understand why—it was an emotionally taxing job. Being around people whose mental states are deteriorating more with each passing day, watching as they slowly forget their loved ones, is heartbreaking. There's nothing you can do to stop the process.

But I tried not to focus on that. I'd talk to them even if they didn't respond to me, hoping that the sound of my voice was soothing in a way. And if they did reply, I'd pay attention to whatever seemed to make them happy—their favorite snack, a song, a joke, or some random memory. Even if I had no idea what they were talking about, I'd smile and laugh and nod along. I'd let them talk and ask them questions, anything to keep them in that happy state.

It's a skill I've kept up as a chaplain that works well the times I interact with those patients again.

"This poor guy seems so distraught seeing his grandma in this state," Arlene says. "I thought that maybe if you went in there and talked to them both, it would help."

"Absolutely. I'll head over there right now."

As I walk down to Opal's room, I think back on all the dementia patients and families I've sat with during the five years I've worked here. I thought that since I'm older than when I worked at the memory care facility, it would get easier observing them. It hasn't. To watch families as they witness their loved one's mind decline to the point that they forget everything from their memories to basic motor skills rips my heart out every time.

When I reach the room, the door is cracked open. I take a deep breath before knocking softly.

"Come in," a low, strained voice answers.

I walk into the room and promptly freeze. The guy from the elevator is sitting in the chair next to the hospital bed.

I close my mouth quickly. Judging by his wide, unblinking expression, he's just as shocked to see me.

For a few seconds, we just stare at each other without saying so much as a "hi." All the anger and frustration in his expression and body language from half an hour ago when we first saw each other has disappeared. Right now, with his bloodshot eyes, his crinkled brow, and his shaky lips, he is the picture of distraught.

"Um, hi," I manage to mumble.

"Well, hello there, dear!"

I twist my gaze to the elderly woman sitting up in the hospital bed, smiling at me. "Opal. Hello."

She lifts her delicate, wrinkled hand and waves at me. It takes a second, but I rein in my expression so that I'm hopefully displaying a convincing smile.

"I've been wanting to chat with you for a while," she says. "Come sit, come sit!"

She motions for me to take the chair on the other side of her bed, which I do. And then for a second, I wonder what the hell I should do. Should I pretend like nothing happened between Elevator Guy and me? Should I apologize to Opal's grandson for getting into an argument with him? Yeah, he was rude, but I understand why now. His grandmother is in the throes of dementia. He's clearly devastated by it and is struggling to process it.

Opal starts chatting before I have to decide.

"It's so lovely to see you again, dear," she says, her hazel eyes shining.

"Oh. Well, thank you." I clear my throat and refocus. It seems like Opal wants to talk for a bit, so that will be my immediate focus. "It's nice to see you too. I just wanted to stop in and check on things, see how you're doing."

That smile of hers doesn't budge. It's weirdly comforting to see. It softens the despair and awkwardness of this situation the slightest bit.

She shifts to face me, then reaches out both hands. I freeze once again. Normally I'd be happy to hold a patient's hand in a setting like this. It's clearly something she wants and would give her a lot of comfort. But this is a unique circumstance. I just had an argument with her family member thirty minutes ago. Will he be upset if I hold his grandma's hand? I don't want to upset him more.

Opal looks at me expectantly, still smiling.

"Um . . ." I glance at her grandson.

"Oh, don't mind him." She shakes her head, frowning slightly. "Patrick, you don't mind her holding my hand, do you?"

I don't miss the way he flinches.

"My name's Evan, Grandma," he says, his voice steady and gentle. "Remember me? Evan?"

A phantom ache settles in my chest at the pain in his eyes, the gentle pleading in his tone.

Moving her hands to her lap, she squints at him for a few seconds. "Oh, right. Evan. Of course." She nods once. "Evan."

He nods, his lips pursed. Like he's trying to smile.

Then he turns his focus to me. "It's fine. You can hold her hand."

I say a quiet thanks and reach out to Opal. She smiles widely and takes my hands in hers.

"Well, look at you. Vibrant as ever. How do you manage it every single time I see you?"

I tell her thanks, feeling Evan's eyes on me. It's likely that her dementia is causing her to confuse me with someone else, which is fairly common, but that probably doesn't make it any less upsetting for Evan to witness. Here I am, a complete stranger who's the focus of his grandmother's attention, and yet she can barely remember his name.

After giving my hands another soft squeeze, she folds her hands in her lap and gazes between Evan and me.

"You two are doing such a great job. You know that?"

"Thank you, Opal."

"Thanks, Grandma."

When she glances down and starts fussing with the sheets on the bed, I make eye contact with Evan.

"I'm so sorry. About earlier," I say, then dart my gaze to Opal. She's fiddling with something on the side table now and doesn't seem to hear me.

His eyebrows bunch together slightly, like two blond caterpillars. "It's okay. I'm, uh, I'm sorry too."

"Is there anything you need?"

His shoulders fall forward slightly, like the energy is being zapped from his body.

"I don't really know what I need," he finally says, his voice shaky.

Moments pass, and the air in the room thickens. It doesn't feel tense, though, just different.

"One of the nurses, Arlene, thought it might help if I stopped by to check on you," I say, then immediately regret it. That sounded weird. Like we're his babysitters or something.

"If you want to talk, I'm here to listen," I say. "Or if you'd rather talk to someone else, that's fine too. I can connect you with a different chaplain. Or a counselor or—"

He shakes his head before I even finish.

"No, this is . . ." He turns his stare back to Opal, who's looking at me expectantly again. "Just, is it okay if you keep talking to her? She seems to really like it, talking to you."

"Oh. Sure." I smile at Opal. "How are you feeling?"

She runs a hand over her shock of wavy white hair and chuckles. "I've been better. Staying in a hospital is never very fun. But the people here are so lovely. So caring and welcoming."

I nod along as she rattles off the names of people I don't know, explaining that they're due to visit her.

"I won't get to see all of them for very long, of course, but when I go home, we'll have a proper catch-up. And the ladies at bridge club too."

For a few minutes, she talks about how she plays cards once a week with a group of her friends. I silently hope that she gets to see everyone she's talking about. They all seem to make her so happy.

"Oh, and that nurse! Annette?"

"Arlene."

"That's right! Arlene! What a sweetie. If I had a figure like that and was about fifty years younger, I'd clean up."

Out of the corner of my eye, I catch Evan smiling slightly.

"Opal, I think you look pretty darn good right now."

"My dear, you are too kind."

Just then, another nurse walks in and checks her vitals, then mentions that the doctor will be in soon.

I take that as my cue to leave. "It was so lovely seeing you."

"You too, dear. Will I get to see you again soon?"

"Absolutely."

Even though I have no idea if that will ever happen, it's better just to say yes to keep her mood up. I wouldn't normally outright lie to a patient, but dementia requires special consideration. I've learned that it's best to go along with whatever is making the patient happy, as long as it's not hurting them or anyone else. At my old job, I witnessed countless times when patients' loved ones tried to correct them whenever they forgot a name or couldn't recall an important detail. I understand completely why they do it—it's wrenching to see the person you love forget you or your other family members. They press the issue out of desperation because they want more than anything for the patient to just remember again, and they think that persisting will help trigger their memory. But so often, it just leads to the patient becoming upset or distraught, which sometimes worsens their condition. There's no point in potentially upsetting Opal by trying to explain that we may not see each other ever again after today.

I'm about to walk off when I notice the smile on her face slowly fading. She squints at me, like she's studying my face, like my presence has suddenly triggered something in her.

Then she claps her hands, and her eyes go wide with recognition. "That's it! That's where I know you! You look just like her!"

She clasps her hands to her chest as she gazes at me.

"Who do I look like?" I phrase it gently, keeping my tone light and happy.

"Edna from upstairs. She's a hell of a card shark, and I swear she's cheating half the time, but I've beaten her twice. You're much nicer, though."

When I hear Evan laugh softly, I look over at him. That's when I notice the shape and color of their eyes are exactly the same. Large and on the greener side of hazel.

"Well, if you see Edna, tell her hello from me," I say.

She nods excitedly.

"I'll see you next time, okay?"

She waves goodbye. When I glance at Evan, I notice the anguish has melted from his face. He's not smiling, but that pain in his gaze that I noticed when I first walked in has disappeared.

"Thank you," he says.

I say, "You're welcome," and then leave the room.

Chapter Three

When I pull into my driveway after work, I freeze. There's my mom, sitting on the steps of my porch, a foil-topped casserole dish in her lap.

For a fleeting moment, I contemplate throwing my car in reverse and speeding away. It's been almost five months since we've seen each other—and the last time we did ended in tears. Hers, not mine. There's little worse in this world than watching your mother cry and knowing that you're responsible for her pain. I'm not eager to do it again anytime soon.

That's why I stayed away, even though she lives less than an hour from me in Lincoln. That's why I ignored her calls and most of her texts, only messaging her a handful of times in response when she inquired if I was alive, if I was eating enough.

Because every time we get together, there's tension. There's always an argument. And there are always, always tears.

My hands cramp as I tighten my grip around the steering wheel. Leaving will only postpone the inevitable.

Mom stands when I don't get out of my car right away. I turn off the engine, grab my purse, and step out of the car. I take a long, silent breath and walk toward her.

She flashes a smile that's as relieved as it is happy. "*Anakko*. Hi. How are you?"

I force a smile of my own, but it feels so fake. "I'm good, Mom. Thanks."

I stop just before I reach the porch, unsure of what to do. My instinct is to hug her, but I don't know if she'd want that after the way we left things last time.

But then she focuses her burned-umber eyes on me. The disappointment and hurt are as clear as the unshed tears pooling along her tear ducts. In that moment, I know I made the wrong choice.

Her inky-black waves move as she shakes her head at me, clearly disappointed. Then she bends down to set the casserole dish on a nearby patio chair before yanking me into her arms.

"You always hug me. No matter what." Her voice is a shaky whisper.

I do as she says and squeeze her back. Even though we're technically not on speaking terms, hugging her is heaven. Like coming home after a yearlong trip around the world. When my mother's arms are around me, I feel like I belong again. And for the briefest second, it feels like everything will be okay.

We stay pressed together for what feels like a full minute. When she sniffles, we pull apart.

"I made you *pansit*," she says as she turns away and wipes her nose on her wrist.

"Mom, you didn't have to do that. Especially after what—"

When she whips her head toward me so quickly, I'm afraid she's sprained her neck. But the scowl on her face tells me she's just fine.

"You think I would hold a grudge against my own daughter?" She makes a *pssh* noise before scooping up the casserole dish and motioning for me to open the front door.

I swallow back the lump in my throat as I unlock it, then hold the door open for her. A blast of cold air hits, and I sigh, happy to be out of the stagnant heat and humidity.

"Ay, why so cold?"

She rushes over to the thermostat and turns it off, then marches over to the kitchen and opens the cupboard with all my plates. She scoops a mound of *pansit* onto a single plate and points at my dining table. I sigh and sit down in one of the chairs.

"It's summer in Omaha, Mom. It's sweltering outside. And seventy-eight degrees is not cold. It's actually a lot warmer than the temperature that most people keep their houses at."

She shoves the plate of food into the microwave. "I lived half my life without air-conditioning, *anak*. In the Philippines. Anything lower than eighty-four degrees is cold to me."

"I know. I grew up with you. You'd never turn on the air conditioner."

She tucks a chunk of her hair behind her ear. A few strands of gray shine through in the overhead kitchen lighting.

She sets the plate down in front of me along with a giant glass of water and a fork. "Eat."

I obey her command as she warms up a plate for herself. I hum at the burst of flavor on my tongue. The fatty pork, the crunch of the cabbage and carrots, the salty soy sauce, the umami of the fish sauce.

I've wolfed down half my plate by the time she sits down to join me. Between the small bites she takes, she scans the room in her signature way. Her gaze lingers at each point for a few seconds before she furrows her brow slightly, then moves on to look at something else. Then she focuses back on her plate, takes another bite; then it's back to glancing around. I know what she's doing. She's probably thinking it's gross that I have a trio of half-empty coffee mugs on my coffee table and a bra strung over the back of my couch. She can probably see that thin layer of dust on my flat-screen TV too. And there's no way she misses the smudges on the decorative mirror hanging in the nearby hallway.

I bet she's wondering if I've had anyone over in the months since she last visited.

"Do your friends mind that it's so messy here when they come over to visit?" she says casually before taking another small bite.

I don't miss the pointedness in her question. It's slight and covered mostly by her upbeat tone, but I detect it loud and clear.

"No. They don't."

It's a lie. She knows it is. I wonder how long we'll do this dance—her asking me questions she already knows the answers to, me lying just to keep the conversation going, and then her getting so irritated with me that she calls me out on my lies. Then we argue.

"Huh."

Mom's barely audible response relays her doubt so clearly. I know she knows I haven't had a single person over to my house in two years and two months.

If only Chantel was here. She'd lighten things up with a ridiculous joke or sneak up behind Mom and give her a surprise hug. Mom would shriek, then laugh, and the tension would break.

But part of me is glad she's gone. That means she doesn't have to witness just how much my and Mom's relationship has deteriorated.

"How's Dad?" I ask, changing the subject.

"Good. Spending too much time working, like usual."

Dad is one step below a workaholic. He's been that way my whole life. He runs one of the top accounting firms in the city. Working twelve-hour days is standard for him. But there was always a limit. He was busy during the week, so that meant Chantel, Mom, and I would spend most days together without him. But the weekends were family time, always. Dad would take us on road trips or to the movies or to the park—whatever we wanted, he was game. And he never missed a school play or recital or game.

Mom looks up from her plate, her eyes glistening. "He worries about you."

The sadness of her words halts my fork as I stab at the *pansit* on my plate. But then a second later, my muscles tense. It feels like the organs inside me are hardening. The last time I saw him was months ago, when I saw Mom . . . and he cried too. He cries almost every time he sees me, ever since That Day. And I just can't take it.

I can't stand there and watch him break and know that I'm the reason he's so sad.

"He doesn't need to worry. I'm fine." I shove a heaping forkful of noodles into my mouth even though I'm full, just to avoid saying more. "So what's the surprise visit for?"

A sharp sigh rockets from her. "To make sure you're alive. You're not returning my calls. Or texts." She speaks to her *pansit*. "Clearly I waited too long. You're wasting away."

"I'm not wasting away."

My rebuttal is automatic, even though it's a lie. I've never been a very skilled cook, unlike her. My diet consists of takeout and whatever is on sale at the grocery store that I can either microwave or toss into a Crock-Pot if I'm feeling ambitious. I'm one of those annoying people who lets their pantry and refrigerator dwindle to the absolute bare necessities before I finally break down and make a run to the grocery store.

The clank of Mom's fork hitting her plate jolts me. She stands up and walks over to the fridge, yanks open the door, and looks inside.

"Half a stick of butter. A block of cheese with mold on it. A few slices of crappy bread. Two eggs. And a million condiments. I don't know what for, though. It's not like you have enough food to eat them with."

Instead of snapping back, I shove more food into my mouth.

"I haven't had time to shop," I lie again after a long pause. "I've been busy."

"With what exactly?" Mom swipes her fork from her plate like a weapon when she sits back down at the table. "Living like a hermit? Avoiding everyone who cares about you and wants to spend time with you? Hurting the people who love you?" Her mouth purses as she looks at me. "I swear, *anak*. You must get some sort of joy out of ignoring your dad and me for how easily you do it."

My blood turns to ice. The now-stagnant air in my house turns frosty.

"It's not just us, *anak*. Your *apong* asks about you all the time, wonders when you'll be back to the Philippines to visit her. It's been years since you've seen her. Not since you were in college. Or your cousins and aunties and uncles on that side of the family. So many years since you've seen them too."

The scolding lilt to her voice burns like a hot iron to my ears. As if I don't already know this. As if I don't already know how I'm failing my entire family because I can't function like a normal human being anymore.

"*Apong* is pushing ninety, Isabel," Mom says. "You realize that, don't you?"

She shakes her head before stabbing at the pile of food on her plate. The sound of the metal hitting ceramic over and over pricks my ears. It's worse than nails on a chalkboard.

"Oh, but you don't care," she bites. "You don't even care about seeing your dad and me, so why would you care about traveling to the Philippines to see the rest of your family?"

I sink my teeth into the inside of my cheek instead of lashing out. It hurts, but not as much as the dismissiveness in her tone. Not as much as the outright disdain that coats every word she speaks. I'm the biggest disappointment. I'm everything she wishes I weren't.

My hands tremble as I set my fork down onto my empty plate. "Mom. I've told you so many times. This is what works for me. I don't like being around lots of people. It upsets me. You know that."

Her chest heaves with the shaky breath she takes. She slides her hand across the table to reach for mine, but I quickly pull it away before her fingertips can make contact with me.

Her perfectly thick, perfectly penciled eyebrows furrow the slightest bit. Under the kitchen lighting, her eyes shine. She's clearly hurt that I don't want her to touch me. But she can't be surprised by my reaction after what she just said.

"*Anak*. I know that. And I want to help you. Your dad and I both do."

I scoff despite the softness of her tone.

"Right," I mutter. With my fork, I move the leftover noodles around my plate. "Just like you tried to help me last time."

Another heavy sigh shoots from her before she leans in closer to me. "Yes. That's what we were trying to do. And if you had just stayed and listened to what Father Leonard and Dr. Milbanks had to say—"

I throw my fork onto my plate. The harsh clanking noise causes her shoulders to jump. She falls back into her chair.

"I'm sorry I wasn't over the moon that you had orchestrated a surprise intervention under the guise of a family dinner."

The bitterness of my voice as I speak rivals how it sounded that day when I walked into my parents' house and found two people sitting in their living room along with them. I recognized Father Leonard right away. He's from my parents' parish, and I had seen and chatted with him the times I went to Mass with them. I had no idea who Dr. Milbanks was, though, until Mom introduced me. She looked vaguely familiar, but I couldn't place her. Somehow, even before anyone had explained what was going on, I knew what was happening. And I was livid.

When I blink, I'm transported back to that late Sunday afternoon. I walked through the front door and stepped inside the living room, only to find two people sitting on the couch. I froze. And then I looked at my parents, who were standing next to me. Raw pity emanated from their gazes as they focused on me. My legs twitched with the urge to dart out of their house and back to my car so I could speed as far away from them as possible.

But Mom grabbed my hand. "Come sit down, *anak*," she said. "We thought it would be nice for you to chat with Father Leonard and my friend Dr. Milbanks."

"Who's Dr. Milbanks?" I snapped as I pulled my hand from hers.

It was then that Dad moved to stand behind me. It was such a casual action in the moment. I didn't think anything of it right away. But when Mom scooped my hand in hers again, it hit me why he did that, why he stepped around me to stand between their front door and me—so I wouldn't leave right away.

"She's a therapist," Mom said. "We think it would help if you talked to her. And Father Leonard too."

"I see." For a full minute after I said that, no one said a word. Everyone just stayed in place and quietly stared at me. It's like we were actors on a stage holding our places until the curtain rose.

The warmth of Dad's hand on my shoulder broke the moment. "It's just that you've been so isolated for so long, sweetie," he said in a soft voice. "We don't think that it's good for you to be away from your family and your friends anymore."

"I see."

Those were the only two words I could muster in that moment, when shock and disbelief consumed me, like a massive ocean wave decimating a sandcastle.

"You need help," Mom said. "You can't keep shutting everyone out. And we thought that if you talked to someone about it, it would make you feel better."

"It could help you start processing the pain and the grief . . . what you went through."

"It was hard for all of us, what happened. I still can't believe—"

"Stop!"

My shout was enough to jolt everyone in the room. Father Leonard and Dr. Milbanks jumped in their seats. Both Dad and Mom jerked their hands off me. And I took that as my opportunity to escape.

I stepped around Dad and stormed out the front door. I was half-way down the driveway by the time they made it to the porch.

"Isabel, stop," they called after me. "Please."

And for some reason, that set me off. I still don't know why. They've yelled at me to stop loads of times my whole life. When I was a kid or teenager doing something I shouldn't be doing, they recited that word millions of times. It never fazed me. But in that moment, I lost it.

I spun around to face them. "No. *You* stop. How many times have I told you I don't want this? I don't want to talk to anyone about what happened. And you go behind my back and do the one thing I asked you to never, ever do?"

They stood on the steps of their porch as I spewed my angry words at them. I didn't miss the way their eyes watered. I didn't miss the pained twist of their expressions. I didn't miss the way Dad blinked and tears stumbled down his cheeks. I didn't miss the way my mom's mouth quivered as she tried not to cry.

But I didn't care. They went behind my back to arrange something they knew would destroy me. In that moment, I was done.

"I don't want to see either of you again."

I hopped in my car, drove home, and ignored their calls and texts. That was five months ago. And now, I'm sitting at my kitchen table with my mom as she tries to shove her way back into my life. But I just can't, not if she's going to push me to do something I've repeatedly told her I'm not able to do.

Her hand on my hand jerks me back to the moment.

"You're not okay, *anak*. Not even close," she says, her voice breaking.

"I'm fine, Mom."

She flinches at my hard tone. Her stare turns watery the longer she looks at me. "You don't spend time with your friends anymore." She squeezes my hand tighter. "I ran into Keely a few weeks ago and asked if maybe you two had gotten together, and she said no. She said it's been years since she's even seen you. Talked to you."

"Two years and two months." I say it through gritted teeth.

Mom's expression crumples to something even more desperate and pained.

"Mom. Please stop meddling in my life. I don't need you calling my friends to see what I'm up to. That's humiliating."

"You're hurting. I can see it so clearly. Keely, your other friends, your dad and me. Everyone can. That's why we want to help you. So you can get better. So you can be happy and whole again."

"Whole? Really?" I jerk my hand out of her hold.

She shakes her head and looks off to the side, like she's overwhelmed with frustration. "I didn't mean it like . . . Come to Mass with me."

I almost laugh at her persistence.

"Mom, no."

"I just don't understand why you won't. You used to be so happy to go with me." She throws her delicate hands in the air. "Or we can go to any kind of church, whatever you want. It'll help you."

"I won't ever go again. Those places are absolutely worthless to me."

Mom scoots her chair closer to me on my side of the table. "I'm sorry, *anakko*," she says, her eyes glistening with tears. "You're right. What your dad and I did that day, surprising you with all that, it was wrong. We shouldn't have done it."

I soften the slightest bit.

"But we're just so desperate for you to get better, for you to be happy again, like you were before . . ."

She clamps her mouth shut, catching herself. It still stings, though. Because that's the whole problem. My parents want me to be the person I was before—before That Day. Happy and social, surrounded by friends and family always. But that person is gone forever.

"Mom, listen to me. I won't ever be the way I was before. No matter how hard you and Dad wish, no matter what you do, it won't happen. I'm different now. This is the only way I know how to be. I'm sorry that's not good enough for you."

Her mouth wobbles as tears tumble down her face. She swipes the napkin from her lap and dabs at her face. My chest throbs. I'm making her cry again. Like always.

She stands up and clears the dishes from the table and sets them in the sink. She covers up the dish of *pansit* with foil. I start to tell her she doesn't have to, but she ignores me and sets it in the refrigerator. Then she walks over and bends down to hug me and kisses my cheek through my hair.

"I love you, Isabel. Always. No matter what."

Her whisper echoes in my ear long after she's walked out my front door and backed out of my driveway. I hear it as I go through my routine of tidying up the kitchen and living room, going for an evening jog, showering, and getting ready for bed. When I close my eyes and drift off to sleep, I still hear it.

Chapter Four

When I knock on Dr. Walder's office door, there's no answer. But I can hear papers shuffling through the walls.

It's the day after Martha asked me to reach out to Dr. Walder and Dr. Inuie about their impending divorce and how it's affecting their behavior at work. I tried getting ahold of Dr. Inuie, but she's in the middle of an hours-long trauma surgery and won't be available anytime soon. So Dr. Walder is up first.

I knock again, but still no answer. Only more papers shuffling.

I take a breath when I notice just how hard my heart is beating. I don't know if it's the fact that Dr. Walder is clearly ignoring me or that I'm still reeling from Mom's surprise visit and our subsequent argument last night, but I'm feeling especially on edge today.

"Dr. Walder, are you in there? It's Isabel, the chaplain on staff for this shift."

"Go away!" he barks behind the door.

I jolt back a step in shock. Until today, I've only seen Dr. Walder in passing. We say a quick hello to each other sometimes when we pass each other in the elevator or in the cafeteria. He's always been polite and professional, never hostile like this.

"Dr. Walder, I—"

Just then, the door flies open, and his scowling face greets me.

"What don't you understand about 'go away'?"

I breathe in slowly and silently exhale, hoping that extra moment eases the adrenaline coursing through me.

"If this is a bad time, I can come back later," I say. "But it's been brought to my attention that you've been having outbursts while at work due to some personal matters, and I'm here to check on you and see if—"

He slams the door in my face so hard, the walls rattle. For a minute, all I can do is just stand there and stare at the slab of dark wood as my heartbeat rebounds. Behind me, I hear whispering at the nurses' station just a few feet away. My face heats as I soak in the moment, how everyone on this end of the floor just witnessed a literal door being slammed in my face.

I start to walk away, but I stop myself. No. I can't just leave this. Yes, the professional thing to do would be to have a chat with Martha the next time I see her and figure out if there's a different way we can approach this. Maybe we could have another chaplain try. Or maybe HR could mediate a meeting.

But something inside me snaps. It's like my patience is a long, brittle twig tied to a brick. The weight is too much to bear, and finally that flimsy piece of wood snaps.

When I throw open the door to Dr. Walder's office, he's sitting at his desk, staring at me with bulging eyes.

"What in the world—"

"You will not slam the door in my face, do you understand?"

He stammers something.

I walk up to his desk so I'm leaning over him. "Do you understand, Dr. Walder?" My volume is a few notches under a shout.

He clamps his mouth shut and nods.

I swallow to reel in the volume of my voice. "Now, I feel for what you're going through. It's clearly a very difficult time for you, and you're struggling. But acting like a petulant asshole isn't the appropriate way to deal with it. You absolutely will not lash out at me or any other staff member at this hospital. Nor any patients. Is that clear?"

Still nothing. Dr. Walder just sits there, his jaw now on the floor, his wide, unblinking eyes fixed on me.

"Is that clear?"

It's not till the words leave my mouth that I realize I'm shouting.

His eyebrows crash together as he quickly nods. "Y-yes," he stammers.

When I step out and shut the door behind me, I have to grip the knob extra hard. It's like all the energy has jolted from my body. My legs wobble as I walk by the nurses' station in the direction of my office. A dozen wide-eyed stares surround me. No one says a word.

When I'm down the hall, I hear the faint sound of applause. I'd laugh if I wasn't so panicked.

I just yelled and swore at an attending physician. Yeah, he was a jerk, but that doesn't excuse what I did.

When I get back to the office, I collapse into my chair, my head spinning. I'm in deep shit.

~

"I think you know why I called this meeting with you, Isabel," Martha says.

I nod as I sit across from her in the chaplain office. "Yeah. I do."

I'm gripping the arms of my chair so hard, my knuckles ache. I wiggle them out, then fold them in my lap.

"It's come to my attention that you had a verbal altercation with Dr. Walder."

I knew this was coming. I shouldn't be sweating through my blouse or death-gripping my chair. But it's one thing to expect to get fired. It's an entirely different thing to go through the actual process of it. To hear your boss tell you that you're no longer welcome at this job, to go through the mortifying act of cleaning out your desk, tossing everything in a box, and walking out of the office as everyone around you looks on. To accept that your source of income is gone.

"Yes, um. That h-happened," I stammer. "And I'm very sorry. I let my frustration get the best of me. I do feel that Dr. Walder was out of line, but how I responded was unprofessional."

A sad smile appears on Martha's face. "You're not getting fired, Isabel."

I sit up in my chair. "I'm not?"

She shakes her head. "The fact that the entire nurses' station witnessed this incident turned out to be a good thing. They reported to HR that Dr. Walder was being equally hostile to you. He's being suspended for ninety days."

"Oh." I make a mental note to order cupcakes for the entire nurses' station for backing me up.

But then Martha's face falls slightly. "I'm sorry to say that you're being suspended for ninety days as well. Without pay."

I try not to choke when I swallow. That's not nearly as bad as being fired, but it's definitely not ideal.

Martha starts to explain that this is all part of the hospital's HR policy, but I can't really focus. I'm too busy thinking of how I'm going to budget properly for the next three months so I don't have to drain all of my savings to cover my bills.

". . . and at the end of the ninety-day period, you and I will have a review. And as long as that goes well, which I'm sure it will, and you agree to complete an online workplace conflict resolution module, you'll be able to start up again here at the hospital."

"Oh. Okay."

She leans over to pat my hand. "I know this isn't ideal, but I want you to know that your job will be waiting for you when you get back, Isabel. No one is holding this incident against you. In fact, Arlene came to me and told me that she and the other nursing staff were behind you one hundred percent. She even said a few of the nurses toasted to you when they went out for drinks at the end of their shift that day."

I smile slightly.

"The suspension is essentially a formality, so that the hospital shows that they follow proper procedure when an incident occurs."

"I understand." I glance around the tiny office. "So, um, I guess I should just head home now?"

She nods, the look on her face regretful. "I'm afraid so."

I stand up and gather my things and stand by the door.

"Thanks for everything, Martha."

"I'll be here when you get back, kiddo."

I reach for the knob, but she stops me. "Oh! I almost forgot." She grabs a small blue envelope from the desk and hands it to me. "A patient's family wrote you a thank-you card. Arlene gave it to me to give to you."

I tell her thanks, tuck the card in my purse, then leave.

As I drive home at nine in the morning, a ball of nerves lodges in the pit of my stomach. What am I going to do for money for the next three months? As much of a relief as it is that I didn't end up losing my job, three months without pay is scary as hell. I have savings, but not enough to let me coast for three months.

That head-spinning feeling hits as I make my way through traffic back to my house.

Why did I make that extra payment on my house in the spring? If I hadn't done that, I'd have an extra month's worth of expenses. And what was I thinking paying off my car loan earlier this year? I'd have had a few thousand bucks left in my bank account. That would have been the perfect buffer.

Well, maybe you shouldn't have lost your shit at work.

I groan at my self-scolding.

I grab my phone and call Chantel, hoping that she just happens to be on break and can talk to me.

"Bel! How's it going?"

"Fine. Actually, it's not fine. It's really, really not fine."

"Okay, I'm gonna need you to explain."

"I will, just . . . how are you?"

"Seriously? You just kicked off our conversation with the most cryptic opening line and now you're asking me how I'm doing?"

I let out a small laugh. "Yeah. I am. I need a distraction before I dive into my crap. So tell me. How's Phoenix?"

"Hot. Like, hell isn't even this hot. It can't be."

I honk out a laugh.

"Oh, you think that's funny?"

"I needed that. Thanks."

"It's so hot, I need oven mitts to touch the steering wheel of my car after working a twelve-hour shift."

"You're kidding."

"I wish I was."

"Holy hell."

"It's so hot, I walk around naked in my hotel room with the AC on full blast because I soak my clothes through with sweat otherwise."

I'm giggling.

"It's so hot, I spent my day off yesterday at Kmart for five hours because their AC is the coldest of any department store I've been to. I took a nap on a plush couch in the home goods section. One of the employees woke me up and asked me to leave."

I'm laughing so hard, my stomach aches.

"Oh my god, stop," I say as I wipe my eyes. "That's about all I can take. I'm driving, and I can't pass out due to laughter. I'll crash my car."

Chantel chuckles.

"Okay," I say after catching my breath. "Here's what happened."

I spend the next few minutes giving Chantel a rundown of my meeting with Martha.

"Well, that's not so bad. You're not jobless," she says.

"I am, though. I'm out of work for the next three months. I need to figure out a temporary job. I just . . . who would even hire me? No business owner is going to hire someone who's planning to quit in three months."

"Are you worried about money?"

I purse my lips together, knowing I can't lie. She'll see right through it.

"A little."

"Let me float you some."

"No way."

"Bel, come on. This isn't the time to let your pride get in the way of your livelihood. I can help, it's no problem."

"I'm not taking money from you, Chantel."

"You take money from me every month that I'm home from traveling. What's the big deal if I offer to give you more?"

As valid as Chantel's points are, there's no way I'm accepting money from her. She's been working so hard to earn enough money to pay off her debts and save a sizable down payment for a house. I don't want to be the reason why she stalls on either one of those goals. I'm her big sister; I shouldn't be a burden on her.

"It's a no-go, Tel. I appreciate the offer, but I'll figure this out myself."

I can tell by the long silence that Chantel has accepted the finality in my tone.

"Okay, fine," she says after a moment.

"I just need to find another job to get me through the summer."

There's another long pause on her end of the line. "I know someone who'd be happy to help you."

As soon as she says it, I know exactly who she's talking about.

"No way. I can't."

"Why not?"

"Because. Just thinking of asking her for a favor makes me want to crawl out of my skin."

Chantel sighs. "I don't know why you think that, Isabel. You know she'd be happy to help. Even after everything that went down."

"That's just it. I'd feel like the biggest piece of shit reaching out to her after the way I've treated her."

"Then make it right." She says it so resolutely, so firmly.

For a few seconds, neither of us says anything. It's just the sound of traffic on my end and the sound of medical equipment beeping on hers.

"Look, there are a lot of options for you, Isabel. You don't have to do this one. But I think you should. Not only would it help you out with job stuff, but it would help you start to work your way back to your friend."

I start to speak, but she talks over me.

"I know you're not into seeing people anymore. But this isn't just anyone. This is Keely. She was your best friend. And you *were* going to see her the other night anyway if it hadn't been for your pitiful alcohol tolerance."

I let out a soft chuckle. And then I take a few moments, Chantel still on the line, and think about the prospect of reaching out to Keely.

"Okay. I'll do it."

~

I sit alone at a table for two near the back of the Grey Plume and try to remember how I used to act when I'd arrive at a restaurant, the first person in my party.

Despite that considerable two-plus-year gap, it comes back to me relatively easily. I'd normally sip water, then read a book or look at something on my phone. But now I'd rather people watch. Maybe it's because it's been so long since I've been out like this, but watching people is fascinating. Why did I never pay attention to the people around me before? Like that couple at the table next to me who's clearly on their first date. They both flash nervous smiles at each other between glances at the menu. He keeps stammering, then asking her what food preferences she has. She keeps repeating that she likes everything.

There's that guy by the bar who is clearly super into the incredibly handsome bartender. He keeps asking him to take a shot with him, but the bartender politely declines, always with a smile. God, that probably gets old, having to deflect unwanted attention when you work in a restaurant.

When the server drops by to ask if I want something else to drink besides water, I tell him no thanks.

"Oh, but . . . the person I'm waiting for might."

He starts to drop off a menu, but I stop him.

"Oh! Actually, can I order a lemon drop?" Keely's favorite drink.

He says of course and darts off to the bar. And then I silently second-guess myself into oblivion. Was that too presumptuous what I just did? To assume that she'd even want a lemon drop? That was her go-to drink when we'd go out together . . . but maybe it's changed in the past couple of years.

I thought it would make her smile, though, to see her old favorite sitting at the table and waiting for her. She'd think it was a sweet gesture.

But then I tell myself that no, it's not such a sweet gesture. A sweet gesture would have been showing up to her birthday last week. Or texting an apology instead of never responding to the messages she sent me on her birthday because I wasn't sure how to explain that I really was planning to see her, but I let my nerves and my low alcohol tolerance get in the way.

A sweet gesture would have been to bring her a gift as a thank-you for even answering my text yesterday and agreeing to meet up with me after two years and two months of radio silence from me.

My skin pricks with the heat of regret as I gaze around the dimly lit space. I'm so bad at this, at being a friend. At being a decent person.

The server sets the lemon drop at my table. I thank him, then stare at the yellowy liquid as it ripples against the martini glass. Sugar crystals adorn the rim. Under the mood lighting, they shine like diamonds.

"Isabel."

I look up to see a smiling Keely standing above me. She doesn't wait for me to stand up before she leans down and pulls me into a hug so tight, I lose all the breath in my lungs. I can't help but laugh, though, as I squeeze my arms around her. It's several seconds before she lets me go, and even when we break apart, she keeps hold of my shoulders, her eyes bright and her smile wide.

And that's when I notice her stomach.

My jaw falls as I gaze at the black fabric stretching across her swollen belly.

"Oh my god."

Keely's arms fall to her sides, her smile turning sheepish. She shrugs. "Surprise."

I don't know how long I gawk at her, but it feels like a while. Eventually, she sits down in the chair across from me.

"Congratulations," I finally say, instantly annoyed with myself that I didn't think to say it sooner.

That sweet, tender smile tugs at her full pink lips. "Thanks. I, um, I thought about texting you, but . . ." She fiddles with the stark-white napkin, pulling the silverware out of it and setting it aside. "I was going to tell you in person. Last week. On my, um, birthday . . . I know that was kind of silly, but I was being hopeful . . ."

My throat aches as I take in the reluctance in her tone. Even after everything I've done, she still wanted to share this news with me.

My eyes water, but I blink furiously until they're dry again.

"I'm so sorry, Keely. I swear, I was gonna come out and see you, but . . . I was nervous, so I had a bit to drink to work up the nerve, but I passed out, and . . ." My voice shakes so hard, I have to stop talking or else I'll lose it.

I don't want to cry. Not here, not in this fancy restaurant where patrons are meant to enjoy Michelin-starred food and pleasant conversation. Not when I should be focusing on reconnecting with my best friend. Not when I should be focused on the joy of her pregnancy.

"Keely, I . . . I'm so . . ."

With her lips pursed, she shakes her head and looks off to the side. It's such a slight tell, but I notice it right away. Her "I'm so mad, I could cry" move. By the way her eyes glisten and the slight furrow in her brow, I can tell she's gutted at how I ignored her. I can tell that my babbled explanation for missing her birthday is nowhere near good enough.

And in the seconds that pass, I wait for her to turn back to me and let me have it. I deserve it. I spent so much time ignoring her, I missed so many things in her life . . . I deserve, at the very least, an earful. Maybe even a drink thrown in my face.

But Keely just keeps staring off to the side, swallowing hard and blinking furiously. Watching her struggle makes me want to melt into the marble floor beneath us and disappear forever.

But I stay seated, resisting every muscle twitch in my arms and legs, every urge to bolt. I deserve this discomfort. After how I ghosted Keely, I deserve every second of this.

"You were the first person I wanted to tell when I saw the positive on my pregnancy test." She stares at her lap as she speaks. A sad chuckle falls from her lips before she sniffles. "I thought of you even before I thought of Theo. Weird, huh?"

I bite my quivering lip. For a moment, I wonder how her husband, Theo, feels about her meeting me. No doubt he's pissed at me for icing out his wife for so long.

"Keely."

It's a second before she looks up at me.

"I don't deserve how good you're being to me right now. I could say sorry a million times, and it still wouldn't be enough. And I want you to know that as happy as I am that you're here with me right now, you have every right to walk out on me. No one would blame you, least of all me."

Her chest heaves as she takes a shaky breath. Then she does something I don't expect. She reaches across the table and places her hand over mine.

"You're right. Maybe I should walk out. But I'm not going to." Her grip on my hand tightens. "Yeah, I'm still hurt at what you did. But . . . then I remember all the times you were there for me when no one else was. Like when you threw a glass of punch at Seth Slater's head junior year when I caught him making out with Lacey Showalter at the prom."

"I can't believe you remember that."

"How could I forget?" Her trembling lips curve upward into a smile. "It was one of the greatest things a friend has ever done for me."

"He was your prom date and ditched you to make out with someone else. Throwing punch on him was the least he deserved."

Her laugh sounds lighter, happier this time. She dabs her napkin against her cheeks. "I remember how you took the blame when Mr. Meister caught us smoking behind the bleachers freshman year after ditching gym class."

The memory of Keely and me running off when he shouted at us flashes in my mind, like a highlight reel. This time I let out a laugh so loud, several patrons at a few tables turn to look at us.

"I still can't believe he bought it when I told him I was the only one smoking and that you were trying to talk me out of it," I say.

Her head falls back as she laughs. "You were such a quick thinker. You saved my ass, though. My mom would have grounded me for life, and I wouldn't have been able to go on that trip to Paris with my cousin had she found out that I had been smoking."

I smile at Keely. A million more memories of us together flip through my head, like a movie reel of our friendship. Of Keely asking me if I wanted to play tetherball with her in third grade as I stood alone on the playground, the new kid in school with no friends. Of the two of us shopping for homecoming dresses together. Of her letting me bring Chantel along to most of our hangouts when we were teenagers because my parents had to work and I would have to watch her. Of her coming with me to the pharmacy for the morning-after pill when my birth control failed when I was twenty, holding my hand, reassuring me that everything was going to be fine.

"You've done a million things for me, Keely. You've been there for me so many times."

Her smile turns wistful as she gazes at me. "Just like you have for me. And that's what matters. It's okay. You're here now, and I'm so happy."

Her light-brown eyes glisten. Unshed tears. Of joy. At seeing me.

I nod quickly and let out a watery laugh before sniffling. "Thank you, Keely."

She glances down at the lemon drop.

"I guess you can't drink that."

She shakes her head. "Sorry, no."

"I shouldn't have it either." Just the thought of anything alcoholic touching my tongue has my stomach curdling. I hop up with the drink in my hand, then step over to the table with the first date couple.

"Free lemon drop on me. Enjoy!"

The couple flashes a dazed look at me as they mumble a thanks. When I sit back down at the table, Keely is giggling.

"That was sweet of you."

"I hope it's okay that I suggested meeting here," I say. "I guess I figured you'd be okay coming here, since you came here last week."

I fight the cringe that hits me. It's also a reminder of how I hurt her—how I ignored her.

"It's okay. Really." She shakes her head quickly, as if she can sense what I'm thinking.

The server stops by and asks if we're ready to order. We're obviously not, since we haven't even looked at the menu yet, so we ask for a few minutes.

There are a million things I want to say, but I want Keely to figure out her order first. She's eating for two, after all. When she closes her menu and looks up at me, I take that as my cue.

"So you and Theo are gonna be parents. I'm so, so happy for you."

She nods, her wild, curly chestnut hair bouncing along with the movement. She rests a hand on her stomach. The hesitation she displayed before is long gone at the mention of her baby. "I'm six months along and counting down the days. This little one, let me tell you. Already so huge and active. They kick my bladder like they're training for the World Cup."

I let out a laugh. In this moment, it feels like old times. Another wave of memories floods me—of happy hours, weekend getaways, road trips, and late-night karaoke sessions that turned into dancing into the wee hours of the morning.

And then nostalgia hits. The memory of attending Keely's wedding tumbles into my brain. She wanted a veil as long as Princess Diana's. I can recall perfectly even now how insistent she was at the bridal boutique.

Then another memory of Keely dressed in all black, of her telling me how sorry she is, that she's just one phone call away, that she's always here if I ever want to talk about what happened, of her saying over and over that it's not my fault . . .

My shoulders freeze like they're made of stone. I swallow before downing half my glass of water.

No. Not here. Not now. Please.

Thankfully, focusing on Keely's smile and her excited chatter grounds me in the moment. Then the server is back, and we place our order.

"I'm having my baby shower here in a couple of months, actually," she says.

"Oh, wow. So fancy."

"I know this is probably a weird place to have it, but Theo's mom wants to throw a bit of a lavish shindig, since this'll be their first grandbaby."

I smile when she says the word *shindig*. No one under the age of sixty says that word. Except Keely.

She opens her mouth, but before she says anything, she clamps it shut and shakes her head.

"What is it?" I ask.

She shakes her head again, but when she focuses back on me, her expression turns tender and determined at once. "I know it's a big ask, but I wanted to say that you should come to my baby shower. If you want to. I'd love it if you were there."

"Oh."

"No pressure, though," she rushes to say. "Promise, I won't get upset if you don't come. Just know that you're welcome. Always."

Instead of the wave of nerves I expect to hit me at the thought of attending a party and seeing Keely's family, who haven't seen me since before That Day, the strangest thing happens. I'm calm. Maybe it's because Keely has made it clear there is zero expectation for me to attend. Maybe it's the comfort I feel from being with her right now.

"I'd love to come. Thank you."

Keely's eyes go teary once more as she beams at me. The server stops to drop off our plates.

"So what's new with you?" Keely asks as she digs into her smoked duck.

I set my fork down, remembering why I asked her here in the first place.

"Um, it's kind of a funny story. Actually, not really."

Her saucerlike eyes go wide as she chews. I give her an abbreviated version of the incident at work and my suspension.

"And, well, um, I figured since you're a recruiter, I could get your advice on where to look for jobs. Or maybe you know of something temporary I could do over the summer."

"Oh."

When she hesitates, I bite the inside of my cheek, ashamed at how I must come off to her in this moment. I'm her estranged friend who got in touch with her so that she could help me find work. I'm such a leech.

"I know how this must look . . . like I only wanted to meet up because I need you for job help."

Another hard swallow moves along her delicate throat. That's exactly what she's thinking.

"I swear, it's not, though. I wanted to see you, Keely. I miss you. And I want to try to make this right between us. I want to be your friend again."

She nods, clearly processing what I've said. After a few seconds, her expression turns focused. "I want that too." She smiles slightly, then nods once. "Okay, well, first of all, that doctor sounds like he was being an absolute dick. You were justified in standing up to him. You shouldn't have gotten in trouble at all."

I chuckle, heartened at her defense of me.

"But I guess that's neither here nor there," she says. Then she smiles at me. "Of course I'll help. Next week, I'll put some feelers out. Promise I'll find you something."

"Thanks, Keely."

She waves her hand as she holds her fork, like it's no big deal. I gently touch her arm to get her to look at me.

"I mean it. You don't have to help me." I swallow back the lump that's lodged in my throat. "No one would blame you for never wanting to see me again after how I dropped off the face of the earth and didn't bother to reach out to you. And here you are, still wanting to be my friend. Still wanting to help me. I just . . . it's more than I deserve."

"Hey." Her firm tone catches me off guard. "I won't lie. I'm still hurt. And a little upset." Her voice, along with her expression, softens. "But I still want to be your friend, too, Isabel."

This time, when I blink, a tear falls. "You're the best."

She sniffles and dabs a napkin under her eyes. "Dammit, don't make me cry. It doesn't take much to get me going these days."

We share a snotty laugh, then get it together and finish our meal. I leave to use the restroom. As I snake my way through the configuration of tables toward the back of the restaurant, I turn the corner and bump into someone.

"Oof," a low voice grunts.

"Oh, sorry, I—"

And then I go silent. Because Evan is standing right in front of me.

Chapter Five

"Isabel. Uh, hey."

"Hey."

Evan wears a white chef's jacket, the sleeves rolled up to his elbows. Grease and food stains dot the fabric.

"You're a chef." Why did I say that? What a random and obvious observation to verbalize.

He half smiles and looks down at his jacket. "What gave it away?"

I let out an awkward-sounding chuckle and shuffle my feet, then look down at my heels for a second. When I glance up at Evan, his expression is something between strained and unsure. I bet mine is too. This is a strange space we're occupying. Running into each other randomly and attempting to have a normal, pleasant interaction after the way we met is awkward, to say the least. I can feel my muscles tense the slightest bit, like I'm bracing myself just in case this turns into an argument. After a second, I let out a slow, quiet breath and relax.

"Sorry, I, uh . . . I guess I'm a little surprised to run into you here," I blurt.

"Same."

For a moment, we just stand there and look at each other. It's clear neither one of us knows how to navigate this.

"How long have you worked here?" I say when I can't think of anything else.

"I opened the restaurant just over five years ago."

"Oh. Um, how's your grandma?"

His eyebrows furrow. I can't tell if he's annoyed or sad that I asked. "Overall, she's okay. She can remember some people still, like my mom. But she's struggling to remember a lot of other things. Including me."

The defeat and sorrow in his softly spoken words are an arrow to my heart.

"I'm sorry."

"No. I'm sorry"—his chest heaves with a sigh, and he rubs the back of his neck—"for the way I spoke to you in the elevator at the hospital the other day."

"It's really okay—"

"It's not." He bites the side of his cheek as he glances off to the side, like he's thinking about what he wants to say. "My grandma had a bad fall and hit her head. That's why she was in the hospital. And even though she wasn't seriously injured, thankfully, I think the stress of it seemed to worsen her memory somehow. She was more confused than normal. I don't really understand it. The doctor explained, but I had a hard time following."

"Evan, that's terrible. I'm sorry."

"She was having a hard time remembering me before this happened, but when I came to visit her at the hospital, she started calling me by different names."

He pauses to swallow, like it's taking everything in him not to break down as he tells me this.

"Before then, with her dementia, it would always take her a bit to remember me. But she never called me by the wrong name. I know that her situation isn't unique. So many people with dementia experience that. It just . . . it hit me really hard for some reason. I know she can't help it. And it's not anyone's fault. That's the nature of this disease. But I was still angry about it. Angry at the situation. And sad too. Clearly I did a terrible job of keeping that in check. I'm really sorry for how I spoke to you that day in the elevator." His voice goes soft at the end, like he's scared of how I'll react to what he's said.

At first I say nothing. I just soak in the impromptu apology from Evan as we stand in the darkened hallway in the back of this restaurant.

"I appreciate that," I say. "And I'm sorry for what you and your family are going through. That must be so difficult."

"It is," he mumbles.

The kitchen door swings open, and a guy also wearing a white chef's jacket steps out. "Chef, you coming? We're slammed in here."

"Yeah, sorry, Miguel. One sec, okay?"

The guy nods and darts back into the kitchen.

Evan turns to look at me again. "I wanted to say thank you too."

"For what?"

"For how happy you made her when you came to see her. I think you remind her of someone she really likes. Or maybe she just really likes you. She was in the best mood that day."

I can't help the lightness that washes over me at what Evan has said. Considering I'm officially suspended from my job for the entire summer for losing my cool, it's heartening to know I did one good thing.

"You don't need to thank me," I say. "I was just doing my job."

"Even my mom noticed it when she came to the hospital later that day. When I told her it was you, the chaplain, who put Grandma in such good spirits, she was so happy. Did you get the card she wrote you?"

I frown, shaking my head. "No, I . . ."

Then I remember the blue envelope Martha gave me on my last day of work at the hospital. I was too overwhelmed to read it then, but it's still in my purse.

"I haven't read it yet. Sorry, it's been kind of a weird and busy week." I opt not to share the details of my professional low point with Evan. "But I'm going to read it later. I promise."

He scrunches his lips, almost like he doesn't have the energy to smile.

"I'd better get back to work," he says through an exhale. He gives me a quick head nod, like he's dismissing himself from the conversation. It comes off weirdly detached, considering what we just talked about.

"Of course. It was nice seeing you."

"You too," he says as he turns away from me.

He disappears behind the kitchen doors, and I make my way back to my table. When she jokingly asks why I was gone for so long, I mumble that I ran into a guy I know.

"A guy?" Keely grins as she wags an eyebrow.

"Oh, um . . . he's the grandson of a dementia patient I saw the other day at work."

"Oh." The amusement in Keely's face quickly melts away. She doesn't press further, probably because it's a hospital-related matter, and she's aware that I can't talk too much about patients and their families due to HIPAA.

I'm quietly relieved. I don't know if I have the energy to retell my and Evan's short yet very awkward history on top of the emotional night Keely and I have had already.

We pay the bill and walk outside together. She pulls me into another deathly tight hug that makes me warm all over. When we pull apart, she promises to contact me next week with news about any job leads. I thank her, we tell each other good night, and I walk to my car.

As soon as I'm inside, I open the blue envelope from my purse and read the card.

Isabel,

Thank you so much for stopping in to visit with my mother. Our whole family noticed what a great mood she was in that day because of her chat with you. I know it's a bit of an imposition and please don't feel like you have to, but if you ever want to visit her again, she'd love that. We would too. She's been transferred to a memory care facility to complete her rehab. Please drop by for a visit anytime you'd like.

April Sanderson

At the bottom of the card is the name and address of the memory care facility.

A strange mix of relief and determination hits me at once. Relief that despite my recent professional failure, I'm still good at this—at being a comfort to someone in their time of need. And I'm more determined than ever to keep that up, to continue being a support to Opal and her family in this small way. I save the address in my phone and look up online when visitors are allowed. Tomorrow, I'm going to see Opal.

~

When I walk into the memory care facility, I check in with the receptionist. He lets me through, and as I make my way down the hall to Opal's room, I take in how lively the decor is. The walls are beige, but there are colorful decorations throughout. A bulletin board with bright-orange sun decals displays each of the residents' names. Wreaths with blossoms of every color adorn almost every door. When I walk by the dining hall, vibrant green aloe sits in the middle of each table.

As I turn the corner, I spot a chubby tabby cat lumbering through the hallway. It stops, then turns right into the nearest resident's room. I smile the rest of the way to Opal's room. I notice that each of the doors on the residents' rooms has a decoration on it—one door has a photo of a dog, one has bright-yellow happy-face stickers on it, one has a photo of a mountain taped to it. It reminds me of when I worked for a memory care facility and they used photos that were personal to each resident and that they could easily recognize as a way for them to remember which room was theirs.

When I make it to Opal's door, it's open, but I still knock. "Yes?"

She's seated in an armchair near the window. I stop a few feet from her, wondering if she'll be able to remember me.

After a few seconds, her thin pink lips turn upward. "You! Hello! Oh, I knew you'd come visit!"

She gestures for me to take the other armchair across from her. When I sit, she reaches her arm out to me. I stretch out my hand to her, and she grabs it tightly in hers.

"Oh, my dear. You're looking lovely. Not a day past seventy."

"That's kind of you to say, thank you."

She gives my hand one more squeeze before letting go. Her eyes practically sparkle as she stares at me, like she can't believe I'm sitting here.

"You're looking so good, Opal," I say. "How are you feeling? Is the bump on your head okay?"

She taps her temple. "This old thing? Good as new. I even took a walk out in the garden earlier with that nice young man in the green uniform."

"That's great."

She glances out the window. "I miss seeing those babies, though. They were so cute."

"What babies?"

"The ones in the hospital."

It takes me a second to understand what she's saying. "Did you visit the nursery while you were there?"

"I sure did. They were adorable. I wish I could cuddle all of them."

"Oh, yes, I'm sure that would have been so nice."

She turns to stare out the window of her room.

"Enjoying the view?" I ask.

For a second, she squints at me; then that upward curve widens into a smile. "I sure am, dear. A crystal-blue sky is something I always have to stop and take in."

"You and me both."

"You know, I remember you from the last time we chatted."

"Well, I'm glad, because I definitely remember you. I'm so happy we get to chat again."

Just like the first time I talked to Opal, I stay as open-ended in my responses to her as I can, stick to topics that seem to make her happy, and keep a positive demeanor. I want to keep this interaction as pleasant and low-stress as possible.

"You know, I saw this very handsome young man with long hair this morning," she says out of the blue.

"Oh, really?" I wonder if she's talking about Evan.

When she fans herself and says, "My, oh my," I laugh.

"It's a shame the men back in my day didn't wear their hair long," she says. "It's quite dashing."

She tilts her head at me, and the look in her blue eyes takes on a tender sheen. "You must have been a beautiful baby."

"Maybe? I guess I was. Some of my baby pictures are pretty cute."

"Cutest baby ever. I'm sure of it."

I smile at the conviction in her voice. "That's kind of you, Opal. I'm pretty sure my little sister was cuter, though. Everyone thought she was the cutest baby."

As she nods at me, her gaze turns focused. Determined, almost. "You two are really close, aren't you?"

There's a pulse in my chest that hits hard. It comes suddenly, like a hiccup or an eye twitch. How could she know about Chantel and me?

But then clarity sets in. She doesn't know. She's just saying random things. And this one thing just so happens to resonate.

"Yes," I say after a moment, trying to keep that same light tone. "We are pretty close, actually."

"That's good. Although it'll be hard when she leaves, won't it?"

I don't say anything for a few seconds. "What do you mean?"

Opal waves a hand. "We're all gone. I left. That handsome young man with the long hair left." She points to the hallway as someone decked out in green scrubs walks by. "She left. They left too. Everyone and everything and every . . . every . . ."

Her eyes go from focused to darting across random points in the room. I open my mouth but don't say anything. She's clearly confused.

"You're right. My sister does leave sometimes. She's a travel nurse, so she's gone a lot."

The confusion melts from Opal's hazel stare. She's more focused now, like she's enraptured by what I've said. I take that as my cue to keep talking.

"I miss her sometimes. She's my best friend."

Opal smiles. Something about it makes me go warm inside.

"But she always comes back. And stays with me at my house. I get to hear all about the place where she stayed, the hospital where she worked, what the people were like, how she liked the work. Sometimes she brings me souvenirs."

"What kind of souvenirs?"

"Rocks if she goes on a hike somewhere. Sometimes shot glasses."

"Oh, what I would give for a gin martini right about now."

I laugh again. She closes her eyes and shakes her head while smiling. "What else, dear?"

"She always gives me the best hugs when she comes home," I say. "Like she's trying to squeeze all the air out of me. But in a good way. It's like I can tell how much she missed me by how hard she hugs me."

Opal opens her eyes, her smile wide. "We all leave. It's such a shame. But until then, we have each other," she says.

"I guess that's true."

Her gaze glides to the window once again, and I remind myself that it's normal for dementia patients to speak like this, to go off on random and confusing tangents. It's sadly evidence of the brain deteriorating due to the disease.

I sit there silently and let Opal enjoy the view in peace.

A minute later, I hear someone enter the room. I look up and see a woman in her sixties with gray-brown hair dressed in a sweater and loose-fitting jeans. She's got the same more-green-than-hazel eyes as Opal and Evan.

She smiles at me. "You must be Isabel. I'm April."

I stand up and reach my hand out to her. She shakes it.

"I hope it's okay that I stopped by," I say when we release our hands.

The woman smiles that same gentle upward curve I saw on Opal's face. "Of course. I'm so happy you came. We'd love for you to visit as much as you'd like."

I gesture for her to take the seat next to her mom. I sit on the ledge along the edge of the window.

Opal grins at April. "Hi, Bunny."

"Hey, Mom." April twists to me. "Childhood nickname."

"Very cute."

April digs a folded piece of construction paper out of her purse and hands it to Opal. "Jonah made you a card, Mom. Wanna see?"

Opal nods, reaching her arms out and making a grabbing gesture. She clutches the card in both hands, her eyes wide as she looks it over. I catch a glimpse of it and smile at the drawing of what looks like a lizard in bright-green crayon against the yellow construction paper.

Opal runs her finger along the border of the card, which is lined with smiley faces in a rainbow of colors. "So very pretty," she says.

"Jonah is my grandson," April says to me. Opal is so fixated on the drawing, she doesn't seem to hear April speaking.

April sighs, her smile slowly fading. "I feel bad that I can't be here all the time for her. It's just so hard with work and Jonah. I watch him a few days a week to help out my daughter and son-in-law."

"I'm sure she understands."

She nods at what I've said, even though the sadness on her face conveys she doesn't truly believe it.

April focuses on her mom. "It's just one more thing it feels like I'm failing at."

"I'm sure you're not. I'm sure you're doing the best you can."

I can't help but fall into chaplain mode, even though I'm technically suspended. But whenever I hear a family member of a patient disparage themselves, I make it a point to try to gently support them. I can't know the pain and stress they're enduring as they watch their loved one go through a medical emergency, but I can offer kindness. I can be a sympathetic listener for them.

April shakes her head. "It's just . . . god, it's so hard right now. I can't . . ." Her sigh shakes her entire body.

"It seems like something's bothering you," I say. "Would you like to talk about it?"

She hesitates. "I don't want to burden you."

"You're not. I'm a chaplain. I enjoy listening to people. And offering whatever support I can."

The worried lines in her forehead ease.

"This memory care facility is wonderful, but it's quite expensive. I won't be able to keep her here much longer."

"Oh. I'm sorry." Crap. That must be so stressful for April and her family to deal with, especially right after Opal's hospital stay.

"The good news is that I've found another facility in town for her to move into. But they don't have an opening until the end of the summer. That means she'll have to live with me for the next few months, but . . ."

April's eyes start to water. Just then, Opal looks up. "What's wrong, Bunny?"

She offers a shaky smile, then sniffles. "Nothing, Mom. Just allergies."

Opal nods, then goes back to gazing at the drawing.

"Her staying with me temporarily for the next few months would be fine if I didn't work so much. But I have to. I can't afford not to. And I don't have enough in my savings to cover expenses if I take months off to look after her."

I grab a tissue box, then hand it to her. She thanks me as she dabs at her eyes.

"I looked into hiring a home health aide, but they're so expensive. I mean, I understand why. They're providing such an important service, and they deserve to be paid well. I just can't afford to pay that if I'm going to also pay for the new memory care facility. My son and daughter offered to take off work and watch her during the day, but they're so busy with their own lives. I can't ask them to do that. It's just . . . this is all so overwhelming. And I don't know what to do or how I'm going to cope or—"

"I'll do it."

The shock in April's wide-eyed stare matches the shock I'm feeling. Did I really just say that?

Yeah. I did.

April squints at me. "Sorry, dear, but what was that?"

I take a few moments to gather my thoughts. I can do this. I can help Opal and April temporarily while at the same time earning some money to float myself until I can go back to work.

But more than that, I really *want* to do this—I want to help Opal and April. Something about being with Opal is so heartening. And she seems happy when she's around me, which is ultimately good for her overall well-being. And if I do this, I'll be doing something good to help someone else—like I would have been doing as a chaplain. Except I won't have to hide any part of myself to do this job.

"I can be Opal's home health aide," I say.

"That's nice of you to offer, dear. But don't you have a job?"

I shake my head. "I'm taking the summer off." I opt to leave out the reason why. I'm sure she wouldn't be thrilled to know that I'm suddenly available because I lost my shit on a doctor at the hospital. "This would be good for me to do on my free days during the week."

"Oh. Well then."

April's expression shifts from surprised to thoughtful, like she's seriously considering what I've offered.

"I don't think I have enough money to pay you, though."

It's like the gears in my brain kick in all of a sudden. "It's okay. You won't have to."

I explain that at the hospital, I work with social workers who help secure grants and state funding for people like April and Opal, who qualify for financial assistance for things like medical care and temporary home health assistance. I'm sure this setup would qualify.

April's brow raises. "I didn't know such a thing existed."

"Most people don't. They're wonderful programs but not well publicized, unfortunately."

I sit silently and wait as April takes a minute to think over what I've said.

"I'm also first aid and CPR certified," I say after a while. "I've always kept those current, since I work in a hospital. I mean, hopefully I won't have to use them. I just mean that I'm prepared. Just in case."

April smiles. "Of course."

My heartbeat quickens as she goes quiet once more. It's difficult to explain why I'm so invested in this, why it means so much to me for April to say yes to my offer so I can be Opal's temporary caretaker.

But there's an urge inside me. To help. To offer assistance to someone who clearly needs and deserves it. To do something other than be a shut-in for the next three months.

To show that I can do something honorable and true—to show that I can help someone in their time of need.

As much as being a chaplain means to me, I have to hide a huge part of myself in order to do it. I have to hide that I don't truly believe in anything anymore.

But I wouldn't have to hide with this. Yeah, I don't plan on telling April about my suspension from the hospital, but that has nothing to do with the actual task at hand—being Opal's caretaker.

April gazes at Opal before she turns back to me. "Are you sure? I'd need someone from eight to five most weekdays. I can take probably one day off during the week, since this is temporary, but I'll need some-one with her the rest of the days."

"I'm certain."

"And I wouldn't need you to do anything medical for her, of course," she quickly reassures me. "I'm able to give her all her meds before and after I get done with work. I just need someone to physically be around her for the day. To chat with her and make sure she eats enough. Maybe go for a walk and drive her places if she feels up to it. Just make sure she's safe and as happy as possible."

"I can do all of that, no problem."

I tell her, too, that I used to work in a memory care facility when I was in high school and college.

"I've had a lot of experience working with people in Opal's condi-tion. I really enjoy it. I can give you references if you'd like. And in order to qualify for the state funding, they'll run a background check on me, but I can promise you there won't be any issues there. I've never even gotten a speeding ticket."

Relief washes over her face. When she smiles, it looks different this time. It's light and without the strain that was etched on her face just seconds ago.

"Okay. Thank you, Isabel. I'd love it if you could watch my mother."

I tell her I'm happy to. She asks again if the grant and funding will work out, and I reassure her that it's worked out for other patients' families.

"I just want to make sure you get paid for this," she says.

"I'll make sure of it."

I'm about to ask if she'd like me to give her my phone number so we can arrange things, but she pulls me into a hug. I'm caught so off guard that it takes a few seconds before I wrap my arms around her.

"Oh, Isabel. Thank you, thank you, thank you," April says, her voice shaky. "You have no idea how much you're helping us."

When she sniffles, my eyes start to burn. I blink quickly.

"It's really okay. I'm happy to."

She squeezes me for a few more seconds, then releases me. We both look over at Opal, who's smiling at us.

"Aww, hugs," she says.

April grabs my hand and flashes a smile at me before she looks over at Opal again. "Mom. I have some news."

When April finishes explaining that I'm going to be Opal's caretaker for the summer, Opal's expression goes blank for a few seconds. Then she looks at me and starts to smile.

"You're going to visit me every day?"

"Yes, during the week," I say.

Opal claps her hands and beams. "Oh goodness, how fantastic!"

April walks over to give her mom a hug. I write my phone number on a piece of paper and leave it with her. Then I stand up and start to leave so they can have some time alone.

"Call me and we'll work out when you want me to start," I say.

April says of course. Her eyes are misty as she smiles at me. "I can't thank you enough."

When I'm back in my car, I dial Chantel. She picks up right away.

"Hey, Bel. I'm melting. Like, I'm the wicked witch slowly liquefying into a puddle in my hotel room."

"Still hot?"

"As hell. Remind me never to take a contract in the southwest during the dead of summer. How are you holding up?"

"Pretty good, actually. I, uh, did a thing."

I can picture the tic in Chantel's eyebrow perfectly. She knows that phrase well. I utter it every time I've done something big.

"Good thing or bad thing?" she asks without missing a beat.

"Good. I think."

"Spill."

Chapter Six

When I knock on the front door of April's house, my hand is shaking. How ridiculous.

I shouldn't be so nervous. April wants me to be here, taking care of her mom four days a week while she's at work. *I* want to be here. We've talked on the phone multiple times to iron out the details. Funding has been secured after talking to a social worker friend, so I'm getting paid. April no longer has this financial burden hanging over her head, and I don't have to worry about how I'm going to cover my expenses for the summer while I'm away from the hospital. I've even been by once before so she could show me where everything is, how the appliances work, and so I could get a feel for things before my first official day as Opal's caretaker.

Still, though. My palms are clammy with sweat. First day of work jitters are hard for me to shake, I guess.

But as soon as I see April's smiling face when she opens the door, my heartbeat eases.

"Come in, come in." She steps aside for me to walk into her small-ish two-bedroom home in the Benson neighborhood of Omaha.

"Mom, look who's here."

April walks over to a plush recliner in the corner of the living room where Opal is sitting. I smile at the pink sweatpants and sweater she's wearing today. She takes a second to squint at me before slowly smiling. "Oh! Hello, dear!"

I walk over and touch my hand to her arm, but she pulls me into a hug. I stay hunched like that for a few seconds while April whizzes around me.

"Help yourself to anything in the fridge, Isabel."

When Opal releases me, I turn to April, who's standing next to the recliner, her purse in one hand, a lunch bag in the other. "I'll be home at five-thirty sharp, Mom. Okay?"

"Okay, Bunny," Opal says as she smooths a hand over the front of her sweater.

"I know it's gonna be hot today, but Mom insisted on wearing her favorite sweat suit."

I tell her it's no problem and that I'd be happy to help her change into lighter clothing whenever she wants.

"She normally wants to spend the mornings watching her favorite news show, then a couple of game shows. Then she should be up for some coffee or tea, then a walk around the neighborhood, then lunch. I've written the schedule and all the key numbers down in the kitchen."

I nod along. April's also told me all of this before, but I know she's probably nervous about someone else taking care of her mom.

She presses a kiss to the top of Opal's forehead. "Love you, Mom."

"Love you, Bunny," Opal says, her gaze glued to the television screen as a cheery weatherman details the day's forecast.

April says goodbye and is out the door. I sit on the edge of the couch near Opal, and for the next hour, we watch the news together. Opal is mostly quiet save a few chuckles whenever one of the anchors makes a joke.

When she empties her water glass, I hop up to refill it and fetch a glass for myself. When I return to the living room, she's frowning at a game-show contestant on TV.

"Why in the world did he bid that high? It's a bicycle, for goodness' sake."

"Some models can be pretty expensive these days."

"Ridiculous," she mutters and continues watching. I turn to set my glass on the nearby side table and spot a stack of colorful drawings scrawled on construction paper.

"More drawings from Jonah?" I ask her.

Her face twists in confusion. "Who?"

I work to keep hold of my smile. As sad as it is that Opal has trouble remembering her own great-grandson, I need to get used to it. I don't want to upset her with my reactions.

"Your great-grandson. His name is Jonah," I say with a forced cheeriness to my tone.

I wait quietly for the next several seconds as she turns away, clearly lost in thought.

"That little one April brings around sometimes? With the blond hair and chubby cheeks?"

"Yes. That's him. He's your great-grandson."

Her brow raises all the way to her silver hairline. "I have a great-grandson?"

My mouth twitches for a second, but I catch myself. The slightest hint of guilt seeps through me. Even if she sometimes doesn't remember my name, she clearly has a pleasant memory that she associates with me. But I'm not her family. The fact that her dementia prevents her from remembering her own great-grandson nearly breaks me. It doesn't seem the least bit fair. I'm practically a stranger. If memory were loyal, she would remember him first, not me.

I swallow and steady my smile as I nod. "You have a very adorable great-grandson. April showed me photos."

I point to the wall, where there's a trio of floating wooden shelves adorned with framed photos. On the top is a smiling Jonah.

"That's him."

"Huh." Her eyes take on a faraway look as she gazes at it.

She pivots back to the TV, and for a few minutes we continue watching the game show.

Suddenly, Opal whips her head to me. "I wonder if my parents know about Jonah."

"I'm sure they do."

She's quiet again as she watches the TV screen. I can't help but wonder what she's thinking, how her brain is processing all this information.

It's typical for those with dementia to forget the people close to them, to mix living relatives with ones who have died, to forget who's passed and who's alive, to feel like they're currently living in an event that happened decades ago.

Since Opal is eighty-eight years old, it's likely her parents are gone. But maybe, in a way, it's good that she can't remember they've died. Maybe it's good that she thinks they're still here. There's joy in that—there's hope in that. And she deserves to feel both of those things.

She tilts her head to me, and the expression on her face turns the slightest bit conspiratorial.

"You know, my parents never wanted me to marry Hugh. They thought he wasn't good enough. But I knew better. I knew what a catch he was. So I went ahead and married him anyway." Her head falls back as she laughs. "They were so mad when they heard we eloped. Didn't even come to the reception we had afterwards for family."

"Oh, wow. I'm so sorry to hear that."

Opal waves her hand. "I wasn't. They would have ruined the whole day. But when we started having our babies, that's when they came around. It was a hard road, but we got to a good place eventually."

She sighs, tapping her fingers on her knees. "I should call them. We haven't talked in a while."

"I'm sure they'd love to hear from you."

"Maybe I can ask Bunny for their number later. I can't for the life of me remember what it is."

I tell her that's a great idea, quietly thankful that she didn't ask me to call them for her. I could have fibbed my way through it, like, telling Opal they were busy or to call on a different day, but I don't know if that's how April would want me to handle it. I should ask her later.

"How are your parents?" she asks, catching me off guard.

"Oh. Um, I'm not really sure."

I immediately regret the honesty in my answer, because now she looks worried.

"How come?"

"Just, um, it's been a while since I've seen them."

My mind flashes back to that evening when I came home from work to see Mom sitting on my porch, waiting for me. And then all I can think about is how we snapped at each other, the tears in her eyes, the pleading tone of her voice as she asked me yet again to come to church with her, to get help, to do something, anything so that I could be the person I used to be.

I haven't spoken to her since. She hasn't bothered to call or text. Neither has my dad.

A lump forms in my throat, but I quickly swallow it away, hoping that Opal doesn't pick up on how distraught I am in this moment.

"You don't see them much?" she asks.

"Not really."

"Why?"

I wonder how in the world I can put a positive spin on this so I don't upset her. I want to be honest, but there's no happy way I can describe my relationship with my parents.

"We just get on each other's nerves sometimes," I say after a bit. Not an outright lie, but also a massively oversimplified version of the truth.

I'm relieved when she nods in understanding and pats my hand. "Join the club, dear."

I smile slightly, relieved when she goes back to watching TV. I make her a cup of coffee, and together we sit at the kitchen table as she drinks it.

I'm about to ask if she feels up for a walk when my phone rings.

When I see Keely's name flash across the screen, I tell Opal that I have to take it, but I'll be quick.

"Oh, it's fine. You take your time."

I walk back into the living room and answer, making sure that I can still see Opal in case she falls or wants to stand up and walk around.

"Hey, Keely."

"Oh, wow. You answered."

It shouldn't sting to hear the shock in her voice. I spent the last two-plus years ignoring her. She has every right to think I'd do it again. And even though we reconnected the other night at the Grey Plume, that doesn't erase the rift in our friendship that I caused—that caused her to doubt that I would ever pick up the phone if she was to call me again.

"Of course I answered." My attempt to sound cheery and casual flops. I can tell by the awkward silence that follows.

"Right. Ha. I just . . . I think I just got so used to you never answering," she says before nervously laughing. "I figured I would just leave a voice mail and hope that you'd get back to me."

"Oh, yeah. That makes sense." I try to laugh myself, but it ends up sounding even more strained than Keely's.

"I'm sorry, Isabel," she says. "That sounded terrible."

"No, don't be sorry. You had every right to think that. But, um, I answered." This time when I chuckle, it sounds more flustered than nervous. That's preferable to me for some reason.

"Right."

The fact that I can hear the smile in Keely's voice helps that knot in my throat dissipate.

"I was calling about job leads for you."

"Oh." Suddenly, I realize that I was so focused on preparing to take care of Opal this past week that I forgot I had asked Keely to help me look for a new job.

"Actually, I found a job."

"You did?"

"Yeah, it's kind of a funny story." I fill her in on the situation with Opal and her family. "I'm sorry—I should have told you sooner. I feel so bad." I press my eyes shut, fighting through the wave of guilt that hits me. "You've been spending all this time researching job stuff for me."

"Oh, no worries, it's fine." She says it quickly, with a pitchy lilt to her voice.

Inside, I deflate. That's how she sounds when she's trying to play off that she's not bothered by something. I've heard it when she talked to other people—never me, though.

"Wait," Keely says through a sigh. "It's not fine, Isabel. I'm not mad, but I'm a little hurt. Why didn't you call me to let me know?"

I stammer and fail to think of a single reasonable excuse.

"I just didn't think to call you. I'm sorry," I admit, my face hot with shame.

"I guess I shouldn't be surprised," she says. "Especially after these past two-plus years."

The defeat in her tone slices right through my heart.

"No, Keely, that's not—"

"Can I ask you something?" she says, cutting me off.

"Of course."

"Are you going to disappear on me, like you did before? Because if that's the case, I don't know if I can do this with you, Isabel. I don't know if I can take another instance of you—"

"What? Of course not." My voice squeaks with shock.

"Maybe that's wrong of me to say. I just . . . I guess part of me is afraid that since you don't need my help, you won't want to see me again."

The slight shake in her voice rattles me. Something inside me kicks into gear. I made a huge mistake not keeping Keely in the loop. I need to fix this. I need to make her understand that this was a foolish mistake on my part and I won't do it again—because I can't bear the thought of losing her.

"Keely, I know I messed up a lot of things these past couple of years, but I'm not going to shut you out again. I promise. I made a mistake by not letting you know about this new job, and for that, I'm so sorry. But that wasn't on purpose, I swear."

I wait, my heart thudding in my ears, as the silence on her end of the line stretches for seconds.

"Okay," she says quietly. "I believe you."

"Let's meet up again."

She lets out what sounds like a laugh and a choking sound. "Really? I'd love that."

I tell her I'm busy this week but offer up the weekend.

"I'm gonna paint the nursery this weekend, actually. Theo was supposed to help me do it, but he's out of town on a last-minute work trip. Would that . . . is that even something you'd want to do?"

I smile. "Yeah. That sounds really fun."

We plan for me to drop by Saturday morning. I promise her I'll be there at 9:00 a.m. sharp. When I hang up, Opal is finishing her coffee. She turns to me when I sit back at the table.

"Were those your folks you were talking to?"

I do my best to hold my smile. "No. I'll call them later, though."

She nods once, then lightly taps her hands on the tabletop. "I feel like a walk."

Her cheery tone makes me smile for real this time. "Well then, let's walk."

When we return from a twenty-minute stroll around the neighborhood, I spot April's car in the driveway. I pull my phone from my pocket to make sure I didn't miss a call from her. She wasn't planning on coming home for lunch. I wonder why she's here. Maybe she forgot something.

When I help Opal up the porch steps, I freeze at the sound of April's raised voice coming from inside. A second later, I hear a low voice accompany hers.

It sounds like she's arguing with someone. For a split second, my anxiety spikes. I have no idea what's happening on the other side of the door, and I definitely don't want to thrust Opal into the middle of an argument—that could upset her.

I turn to her before I open the screen door. "Wait here on the porch for a sec, okay? I just have to check something inside real quick."

She says okay. When I unlock the front door and open it, I see April and Evan standing in the living room. Judging by the glare on his face and the furrow in her brow, they're arguing. I glance back at Opal through the screen door to make sure she's still okay standing there by herself, which she is.

"Hi." My gaze darts between them, but they say nothing. "Sorry to interrupt. Opal and I were just coming back from a walk."

Neither of them speaks a word. April nods at me, while Evan aims his glare at me now. I turn around and step onto the porch, then gesture for Opal to come in as I hold the door open for her.

When I lead her back inside, she goes straight for the recliner, not even acknowledging the presence of April or Evan. I do my best to stay off to the side as I help Opal take off her orthopedic sneakers, hoping that whatever Evan and April are arguing about, they can take it elsewhere.

"Could I speak to you for a second? In private."

I glance up at Evan as he looms over me.

"Evan, honey. Don't."

He twists around. "Mom. I just want to talk to her."

"Evan. You absolutely do not need to bother Isabel right now, not when she's taking care of your grandma."

I flinch at the firmness in her tone.

"It's fine, April. I can talk to Evan for a sec," I say quickly, hoping that whatever he wants to talk about with me, I can get it over with quickly and this family dispute can end.

She opens her mouth, but before she can say anything, Evan pipes up.

"Great. Let's go in the kitchen."

He stomps away, and I follow him, still confused as to what's going on.

"What's up?" I say as we stand facing each other.

He crosses his arms over his broad chest. I notice that even though his hair is pulled back like every other time I've seen him, it looks extra messy today. A million flyaways frame his face, and it almost looks like he didn't even bother to brush his hair before tying it up.

"What do you think you're doing?"

I lean back at his accusatory tone. "What?"

"Why did you offer to be the caregiver for my grandma?" His stony expression matches the bluntness of his voice, and it's throwing me off.

"What are you . . . what do you mean?"

"You don't even know her. You're a stranger. But for some reason, you think that qualifies you to be her caregiver?"

My head spins as I struggle to take in the obvious anger Evan feels for me in this moment.

I hold up a hand. "First of all, your mom agreed to this arrangement."

"After you offered it up," he snaps.

My hand falls to my side as my skin turns hot. "What's wrong with that? I was visiting your grandma at her old memory care facility, and your mom stopped by. She was obviously upset and explained the situation. So I offered to help."

A bitter chuckle falls from his lips. "Yeah. So helpful."

All the muscles inside me tense. "Would you like to explain why you're attacking me for helping your grandma right now? I feel a bit out of the loop."

My snide remark earns me a glower from Evan. "Gladly. One, you had no business showing up to visit her at the memory care facility out of the blue."

"It wasn't out of the blue!" My throat aches to keep from shouting. I take a breath. "Your mom invited me. Remember that card you told me she gave me? She wrote in there that I was welcome to visit your grandma if I ever wanted to. So I did."

"Of course she'd do that," he mutters before pinning me with that angry stare once more. "What exactly is your agenda here?"

I almost laugh. "My agenda? What are you . . ."

He darts out and back into the living room.

"Mom, did you know that Isabel is on leave from the hospital for the whole summer?"

I nearly choke. What the hell? I walk back into the living room and march up to him, feeling every one of my five-foot-four inches as I stand next to his broad, six-foot-tall frame.

"How did you know that?" I demand.

"Background check," he says without even looking at me.

My head spins. I didn't even know a leave of absence from work would show up on a background check.

"You ran a background check on me?"

He finally turns to face me. "Of course I did. You're looking after my ill family member, and my mom didn't think to do one herself."

April sighs beside us. She looks more exasperated than surprised at what Evan has said.

"Evan, honey, I told you doing another background check wasn't necessary. She's already had one through the program that's paying her. I saw a copy of it, and it's all fine."

"Mom, come on. Some of those agencies are run on a shoestring budget and probably don't have the resources to do a thorough check. That's why it was necessary to do one on my own," Evan says before directing his glare at me once more. "I tried to get more details about Isabel's situation by calling the hospital. When I asked for you, the person said you weren't available because you're on leave for the summer."

The way he says the word *situation* comes off like he's mocking me.

"Just what kind of person is able to take an entire summer off work on zero notice to help a person they don't even know? You wanna explain that? Seems a little suspicious if you ask me."

I'm clenching my jaw so hard, the back of my skull starts to ache. "You had no right to do that."

This jerkoff. He could jeopardize my standing at the hospital with this amateur-private-investigator crap he's trying to pull. I'll have to call Martha later and explain this whole mess to her . . . and hope that I still have a job to go back to in three months, despite Evan's out-of-line antics.

He turns to his mom, ignoring me. "Is that the kind of person you want looking after your own mother, day after day, week after week for the rest of the summer? Someone who's clearly got something to hide?"

As much as I want to rage at Evan, I can't. It would just make things worse. So I spend the next few seconds unclenching my jaw and accepting the fact that I need to come clean to April about my leave from work. Being honest is the only way to dig myself out of this hole.

"April, Evan is right. I'm on leave from the hospital because . . . well, because I've been suspended until the end of summer for arguing with a physician."

She blinks at me, clearly unmoved. "Okay."

I'm thrown by her lack of reaction but push through to explain. "He's going through a divorce and had been lashing out at staff, so I went to check on him, and he yelled at me before slamming a door in my face. I admittedly didn't handle it well. I swore at him. And yelled back. It was incredibly unprofessional, and I deserved to be suspended. I've never, ever been reprimanded at work before, though. I've never even been written up. This was a onetime incident, not that it excuses my behavior. But I wanted to explain. And I'm sorry I didn't disclose this to you before. I should have."

When April shrugs, I'm speechless.

"I went off on a few doctors myself a couple times when Mom was in and out of the hospital over the years. Some of them can be real jerks. What you did isn't all that bad, dear. I probably would have done the same."

I glance over to Evan, who's staring at his mom with his mouth half open.

She turns to him. "I understand you're concerned about your grandma, honey. I love that you care so much. But I wasn't born yesterday. I wouldn't let just anyone into my home to take care of my own mother. Trust me that I know what's best in this situation, okay?"

Evan lets out the heaviest sigh I've ever heard. "Mom, I really think—"

April waves a hand, like she can't be bothered to listen to her own son for a second longer. I can't say that I blame her.

"Mom, would you just—"

"Evan."

Her normally cheery tone has turn pointed and hard. I don't miss the way his shoulders jerk back in response.

"Isabel is wonderful," she says. "Your grandma seems happy with her. That's all I care about. And that's the end of this discussion. Do you hear me?"

Evan's head droops. He doesn't say a word. April glances at the brass clock on the wall. "I need to get back to work. Don't they need you at the restaurant?"

Evan winces as he checks the time before looking back at April. "I think I should come by the house from time to time," he mumbles. "Just to make sure everything's okay."

My mouth falls open. This guy is beyond brazen, openly admitting that he's planning to keep tabs on me. What exactly does he think I'm going to do to his grandmother? The way he's acting, it's like he assumes I'm going to kidnap her and hold her for ransom.

Before I can say anything, April wags a finger up at Evan. "Did I not make myself clear, young man? You most certainly will not do that. I won't have my own son acting like some sort of deranged bodyguard. Good lord, I raised you better than that."

Evan's hazel-green eyes go wide. I'm guessing it's been a while since he's received a scolding from his mom.

His shoulders hunch forward, like he's barely able to bear the brunt of his mother's disappointment.

April flashes a sad smile at me. "I'm sorry about all this."

"It's okay."

"It's really not, dear. I'm quite embarrassed by my son's behavior." She aims a pointed expression at Evan. "Don't you have something to say to Isabel before you leave?"

He purses his lips before turning to me. "I'm sorry."

I nod once. Fine if he has concerns about me as a caretaker for his grandma. He could have politely asked to talk to me, and I would have happily answered any of his questions—but to drop by unannounced and angrily lob accusations at me is out of line.

I'm aching to tell him off, but I bite my tongue. This isn't the time or the place. And it's nowhere near the appropriate or mature way to handle it. Best to just let it go and hope that I don't have to see him much over the summer.

I stay quiet as he leans down to hug Opal goodbye. But before he can wrap his arms around her, she jerks back.

"Who are you?"

There's a sting in my chest as I observe the pain that plays across Evan's face. A hard swallow glides down his stubbled throat before he speaks. "I'm Evan, Grandma."

Her expression remains blank, even as he kisses her cheek. She doesn't squeeze back when he hugs her. Her arms stay still against her sides. April aims a pitying stare at him as he walks out the door. I notice his shoulders are hunched, like he's defeated.

Once they're gone, I turn to Opal to ask what she wants for lunch.

"Who was that man?" she asks me.

The sting intensifies. As much as I dislike Evan, he doesn't deserve to be forgotten by his grandmother.

"That's your grandson. His name's Evan."

"Evan." She says it like she's learning a new word. "Evan."

She turns to look out the window, and I head into the kitchen to make her lunch.

Chapter Seven

"I just want to make sure everything's okay. I mean, I know it's not . . . since I'm, you know, technically suspended from my job."

I stop to clear my throat and catch my breath. I'm in the middle of doing damage control while on the phone with Martha the week after arguing with Evan, when he admitted he called her in an attempt to dig up dirt on my employment status at the hospital. I still can't get over the fact that he ambushed me in front of his family and accused me of having some deceptive motive in offering to take care of Opal.

I peer from the kitchen where I'm standing into the living room to check on Opal. She's still sitting in her recliner watching a game show. Her green-hazel gaze is fixed on the screen as she watches a trio of people spin a giant wheel for cash prizes.

I force myself to take a slow, silent breath before speaking to Martha again. I probably sound like a frantic, babbling mess. I called her the day this all happened, but she was gone on vacation, so I left multiple messages on her voice mail explaining the situation. This is her first day back, and I'm determined to right this mess.

The only time over the past several days that I wasn't actively worrying about what Evan did to jeopardize my standing at the hospital was when I helped Keely paint the nursery. Those few hours of laughing and catching up were a perfect distraction, but the moment I left her house, it was back to obsessing whether or not I'd have a job at the hospital to come back to.

"I'm just really sorry that you had to deal with Evan calling and pestering you like that," I say to Martha. "He's really protective of his grandma, which I understand, but the way he tried to involve you in this whole situation wasn't right. It won't happen again, I promise."

"Oh, kiddo, it's all fine."

Martha's easy tone is a comfort. I start to feel my muscles unclench.

I'm about to thank her, but she starts to speak. "Really, Isabel, you didn't need to call me. The messages you left me explained the situation just fine. So did your email."

The slight exasperation in her tone throws me off. "Oh. Right. I just wanted to make sure."

"Of course," she says with a sigh. "Look, I know this might be hard for you to hear, kiddo. But you shouldn't really be calling and emailing like this. Your suspension stipulates that you take time away from the hospital. When you do things like this, it interferes with that."

Her gentle delivery does little to soften the blow of her words.

"I guess I didn't realize that."

"It's all right. And you don't have to worry. That young man's call about you didn't affect my view of you in the slightest. But I need you to take this suspension seriously."

A mix of relief and paranoia courses through me. I shove both aside and focus on what Martha's said. I don't want to further jeopardize my standing at the hospital. I need to be able to return to my job at the end of the summer. That means I need to cut off all contact until then.

"I'll do that, Martha. Thank you."

"Hang in there. And try not to stress so much. It'll all be okay."

She wishes me a good week, I tell her the same, and then I hang up. I walk back out into the living room.

"Oh, I love this song!" Opal snaps her fingers as a commercial for a cleaning service plays on TV.

I hand her a glass of water, then stand and listen with her. It's a standard big-band sound with saxophone, trumpets, trombones, and a rhythm section. Opal sways her head back and forth while she sits in her recliner.

"I don't know this one," I say.

She finishes sipping her water and continues grooving along. I set the water glass on the side table and sit down in my usual spot at the end of the couch where we spend the mornings together.

"'My Sweetie Sparrow,'" Opal says. "It's my favorite. I sang it all the time when I was little. Drove my brother crazy."

She sings softly along to the lyrics while I look up the song on my phone. I'm stunned at how well she remembers it. She's getting almost every word right.

But then I remember that musical memories are often preserved in the minds of people with dementia. Areas of the brain that are linked to musical memory tend to be undamaged by the disease, which is probably why Opal can sing along to this song.

The commercial ends, and I skim part of the lyrics as she focuses back on the game show.

> My beautiful darling, so kind, so sweet
> My lovely love, every time we meet
> Every time with you feels new
> Your diamond eyes that shine like dew
> Hair that's soft as a feather
> Scent that's sweeter than heather
> Voice like a songbird
> Most heavenly sound I've heard
>
> My sweetie sparrow
> Please never leave me
> My sweetie sparrow
> I'll love you for eternity

Dreaming of you night after night
Seeing you day after day
It's never, ever enough
I'll want you always, always

My sweetie sparrow
Please never leave me
My sweetie sparrow
I'll love you for eternity

I skim the name of the songwriter at the very end. Evan Conklin. I wonder if Evan knows that he has the same name as the composer of his grandma's favorite song.

Just the thought of him brings back the memory of our blow-out last week. I take a breath to quell the surge of fury inside me. Thankfully, he hasn't stopped by since then. Even though April warned him not to, I wouldn't put it past him. If he was willing to call my boss in an attempt to dig up dirt on me, I'm certain he'd have no problem dropping by unannounced to pick another fight with me in the hopes of getting me fired.

But every day so far has been blissfully uneventful. Just me spending time with Opal, chatting, watching television together, sharing meals, and going for walks when the weather's not too humid and hot and she feels up for it.

A lot of people would probably think it's boring to do this day after day, but there's something so soothing about being here and sharing in these simple activities with her. It's relatively low stress, which counts for a lot. And Opal has been happy to see me every day so far. I'm just now realizing what a positive effect it has on your mood when you're around someone who genuinely enjoys being with you.

The game show cuts to a commercial, and Opal turns to me. "I'd like to call my parents."

"Oh. Okay. Well, um . . ."

I internally scramble to figure out what to do. Opal hasn't mentioned her parents since the first day I started looking after her. Because of that, I never asked April what I should do if she asked for them again.

"Let me see if I have their number." I scroll aimlessly through the contacts on my phone for several seconds to make it look like I'm doing something. I look up. "I'm sorry. I don't have it."

When Opal's face starts to twist in sadness, I hold my breath. Shit. Is she going to get upset?

She nods like she understands, even though her lips start to tremble. I can't think of a single comforting thing to say or do as her eyes water.

"I just wanted to say hello to them. I—I haven't spoken to them in so long." Her voice goes watery and wobbly, and I know there's no way I'm going to be able to just sit here and watch her cry.

"Wait." I recall April pointing out the landline in her bedroom the day she showed me around the house before I started working here. And then I have an idea.

I hand Opal my phone, then grab a tissue from the nearby table and dab until her cheeks are dry. "Your mom is going to call you on this phone in just a sec. I forgot!"

The way her eyes instantly brighten and her mouth curves up into a smile sends an arrow of emotion straight to my heart. I swallow to steady my tone.

"I'll go into the bedroom so you two can have a conversation on your own, okay?"

Her smile widens. "Okay."

I pop into the bedroom, then push the door until it's partway shut. And then I lower quietly to the floor and sit against the bed. If I lean forward, I can see Opal sitting in her recliner through the inches-wide crack between the door and the doorway. Perfect. If I keep my voice down, she won't be able to hear me while I talk on the phone, and I'll still be able to keep an eye on her.

I grab the phone from the nightstand and dial my cell number. Opal answers on the second ring.

"Mom? Is that you?"

I swallow back the ache in my throat. "It's me, sweetie. Hi."

A tinge of panic hits. Did her mom ever call her sweetie? Will Opal even buy this? I didn't bother to ask what pet names her parents used for her. If she finds out that it's me pretending to be her mom, will she get mad? Will she be so upset that she'll refuse to see me anymore? What will April think if she tells her?

But then Opal laughs. It's the lightest, most joyful sound. "It's so good to hear your voice, Mom. It's been so long."

I let out a slow, silent breath as I loosen. "It really has. I-I'm sorry it's taken a while for me to call you. How are you?"

"Oh, I'm good. Same old, same old. Just spending most days at home, watching my shows, going on walks, spending time with a very lovely lady who takes care of me."

"That sounds so nice. How's your family? April and the kids?"

"Oh, fine, fine."

I'm relieved when she chats about April for a few minutes. It gives me a moment to regroup, to think of what I'm going to say when it's my turn to speak.

"I heard that song on TV. My favorite song. You remember it?"

"Of course I do. 'My Sweetie Sparrow.' You used to sing it all the time when you were little. Drove your brother crazy."

A tinge of guilt hits me for using that bit of personal information that she shared with me just a bit ago to trick her into thinking I'm her mom. But when she laughs at what I've said, the guilt fades. She sounds so happy in the moment. All of this is okay as long as she's happy.

Opal starts to sing a few bars of the song just as the front door squeaks open. I lean up and check the clock on the nightstand. It's still three hours before April is due home. But then I hear Evan's voice.

"Hey, Grandma. What are you . . ."

I lean forward to peer through the crack in the doorway and see Opal frowning up at Evan, who's standing in front of her. She presses her index finger to her lips, then points to her hand holding the phone.

"Oh. Sorry."

Inside of me, panic sets in. Evan is going to be pissed when he realizes what I'm doing. He already hates that I'm here watching over his grandma, but when he finds out I'm pretending to be his deceased great-grandmother, he'll probably be even angrier. What if he thinks that's yet another reason to suspect that I'm a dishonest weirdo trying to infiltrate his family? He was hell-bent on getting me fired before, and this is certain to add fuel to that fire.

"Is there someone with you, Opal? Do you have to go?" I say, trying to keep my tone easy.

"Never mind that, Mom," she says.

My eyes are glued on Evan as a confused frown mars his face. He starts to look around.

"Um, Opal. I should go."

"No, wait! Not yet. Please just . . ."

My heart races as I press my eyes shut. The ache in my chest intensifies at hearing Opal's pleading tone.

"Mom, do you remember when you'd take us to the lake and feed the ducks?"

I open my eyes, trying to refocus. "Of course I do."

"Remember how scared I always was at first to feed them? I was so afraid they'd bite my fingers off." She chuckles.

"Yes. You were so little. So cute."

"You'd always hold my hand and walk up to them with me. You'd tell me it's okay, that there was nothing to be afraid of. And then you'd show me how easy it was to feed them bread. And I'd stand there, my hand in your hand, and watch you do it. And then I'd be brave enough to feed them myself. Remember?"

The joy in Opal's softly spoken words hits something deep inside me. A memory I haven't recalled in years.

Closing my eyes, I pull it up in my mind.

I'm six years old. Chantel is three. We're standing side by side near a fountain at a park surrounded by dozens of pigeons. I had a fistful of seeds in one hand and Chantel's hand in the other. Tears streamed down my face. I was so freaked out by the birds everywhere. They kept running up to me, crowding me, clearly wanting the birdseed in my hand. But I was too scared to feed them.

Until Mom walked up and crouched down next to me.

"It's okay, *anak*. Here, I'll show you how to do it."

I remember everything. The crimson color of her lipstick. The way her suede jacket felt impossibly soft when my hand brushed against it. How her black hair was longer then, and how she styled it with hot rollers.

How she kissed my forehead, held her hand underneath my tiny fist, and told me to let go. I did.

All the birdseed fell into her palm. With her other hand, she pinched bits of seed and tossed them toward the pigeons. They happily pecked away.

"Now you try, *anak*."

I did exactly what she did. And then I stopped crying. I watched with wide, unblinking eyes as the pigeons ate the seed. When all the seeds were gone, I grabbed Mom's hand and looked up at her. She was smiling.

"I did it, Mom."

"You did it, *anak*. Way to go."

It's not till I open my eyes that I realize I'm crying. My cheeks are soaked with tears, and my eyes are burning and blurry.

"Do you remember that day, Mom?" Opal asks.

I clear my throat and wipe my eyes with the back of my hand. Then I cover the receiver of the phone so that when I sniffle, she doesn't hear me.

"Yes. I remember. I can picture it right now."

"I can too. It was the best day, wasn't it?"

"It really was." I pause and swallow once more to steady my voice. "You were so brave feeding those ducks. I was so proud of you."

When I look up toward the crack in the doorway, I freeze. Evan stands in the living room, and he's looking right at me.

But his expression isn't what I expect. Instead of a glare, his stare has gone soft. Tender almost.

Opal is speaking again, but I can't focus on what she's saying. My mind is too busy in a panicked scramble, wondering how much he's heard me say.

"Opal, sweetie. It's been so much fun talking to you, but I have to go, okay?"

"Okay, Mom. Call me again soon, will you? I want to talk to Dad too."

"Of course. I promise."

I break eye contact with Evan and gaze down at my knees, which are tucked against my chest.

"I love you, Mom."

"I love you too."

When I hang up, I take a few moments to wipe my face on my T-shirt; then I close my eyes and force myself to take a long, deep breath.

When I walk out to check on Opal, Evan's not in the living room anymore.

I turn to Opal, but before I can ask her about Evan, she starts chatting.

"My mom called me."

I glance down at her. The pure joy on her face grounds me back in this moment. "That's wonderful," I say. "How is she?"

"Really good. It was so nice to hear her voice."

I smile down at her, hoping she doesn't notice how blotchy and red my skin is from crying.

"Have you talked to your parents?"

Her question catches me off guard. I stammer for a few seconds, but before I can answer her, Evan walks out of the kitchen and into the living room. He stops and stands, facing me, that same tender look from before on his face. His gaze is hesitant, though. Almost like he's working up the nerve just to look at me.

"Hey," I murmur.

"Hey." He fumbles with the hem of his T-shirt, like he's nervous to say more. "Can we talk for a sec?"

The muscles in my midsection tighten. Even though his demeanor and tone are gentle, the last time he asked to speak to me, we were nearly yelling at each other. I have every reason to expect that it'll happen again.

I nod and follow him into the kitchen. I roll my shoulders back slightly, gearing up for another fight.

"Are you okay?"

His nearly whispered tone throws me off completely. I wasn't expecting that.

"Um, what?" I almost laugh.

"You were crying while you were talking on the phone, and I just wanted to make sure you were okay."

"Oh. Um, yeah. I'm fine."

He lifts an eyebrow, like he doesn't quite believe me. It doesn't come off as judgmental, though. More like concerned.

"Really. I'm good."

Maybe it's Evan's change in demeanor, how his gaze over me is now watchful instead of angry and suspicious, that has me thinking I should be honest with him in this moment instead of on guard.

Inside, I feel myself loosen. "Okay, I guess I'm a little emotional at the moment. Talking with Opal, pretending to be her mom, was a lot more intense than I thought it would be."

I opt to leave out how our conversation reminded me of my own complicated relationship with my parents. He doesn't need to hear that.

He nods like he understands, and when he doesn't speak right away, I realize he's waiting for me to say more—and that I should probably explain why I was pretending to be his great-grandmother just now.

"Opal insisted on talking to her parents, she was getting so sad, I didn't know what to do," I say quickly. "I'm sorry, I know that was dishonest to pretend to be her mom, but—"

"No." He cuts me off with a shake of his head. "Please don't apologize. What you did just now . . . that was amazing. I'm the one who should be sorry."

I hold back a stammer. That's a shocker.

He rests his hands on his hips and takes a breath. Sunlight streaming through the nearby window paints Evan in a glow. I can see features in his face I haven't noticed before. Dark circles under his eyes and a faint set of crow's-feet. He looks tired. Sad. Beaten up. Stressed.

"I'm sorry, Isabel." When he sighs, his shoulders hunch slightly, like it's taking all his strength to hold himself upright. "I'm so sorry for how I've been acting toward you. I've been an asshole. I know that probably means nothing to you, given I've apologized to you before and then gotten mad at you again."

I think back to that night when he apologized to me for the first time in the back of his restaurant, only to angrily confront me with a background check days later.

"I feel like I need to explain myself to you," he says. "Not that it excuses my behavior, but just so you have the full story. So you know what a mess I am right now." He hesitates, then tugs at his hair. "I was angry before because I was jealous. Of you."

My mouth falls open slightly at his admission.

"I'm jealous of the way my grandma is around you. She's happy. She smiles at you. She hugs you. She remembers you even though she doesn't really know you all that well. And she doesn't do any of that with me. She used to, but not anymore. She doesn't even remember me. And that really, really hurts."

When his eyes glisten, he blinks hard. It's a few seconds before he opens them.

"It's hard for me to grapple with it all. My grandma is . . . was . . . such a huge part of my life. She helped my mom raise my sister and me. Our dad died when we were little, so it was a struggle. But she was always there. And it's the hardest thing in the world to see her fade away little by little . . . to see her slowly forget me and my sister and my nephew."

He scrubs a hand over his face as he looks away for a moment.

"I know that doesn't excuse how I've treated you. But I wanted to explain myself. I had no right to be so hostile to you. And I'm working on sorting my shit out so that I won't be like that around you anymore."

I stay quiet as I try to process what he's just told me.

"I get it," I finally say. "I'd be mad, too, if I were in your position."

A dazed look flashes across his face.

"I'm just trying to do what I can to make your grandma happy," I say. "And to help out your mom. I'm not trying to hurt your feelings or undermine you."

"I know that," he says. "I mean, logically I know that. It's just, emotionally it's been rough having her go cold toward me and then seeing her warm up to a stranger. But what you did with her just now, talking to her as her mom, that was . . ." He shakes his head, almost like he's in disbelief. "She looked and sounded so happy."

"I was afraid you'd think it was sneaky and manipulative."

"I didn't. At all."

There's a conviction in his words that hits me hard.

"I don't really know what I'm doing, Evan. When it comes to taking care of your grandma, I mean." I hold back a wince. God, that sounded horrible.

But he doesn't seem fazed by what I've said. In fact, he looks captivated by what I'm admitting.

"I just mean that I'm trying to do what I can to keep her in good spirits because I know that's really important for people with dementia. I don't know if your mom told you, but I worked in a memory care facility earlier. Random things can set them off sometimes or send them spiraling or make them feel depressed. And I'm terrified of having that happen to your grandma. So I just try to focus on what makes her happy."

"She started talking about her mom and dad a lot these past few months, right before she fell and hurt herself," he says. "She'd mention wanting to talk to them, but we had no idea what to even do. It always made her so sad when my mom or my sister or I would tell her that she couldn't talk to them or see them anymore. But you figured out a way to make it happen. You gave her a way to talk to her mom again. Thank you for that." A hard swallow moves down his throat. "I'm sorry I interrupted your phone call. And that I upset you. I didn't mean to make you cry."

It takes me a second to realize what he's talking about. "Oh. No, you—you're not the reason I was crying."

"Oh."

My face heats as I try to explain. "It was just a really emotional moment, talking to Opal, pretending to be her mom when I wasn't sure if it was even the right thing to do. Even though it made her so happy, it felt so deceptive to pretend to be someone I'm not."

"It was the right thing," he says with kindness.

"And it, um, reminded me of some family stuff I'm sorting out too." I swallow, surprised at just how candid I'm being with him now. But something about the rawness of our conversation compels me to be honest.

"I'm sorry you're going through that," he says. "I hope it all ends up okay."

"Me too."

We share another stretch of silence before he speaks.

"You can do that—pretend to be her mom, I mean—whenever she asks for it. Or whenever you think it would make her happy."

There's a hesitation in his tone, like he's not quite sure he should be saying any of this.

"It's okay with you?"

"Yeah. I just want her to be as happy as possible now." He pauses to clear his throat. "And if I can't be the one to do that for her, I'm just grateful that someone else can."

The way his voice trembles through his last few words lands hard and deep. It's not pity I feel for Evan. It's something else; it makes me ache for him. There's a tinge of pain radiating through me at hearing just how much it hurts him to know that his presence no longer makes his grandma happy.

I can't think of a single comforting thing to say to him. I start to turn away to check on Opal, but he clears his throat. When I look at him again, he's hesitating, like he's working up the nerve to speak. "Can I be here the next time you pretend to be her mom? She hardly ever looks that happy when I'm around anymore, and I just thought . . ."

When he clears his throat again, I notice that glassy look in his eyes. He's trying not to cry again.

My chest squeezes tight as I reach out and touch his arm. "Absolutely. Can you come by tomorrow around this time?"

He blinks a few times before a small smile tugs at his lips. "Yes."

He says goodbye to Opal before heading for the front door. But before he opens it, he turns back to me. "Thanks, Isabel."

"Of course."

When he shuts the door behind him, I ask Opal if she'd like an afternoon snack. But instead of answering, she frowns up at me.

"Have you talked to your parents?"

It's a repeat of her question from minutes ago. And it's a sign that I can't afford to ignore anymore.

"No, I haven't spoken to them," I say. "But I will."

This time, it's not a lie. This time, I mean it.

As soon as I go home that night, I pull my phone out of my purse and dial Mom's cell phone number.

"Anak." She's breathless, like she can't believe I called her.

"Hi, Mom. How are you?"

"I'm fine. How are you? Are you okay?"

"Yeah. I'm good. I just . . ."

I contemplate diving right in to an apology for my part in our argument the last time she came over. But I don't. I ask her something else instead.

"Mom, do you remember when you took us to feed the pigeons? I must have been, like, six. I wouldn't stop crying because I was so freaked out."

There's a long pause on her end. "Yes. I think about that day a lot. You were so little. And so scared of the birds."

I let out a weak laugh. "I cried a lot that day."

"You did." She pauses for a moment. "Do you remember when we flew to Manila to see your *apong?*" she asks after a moment. "You were six. It was a week after that day with the birds."

"Yeah. That was my first time on an airplane—that I could remember, I mean."

"You were so excited. You insisted on a window seat so you could see the clouds."

The smile in her voice sends a throb to the base of my throat.

"Do you remember how excited you were to tell your *apong* about how brave you were to feed the birds?"

The memory surfaces in my mind, like an air bubble slowly floating to the surface of water.

"I remember."

"We were walking by these shops. You were holding *Apong*'s hand. And then a bird flew by, close to the ground. And you pointed at it and said, 'I'm not scared of you, bird.'"

Mom lets out a laugh so soft, so light, I'm jarred. It's been ages since I've heard her make that sound. It's enough to send a wave of emotion crashing through me as that moment replays in my head. I remember the soft feel of *Apong* Marie's fingers wrapped around mine, how the wrinkled skin on the top of her hand looked like tissue paper. I remember how her head fell back as she cackled when I said that, and how everyone around us turned to look, it was so loud.

"I remember," I say quietly, my voice thick.

"She'd give anything to see you again." Mom's tone is hesitant, like she's afraid of how I'll react to what she's said.

But instead of the defensiveness that I expect, instead of the excuses I'd normally have ready to spew at the tip of my tongue, all I feel is that ache in my throat as it spreads down my neck and across my chest. It lands somewhere deep in the pit of my stomach, settling right under my heart. With each beat, the ache intensifies.

And I know without a doubt the only thing that would ever make this ache go away is to see my *apong*.

It's a realization that hits with a gentle impact. It soothes that ache inside me.

Maybe I could do it. Maybe someday soon, I could visit *Apong* and the rest of the family.

The thought doesn't send a tidal wave of panic through me. It must be a sign.

"I miss *Apong* Marie," I admit.

"She misses you too. So much." When Mom says nothing more, when she doesn't press me with a million comments on how I need to drop everything and visit my grandmother and the rest of my family in the Philippines, I'm jarred. I figured she would.

I open my mouth to say the words, but they don't come. Not yet anyway—but maybe soon.

"You were so patient with me that day with the birds," I finally say.

"Of course I was. I'm your mom."

I swallow back the *sorry* that rests on the tip of my tongue. It's not enough. It never will be. Instead, I choose the words I should have said ages ago.

"Thank you for being patient with me that day and every day since then. And before then."

"Oh, *anak*."

The way her voice shakes, it sends instant tears to my eyes. I blink, and they fall one after another down my face.

Always so patient. Every time I had a temper tantrum. Every time I mouthed off to her as an angsty adolescent. Every time I shoved away whatever snack or meal she made me when I was a picky kid. When I stopped and started a million hobbies. Every time I whined and complained about the silliest, most insignificant thing. Every time I pushed her away. Every time I ignored her calls and texts and messages. She was always there.

"Every day with you is a joy. Nothing will ever change that."

Her words settle deep inside me. In the center of my heart, in the deepest recesses of my brain, in every muscle and bone, in every nerve and fiber.

I know without a doubt I'll remember her speaking those words forever.

"I love you, Mom."

"I love you too, *anak*."

That night when I fall asleep, I dream of Mom and me standing on the edge of a lake, holding hands, surrounded by ducks and pigeons.

Chapter Eight

"You know what I'm in the mood for? Red meat."

I smile at Opal as I help her settle back on the recliner and flip on the TV. "What, like steak?"

She shakes her head. "Not quite. More like lamb. Oh!" She points her finger up. "Shepherd's pie! I would love some shepherd's pie."

"That sounds delicious and hearty."

"Mm-hmm." She nods as she focuses on the daytime talk show I've turned on for her.

"When April comes home, I'll let her know that's what you're craving. Maybe you can have it for dinner later this week."

I think about Evan, how he's a chef, and wonder if he'd know how to make shepherd's pie. I check the clock. He's due here soon.

The conversation we had yesterday after he saw me on the phone with Opal was an uncomfortable and emotional one, but I'm relieved it happened. It helped us clear the air, and it helped me understand what exactly Evan is going through. He's clearly hurting. And hopefully what I have planned for today will offer him the slightest bit of comfort.

My phone buzzes with a text. When I see that it's from Keely, I read it right away.

Keely: LOVING the way the nursery is coming together!! Thank you again for helping me paint it!

She texts a photo of the nursery decked out in furniture. There's a crib, changing table, rocking chair, and dresser.

Me: It looks so pretty. Light gray was definitely the right color choice for the walls!

Keely: Aww thanks!

Keely: I think you're right, the yellow, gray, and white bedding and color scheme is perfect, no matter if it's a boy or a girl.

Ever since I went over to Keely's house to help paint her nursery, we've been texting, almost as frequently as old times. Every time I get a message from her, I smile. It's bliss having my best friend back in my life.

Me: I can't believe you're waiting until you give birth to find out the gender. I wouldn't be patient enough haha.

Keely: There are so few genuinely wonderful surprises in life. This is one of them, and I totally want to milk it for all it's worth ☺

I smile down at my phone. That's Keely. So joyful about everything.

Keely: You should come over and hang out on Sunday! I got this sparkling grape juice we can try. Not as good as champagne of course, but better than nothing haha.

I'm texting Keely that I'll be there when the lock on the front door clicks. When I look up and see Evan, I notice just how different he looks today. He's standing taller, and that slight twist to his expression is gone. He's not smiling, but he looks lighter. Happier.

When he walks over to Opal, she squints up at him. He hesitates, and his eyes turn shy and sad.

"Hi, Grandma."

She doesn't answer, instead giving him the same reaction as always: a confused stare while leaning away from him as he stands near her. Then she turns back to the TV. He lets out a sigh, his shoulders slumping. He starts to move like he's going to lean down and hug her, but then she holds up her hand.

"Get away from me."

I hold my breath at the bitterness in her voice. I don't miss the way Evan pulls back slightly, how his mouth parts open as if he's just gotten the wind knocked out of him, how he doesn't blink in the seconds that follow. He just stands back and stares, absorbing the rejection from his grandma.

"Who are you?" She sounds more bewildered now as she gazes up at him.

Evan pulls his lips into his mouth before swallowing. And then I notice how shiny his eyes are, how his breath shudders when he exhales.

Part of me wants to step back into the kitchen so that I'm no longer an observer to the pain of this scene: a grandmother in the throes of dementia forgetting her beloved grandson.

But part of me wants to do something, anything, to help. And I think I'll be able to . . . if I can convince Evan.

I pull my phone out of the back pocket of my jeans and walk over to Opal.

"Opal, guess what? Your dad is going to call you."

Her response to my cheery news is the same impossibly wide smile she made yesterday when I told her that her mom would be calling her.

"Oh my gosh, really?"

"Yes. Just hang on and wait for him to call. We'll leave so you can talk in private, okay?"

I grab Evan by the arm and lead him to April's room, then close the door halfway. When I pick up the landline and motion for him to sit on the edge of the bed, he looks dazed.

"What are you . . ."

"Talk to her and pretend to be her dad, okay?"

He stammers for a second. "B-but I don't . . . I never met him. He died before I was born."

"It's okay. I promise that won't matter."

"But I thought . . . you're the one who was supposed to talk to her today. I was just supposed to hang back and listen."

I shake my head but gently squeeze his arm. "I really think it should be you, Evan."

A moment passes before Evan nods. There's a determined look on his face now, which is a million times better than the raw pain I saw moments ago.

"Just talk to her like you normally would," I say. "The only difference is she thinks she's talking to her dad."

I dial my number and hand the phone to him. The wail of my phone ringing echoes from just outside the door.

"Dad? Dad, is that you?"

Evan cradles the phone to his face with both hands. He opens his mouth, but it's a second before he says anything.

"Yes. Hello, Opal."

I stand near the door, peering through the opening at Opal, holding my breath as I wait for her to say something.

"Dad! Hi! Oh, I've missed you so much! It's so nice to hear your voice."

Evan's mouth slowly curves up in a smile. "I miss you too."

I stand off to the side, trying to stay as quiet as possible while they chat. Evan starts off hesitant, speaking slowly, like he's unsure. He sounds a lot like I did when I talked to her on the phone as her mom.

But the more they talk, the more comfortable he grows. His smile widens. His soft chuckles turn to full-on laughs. His shoulders, which started out hunched right under his ears, ease lower and lower.

When I peer through the crack in the door to check on Opal, she's smiling and laughing too. They're both so happy.

Just then, there's a vibrating sound. Evan pulls his phone from the pocket of his jeans. As he stares down at the screen, a struggle plays out on his face. The sound fades, but it's clear he has to go.

"Opal, I'm so sorry, but I have to go."

"Oh. Okay." Her tone falters the slightest bit. When I turn to look at her, her expression starts to fade.

"But I'll call you again later, okay?" Evan says. "I promise I will."

Opal closes her eyes, smiling once more. She nods once. "I can't wait. I love you, Dad. So much."

For a long moment, Evan doesn't say a word. He just stares at his lap and swallows. "I love you too, Opal. So much, you don't even know."

He hangs up and sets the landline back on the nightstand. For a few moments, he stays sitting, staring at the wall, the corners of his mouth turned up slightly. The look on his face is something between disbelief and joy.

When he stands, he turns to me. "Thank you for that."

There's something about the reverence in his tone. It hits hard, like a shove, but it lands gently, like a blanket skimming my skin.

His eyes glisten again, but this time there's no trace of pain in his expression.

"Of course."

I walk out of the room to give him a minute. When he comes out and Opal sees him again, her smile fades. It's such a jarring transition. Not even two minutes ago, she was overjoyed speaking with Evan. Now it's like she's looking at a stranger. There's zero trace of affection.

I quickly walk up to him and touch his arm. "Opal, this is my friend Evan. It would mean a lot to me if you were nice to him, okay?"

She studies Evan, who stays standing next to me. His gaze darts between us, clearly thrown off by what I've said. He stays quiet as we both wait for her reaction.

After a moment, she nods, then looks back at the TV. "Okay."

I let out a breath before looking up at Evan. I pull my hand off him and step away to give him space.

"I'm going to walk him out; then I'll be right back."

I follow him out the front door and onto the porch.

"Sorry, I know that was weird," I say quickly. "It's just, you two had such a nice conversation, and I didn't want anything to taint that."

That sad smile I've seen before appears. "It wasn't weird. It was perfect."

His phone starts buzzing again, but he silences it.

"Work stuff?" I ask.

"Nope. I, uh, I've got an impatient girlfriend waiting for me at home."

"Oh."

I don't know why I'm so surprised to hear him say that.

"Well, you'd better get going, then." I start to laugh, but he frowns. I immediately quiet.

"I guess I should." He lingers for a second, like he's going to say more, but he shakes his head slightly, almost like he reconsiders. He says goodbye, then walks down the steps and to his car parked along the street, and I go back inside to check on Opal.

~

"God, Maine is so much better in the summer than Phoenix." Chantel's excited voice radiates from the speaker of my phone, which is propped on the dashboard of my car. "The high here today is sixty-five degrees. And it's June. Do you know what the high in Phoenix was today? One hundred and ten degrees. One hundred and ten!"

I laugh, then pull into a coffee drive-through.

"Hang on a sec," I tell Chantel as I get ready to place my order.

When I finish, I pull up to wait in line.

"So you're more into the temperate climates, I take it?" I ask Chantel.

"Oh, hell yes. The air here is somehow moist and crisp at the same time. Like, how is that possible? And the pine cones!"

I choke-laugh as I sip from my water bottle. "Um, what?"

"They're huge! I'm gonna bring you some, Bel. You're gonna freak. They're as big as your forearms."

"That's not saying much. I've got pretty puny forearms."

"Ha. Just wait until you see them. Your head will explode. And their smell! Like a woodsy cologne."

"That sounds amazing. Any way you can send me an air freshener for my car?"

She scoffs. "What about that floral air freshener I gave you?"

"It's great. But honestly? I like pine and woodsy aromas more than floral ones."

"Unbelievable," she teases.

"My nose is probably just used to your floral body spray. I'm in the mood for something different. Floral musk is all I can smell every time I walk by your bedroom, Tel, even when you're not here."

"See? Even when I'm not with you, I'm with you. My perfume will make sure of it."

I shake my head, laughing.

"But seriously, I'm in love with Maine," she says.

"You say that now. If you were there in the winter, you'd change your tune real quick. The snow and ice and freezing temperatures there are no joke."

"Okay, fair point. But I'd rather tough it out in the winter here than go back to Phoenix. No way I'm taking a job in the desert in the summer ever again."

"Not even if the money is amazing?"

She hums. "Okay, yeah, for loads of money, I totally would."

I pull ahead to grab my iced coffee from the barista and drive in the direction of April's house.

"So how do you like being a home health aide?"

"Honestly? I like it a lot."

I just finished my first two weeks working with Opal. As nervous as I was to take this on, I'm hitting a pleasant comfort zone now. I genuinely enjoy spending time with her. And knowing that I'm doing something helpful every day for her—keeping her safe and happy—gives me a sense of purpose I don't remember feeling before.

"That's so great, Bel. And hey, I know that you getting suspended from work was a downer. And total bullshit, by the way. Anyone would have responded the way you did. That doctor was an absolute dick."

I smile at her little quip in my defense.

"But all that aside, what I want to say is that it seems like this break from your job is working out well for you. You sound happier."

"Do I?"

"Yeah. Just something in your voice is lighter."

I mull over what she's said as I weave my way through the haphazard traffic along the freeway. Despite how much I enjoy taking care of Opal, my job at the hospital is a constant worry in the back of my mind. I've made good on my promise to Martha that I'd stop obsessively checking in and commit to this time away, but every day I wonder how my absence is being felt by the hospital . . . or if it's noticed at all. Part of me—the petty part of me—hoped that things would fall apart the instant I left and that Martha would call and beg me to come back.

But that hasn't happened. It's been radio silence ever since she told me to stop checking in. And this is the root cause of my lingering doubt—that they're getting along just fine without me, and by the end of my suspension, they'll realize they don't need me at all and tell me never to come back. And then I'll be left with no job and no purpose.

I shake my head slightly, dislodging the thought from the forefront of my brain to the way back where it belongs.

You're happy right now. Chantel even notices. Focus on that.

"It must be Opal," I say. "I really like spending time with her. And her daughter, April, is so kind and grateful."

"Has her grandson stopped being such a dick to you?"

"Yeah, actually."

I vented to Chantel before about how Evan and I clashed. But since we haven't talked in over a week, I haven't had a chance to fill her in about how things have shifted between us . . . how pretending to be Opal's mom on the phone and convincing Evan to pretend to be her dad has smoothed over that hostility between us.

Even though I'm heartened at how happy it made Opal, I still can't shake the feeling that I've done something dishonest. I'm essentially tricking Opal into thinking I'm someone I'm not. But then I remind myself how Evan is okay with it—how he's happy about it. And I remind myself that I did it for Opal's benefit. I did it to keep her from becoming sad and possibly depressed. Her joy and health are what matter most.

I fill in Chantel about all of it. I finish just as I exit the freeway and head toward Benson.

"Oh, wow," Chantel says. "I'm glad you two cleared the air. That was really kind what you did, thinking to have him talk on the phone to Opal as her dad."

"It just killed me to see how destroyed he was when she rejected him. I can't even imagine. Your own family member not remembering you." I pause as a wave of sadness hits me. "But that's what happens with dementia and Alzheimer's. There's nothing anyone can do about it. You just watch it happen and try to find joy in the time you have left with them. And try to remember what they were like before they got sick."

For a moment, it feels like I'm trying to reassure myself with what I've said.

I try not to think too much about how eventually Opal's condition will worsen, and it will absolutely destroy her family.

"Don't think too much about it, Bel," Chantel says, as if reading my mind. "You're doing so much as it is. You found a way for her to have a positive, loving interaction with her grandson. And it clearly meant everything to them. That's incredible. *You* are incredible."

As I pull up to April's house, I think of Evan, of the joy on his face as he spoke on the phone to Opal, of the tears in his eyes.

I wonder if he'll stop by sometime soon to do that again. It made both him and Opal so happy.

"Thanks, Tel. You're the best."

We say a quick goodbye, and I hop out of the car and walk up the steps to knock on April's door. Humidity is through the roof, and it's not even eight in the morning. Even though I've been standing outside for less than a minute, moisture already coats my skin.

I fan myself with my hand for a few seconds until April answers the door. When I step in, she pulls me into a hug.

"Oof."

"You're an angel, you know that?" Her voice quakes as she hugs me tight.

"Oh, um . . ."

She pulls away but keeps hold of me by my shoulders. "Evan told me what you did for him—what you did for Mom. How you spoke to her on the phone as her mom and suggested that he talk to her as her dad. I just . . ."

Her eyes glisten with unshed tears. The way she shakes her head, it's like she's so overcome with emotion, she can barely speak.

She lets out a breath and nods once at me. "I just want to thank you for making my mother so happy. And for figuring out a way for her and Evan to be good again. Like old times almost."

Seeing April overcome with joy melts away the guilt I've been harboring ever since I made the decision to pretend to be Opal's mom on the phone. If April sees it as all good, then I don't have to feel bad or dishonest about it.

My shoulders feel looser as I smile at April. "I'm just so happy your family is happy."

She gives my shoulders another squeeze, then releases me. I turn to Opal, who smiles and waves at me.

April starts gathering her things to leave for work. Before she's out the door, she stops in front of where I'm sitting on the couch.

"It's probably not my place to even say this, but I've been so worried about Evan," she says.

"Oh?"

She tugs a hand through her gray-brown hair, like she's contemplating if she wants to say more. "He's taking Mom's health situation so hard. They were so close his whole life. And now, she sees him as a stranger. It breaks my heart."

"I remember him saying that."

"It's devastating for him to witness her lose her memory of him, her only grandson." April's expression turns pained. "And on top of that, the stress of running his restaurant. And whatever is going on in his personal life."

I stay quiet, wondering if she's referencing his girlfriend.

"Yeah, that sounds like a lot to deal with," I say when she doesn't elaborate.

"I tell him I'm always here if he wants to talk, but he can be so closed off." She sighs as she grabs her car keys from her purse. "He's a grown man. I have no right to meddle. I suppose that's why I'm venting to you, dear."

I tell her it's all right.

"I'm sure he'll figure it out at some point." When she looks up at me, she flashes a small smile. "I'm just so thankful for the joy you brought him and Mom."

When she leaves, I jump into the morning routine with Opal.

Chapter Nine

"It's hot as hell today. My goodness."

I laugh at Opal's remark as we round the street corner and head back down the block to April's house.

"It certainly is," I say as I lead her up the porch steps.

I hold the screen door open and unlock the front door. When I turn back around, she's frowning. Sweat dots her white hairline.

"You know what, hell probably isn't even this hot," she mumbles before stepping inside.

I let out a laugh and look at her.

"What is it, dear?" she asks, now smiling.

"Nothing, just . . . my sister says that too. She was just in Phoenix for work, and she complained that it's hotter than hell there."

Opal grabs a magazine to fan herself before strolling to the kitchen table and sitting down. "Now, there's a place you couldn't pay me to visit. Too damn hot."

I chuckle as I prep lunch for her. One month into being Opal's caretaker and we've hit a rhythm. Conversations with her feel like talking to a friend. We chat about everything—shows, music, traveling, jokes, our favorite foods, family stories, random musings. She struggles sometimes to remember details and people, but as long as I steer the conversation to what makes her happy, everything is okay.

"What does your sister do?" she asks when I set down a turkey sandwich and carrot sticks in front of her.

"She's a travel nurse."

"Oh my." Opal's expression turns thoughtful as she takes a bite of her sandwich. "You know, Mom wanted me to be a nurse. I told her no way. I can't stand the sight of blood. I would have been the worst nurse in the world."

I laugh, then listen as she chats between bites of her sandwich.

"What's your sister's name?" she asks.

"Chantel."

She pauses for a few seconds, like she's deep in thought again. Then she turns to me. "If I had a sister, I'd name her Chantel."

I don't know what to say at first. It's such a random comment from Opal, but that's to be expected given her mental state. She's said random and confusing things from time to time in the month that I've been looking after her, but usually her comments are easy enough for me to follow.

Something about this thought hits differently.

"Do you have a sister?" I ask.

"No. I always wished for one, though. I tell my brother whenever he's annoying that I'd trade him for a sister if I could."

When she finishes eating, I take her plate to the sink, refill her water, and follow her back out to the living room. I turn on the TV so she can watch her afternoon shows while I tidy up the kitchen.

"It's my song!"

Opal snaps her fingers along with the beat of "My Sweetie Sparrow" when that cleaning-service commercial comes on TV. I smile at her as she closes her eyes and sways along with the music.

"You've got some killer moves, Opal."

I hop up from the couch and head to the kitchen to grab her dessert. I plate up a small serving of rice pudding and deliver it to her. She's chowing down while watching that late-afternoon courtroom drama she loves so much when there's a thud at the front door.

I walk over and answer it. When I see Evan standing there, I don't think much of it. Until I take in his appearance. Those undereye circles are back, only this time they're darker. His beard is scruffy, like he hasn't trimmed it in days. His hair, which is normally pulled back in a smooth bun, is tangled to hell, like he slept on it and didn't bother to brush it or retie it. The T-shirt and jeans he's wearing are rumpled like he slept in them too.

When the stench of alcohol hits my nostrils, I clench my jaw. And then I notice his eyes. They're glazed over. He's drunk.

What the hell is he doing showing up here drunk in the middle of the day to see his grandma?

I twist around to Opal, who's focused on her plate.

"I'll just be a second, okay?"

I step out onto the porch and shut the door behind me. "What are you doing here?"

He stumbles back a step. "Shit. Um . . . I, um . . ."

He takes a second to close his eyes and shake his head slowly, like he's trying to reset his brain.

"You're drunk."

Sadness shines bright in his stare when he opens his eyes. He grips the iron railing with his hand. "Yeah. I am."

A sigh rockets from me as I bite the inside of my cheek to keep from going off on him. When I'm certain I won't yell, I speak.

"What were you thinking coming here like this?"

He hunches over, his head hanging low, his gaze fixed on the concrete steps beneath his sneakers. "I just . . . I wanted to see my grandma. That's all."

"While you're drunk? Are you serious right now, Evan?"

The anger coursing through me causes my heart to race in my chest like I've taken a hit of speed. I don't have the slightest clue how to navigate this awkward and tense situation with Evan. I thought we were in a good place. We stopped fighting, and I figured out a way for him to connect with Opal. But then he shows up like this, an intoxicated mess. If Opal sees him like this, she'd definitely get upset, and all the progress they've made so far will have been for nothing.

"Why would you think of coming here like this?" I snap. "You know that seeing you like this—drunk, slurring your words, barely able to stand up—would upset her. Keeping her mood stable and happy is so important in her state right now. Why you would do something so . . ."

I trail off when I notice the twist in his expression. He looks like he's been socked in the stomach.

"I know. I know. I kn—it's just . . . it's been a shitty day, and I just wanted to see her. I wanted to talk to her, hear her voice."

I inhale and will myself to sound less agitated this time. "I'm sorry you had a bad day. You know you're always welcome to see your grandma. But not like this. Not when you reek of booze and are on the verge of tears because you're so drunk you can't even stand up straight without gripping the wall or railing or . . ." I stop talking and gaze off to the side when I catch my voice turning harder. "How did you even get here? Please tell me you didn't drive."

"Of course not." He scoffs like he's pissed I'd even mention it. "I took a rideshare." He runs a hand over his face. When he blinks, his eyelids move more slowly, almost like he's sleepy.

I wait for him to say more, but no words come. I'm about to tell him to leave when he speaks.

"My girlfriend dumped me."

"Oh." I stammer through an "I'm sorry," which he barely nods at.

"I don't blame her." He mumbles something about how she deserves better.

I stay quiet and let him babble more nonsensical comments that I don't quite understand.

"I didn't even love her." His eyes are watery as he makes the softly spoken declaration while staring off to the side, at the massive tree in April's front yard. "I'm not even that sad about it."

"You sure about that?" I try my hardest not to sound indignant.

His gaze darts to me, and I immediately regret what I've said. His eyes are glassy with tears.

"I just mean that it seems like you're taking it pretty hard," I say. "At least it looks that way to me."

He shakes his head. "No, that's not . . . okay, yeah, I'm a little sad. But th-that's why I came here . . . for the only thing that would make me feel better . . . for her. For Grandma. Just to talk, just for a little bit. The only thing that would distract me from feeling this shitty is her. I just . . . I just want to talk . . ."

"She can't see you like this," I repeat, this time in a more patient tone.

He tugs a hand through his hair, his lip quivering. "What if I call her? Pretend to be her dad again? Wouldn't that be . . . I mean, I could try—"

I shake my head. "You can't, Evan. You're in no shape to have a conversation with her. You know you can't do that with how much you've had. If you try to talk to her like this, you know it'll only confuse her."

He sniffles and nods, his gaze downward, like he knows better— like he's embarrassed even for thinking that he could have any kind of conversation with Opal.

The silence lingers between us. As I stand there and watch him blink back tears and pull his quivering lips into his mouth before swallowing, a part of me cracks wide open. It's the part of me that knows what it's like to fall apart. It's the part of me that knows what it's like to burst into tears at random moments. I went through all of that in the weeks and months following That Day.

The base of my throat aches before I shove the memory to some dark place in my brain where I can't easily access it.

I move forward two steps and touch my hand to Evan's arm. "Let's get you home, okay? And then when you're feeling better, you can come see Opal."

"Yeah. Okay," he says, his gaze glued to the ground, his face twisted in regret, so defeated.

He shoves a hand in his pocket, fumbling for a few seconds before pulling out his phone. It's another several seconds of fumbling before he's able to type in the passcode on the screen. I gently take it from him.

"Here, let me help you."

He nods, then leans his back against the wrought-iron railing that lines the perimeter of the porch. His hands grip the bar so hard, his knuckles turn white. I can't tell if he's struggling to stay upright or trying not to vomit.

Thankfully, the car is less than a minute away. When the blue sedan pulls up to the street, I wrap my hand around his arm and help him down the steps, then walk him to the car.

"Thank you," he murmurs.

I release him so I can open the door for him. He moves to climb in but then stops himself. With one hand braced on the open car door, he looks over at me.

"You're not going to tell my mom and grandma about this, are you?"

I don't answer him right away. I can't. Because in this moment, I'm taken aback. He's an utter mess in every sense of the word. His disheveled appearance, the fear and sadness in his eyes, the way his shoulders hunch over like he's a scared little boy, not a tall and broad thirtysomething man.

I'm not pissed at him anymore. All I feel is raw pity for the guy.

"Of course I won't."

He lets out a breath and hunches even lower. "Thank you."

"Don't come here like this again. Please."

"I won't."

He falls into the back passenger seat. I shut the door and watch as the car drives off. When I walk back toward the house, I notice a small, colorful, rectangular piece of paper sticking up from the grass near the porch. When I crouch down to pick it up, I see that it's a photo of a young Evan and Opal. It must have fallen out of his pocket as he pulled out his phone.

In the picture, Evan looks barely five years old. His hair is a lighter shade of blond. He sports a shaggy bowl cut, chubby cheeks, and a smile that's the exact same smile his grandmother is beaming back at him in this moment. He's perched on Opal's lap, looking up at her as he laughs. She's cradling him in her arms, gazing down at him, the look on her face one hundred percent love.

For a few seconds, I take in this special moment captured so long ago. A familiar ache pulses through my chest, and my smile slowly fades. They'll never have a moment like this again, where the two of them can look at each other with equal affection. Opal no longer recognizes Evan; she looks at him like he's a stranger she's suspicious of. And every time Evan looks at her, even those times when he's happy to see her, his expression is tinged with pain at the fact that she has no idea who he is anymore.

I swallow back the lump in my throat and slip the photo in my back pocket. When I make it back into the house, Opal looks up at me, a curious expression on her face.

"Who was at the door, dear?"

"A friend," I say, forcing my voice to stay steady. "No one you'd know, though."

~

When I walk into the lobby of the Grey Plume, I feel instantly out of place.

I'm underdressed. I knew I would be. This is a Michelin-starred restaurant, and everyone in here is dressed in cocktail or business wear. I'm wearing cutoff jean shorts, white sneakers, and a V-neck gray T-shirt that's so worn, I'm pretty sure people can see my bra through it.

But I didn't have time to change after leaving Opal this afternoon. Not like it matters what I'm wearing anyway. I'm here to give the dropped photo back to Evan; then I'm going to leave.

The college-age hostess smiles up at me from behind the wooden podium at the front of the restaurant. "Just one moment, my apologies," she says quietly to me as she finishes up a phone call.

I tell her it's no problem at all, then go back to staring at the ground and fumbling with the hem of my shirt. I probably should have called or texted Evan before just showing up at his place of work. Too late now, though. It was hard to think straight after what happened. Once the frustration of him showing up shit-faced had passed, all I could think about yesterday when I left Opal after April came home from work was that pained look on his face, how distraught and heartbroken he was. And that question he asked me before he fell into his rideshare and took off.

You're not going to tell my mom and grandma about this, are you?

It's obvious he doesn't want anyone close to him to know about his breakdown. And I get it—I can relate to that feeling of wanting privacy to process your pain.

"Table for one?" the hostess asks when she hangs up.

"No, thank you. I'm here to meet with Evan Sanderson."

"Oh! Of course." When she smiles, her crimson lipstick shines under the dim mood lighting. "Right this way."

She leads me through the dining area to the back and into the kitchen. Immediately I'm hit with how bright and shiny everything is—the stainless-steel appliances, the metal prep tables in the middle of the space, the light fixtures that run along the ceiling.

A half dozen people in white chef's jackets stand in the kitchen cooking and prepping. Servers decked out in black cocktail wear dart in and out, balancing trays of plates on their shoulders.

"Chef, someone is here to see you," the hostess announces.

Evan's blond bun pops up. He's standing over a saucepan in front of one of the stovetops. He twists around, locking eyes with me. There's a second of shock; then he furrows his brow. Clearly he's disappointed by my surprise visit. I can't say I'm shocked, given my reaction when he dropped by unannounced yesterday.

He turns away and says something I can't hear to the guy in the white chef's coat next to him. The guy nods, then takes over for Evan as he darts around the bustling kitchen over to me and the hostess.

"Thanks so much, Moira," Evan says.

She flashes a dazzling smile at us both before walking back out to the front of the restaurant. He gestures to that spot in the hallway a few feet away, near the bathrooms.

"Hey. Everything okay?" he asks.

"Yeah, fine. I just . . ." I dig the photo out of my purse and hand it to him. "You dropped this yesterday when you came by your mom's house."

The lines between his eyebrows and along his forehead disappear as surprise takes over his expression. He takes the picture from my hand.

"Shit. I thought I lost this. I couldn't find it anywhere."

"It was in the front lawn by the porch. I saw it after your ride drove off."

It's another few seconds of quiet as Evan fixes his gaze on the photo before tucking it into his back pocket. Then he crosses his arms over his chest and frowns once again at me.

"You doing okay?" I ask.

"Yeah. Fine."

His curt tone is a clear message that he doesn't want to talk about what he's going through. But a part of me doesn't want to just let this go. Maybe it's the chaplain part of me, the part that's used to seeing people distraught and in pain, and it wants to offer some sort of comfort.

"I don't mean to overstep my boundaries here," I say. "But if you ever want to talk about what you're going through, I'm here."

It's an awkward few seconds of observing as Evan's gaze darts everywhere except me before I accept his rejection. He's clearly not the least bit interested in talking to me.

I nod once in silent acceptance.

"I don't like to talk about the shit I'm going through either," I admit.

Evan's brow lifts the slightest bit. "How do you prefer to handle it?"

"Venting to my sister."

The left corner of his mouth quirks up the slightest bit.

"Long walks at Elmwood Park if she's busy and the weather's nice," I say. "If it's not, then rage-crying into my pillow."

That earns me a barely audible chuckle before he pulls his lips into his mouth, as if to reset himself. "Thanks for bringing me that photo."

"Take care of yourself, okay?"

He nods, and I step away and walk out of the restaurant, quietly hoping that whatever Evan is going through, however he chooses to handle it, he ends up okay.

Chapter Ten

"Oh my gosh! Isabel! This is the cutest!"

Keely holds up the mobile I've just gifted her. She stares at it, her mouth open in surprise. She raves about how adorable the plush animals are that hang off it.

"And oh my gosh!" Her eyes bulge at the stitching along the base of the mobile. "Does that say 'Baby Kingston'?"

"It plays music too." When I twist the crank to the side, Brahms's "Lullaby" plays.

Keely scrunches her face as she rests her palm on her chest. "That's my favorite baby song. Oh, Isabel."

She sets the mobile down and pulls me into a hug. "This is the sweetest gift. It's going to look perfect in the baby's crib. Thank you so much."

When she releases me, she hops up from where we're sitting on the couch and darts into the kitchen, where her husband, Theo, is sitting doing work at his laptop.

"Babe, look how cute this is."

He turns and squints through his glasses at the mobile. "Oh, wow. Yeah, really cute." He leans around Keely to look over at me. A small, tight smile pulls at his lips. "Thank you, Isabel. That's very thoughtful."

I tell him it was no problem at all, but he looks back at his laptop before I finish speaking. Keely doesn't seem to notice his low-key frosty response. She's chatting happily away about what a thoughtful gift this is.

I don't blame Theo for his subtle dismissal of me. I ignored his wife these last couple of years. Even though we're reconnecting and spending more time together, it's only natural that he'd be wary of me. I'm sure he's wondering if I'll disappear on her again.

Despite how justified his reaction is, it still hurts. Theo and I were never good friends, but I always liked him. I remember the night he and Keely met. We were out with Chantel for dinner in downtown Omaha. Afterward, we stopped for drinks at a new tavern on the edge of the Old Market. Keely kept glancing over at the bar from our booth. When I finally caught on that she was checking out a guy, I urged her to go over and say hi. I still remember that shy, scrunched smile she flashed when she shook her head and said no.

"I don't want to bother him," she said, sipping her drink.

At that moment, Chantel rolled her eyes, set her empty glass on the table, then hopped up and marched over to Theo. We couldn't hear what she said to him from where we were sitting, but we could see perfectly as Chantel approached him, smiled, said something, then nodded toward Keely.

Keely's eyes went as wide as saucers as she twisted around to avoid their gaze. "Oh my god. Oh my god. Oh my god . . . Is Chantel seriously pointing me out to him?"

I couldn't help but laugh as I said, "Looks like it."

It's a shame Keely wasn't looking at Theo at that moment, because once he glanced over at her, the biggest, most flustered smile spread across his face. It was adorable. And then he said what looked like "thanks" to Chantel before walking over and introducing himself to Keely. They exchanged shy smiles, their names, and a handshake before Keely invited him to sit with us. The two of them flirted in between chatting with the table. The night ended with them exchanging numbers and plans for a first date.

Ever since then, Theo and I always got along. I hung out with them loads of times when they were dating. I was in their wedding, too, as was Chantel.

But when I began ignoring Keely's calls and texts after That Day, I'm certain that turned him bitter toward me. And I deserve it.

Keely plops back on the couch with me, and I start to tuck away the tissue paper from the gift bag.

"So! How's the temporary job going for you? It's been, what, just over a month since you've been working as a caretaker? Still enjoying it?"

"For the most part, yeah." I catch the lift in Keely's eyebrow. "I like it still. Opal is wonderful and so is her daughter, April."

"What about her grandson?"

"I think he's still having a hard time dealing with everything." I wonder just how much I should divulge. It's not like Evan swore me to secrecy about what he's going through after we talked. But I'm sure he wouldn't like his personal struggles being discussed behind his back—most people wouldn't.

"What did he do this time?" Keely asks. She knows about my and Evan's brief yet rocky history. The few times that we've met up and I've talked about work, I've mentioned how difficult it's been navigating things with him. She knows that Opal has a hard time remembering him and that it hurts his feelings.

I hesitate, but the urge to fully explain the situation wins out. I don't want to leave Keely with cryptic statements. I want to be open and honest with her—I always was before. If this were years ago, I would have told her without hesitation what happened with Evan.

"He showed up the other day drunk at April's house when I was with Opal."

"Oh my gosh. Are you serious?"

"Yeah. It was honestly kind of sad."

I explain that his girlfriend had just broken up with him.

"I think he hit his limit," I say. "First, his grandma, who he's been close to his whole life, has pretty much forgotten who he is and is treating him like a stranger. Then his girlfriend breaks up with him. That's rough."

"Yeah, but getting wasted and trying to see her wasn't the right way to deal with it."

"It wasn't. I told him that."

"What did he do?"

"He cried. He was pretty inconsolable. It was awful to see."

Even now, just thinking back on Evan's heartbroken face sends a jolt of pity to my chest. I wonder how he's doing now. Hopefully better.

"I told him he can't show up like that to see her." I fiddle with the tissue paper before shoving it in the bag and setting it on the coffee table. "We talked about it afterwards. He apologized and swore he wouldn't do it again."

"Good. Hopefully the guy sorts his stuff out," Keely says.

"Maybe I could have been nicer about it at first. I was pretty angry when he came by the house. I just didn't want him to upset Opal."

"You handled it perfectly."

Her reassurance settles the lingering doubt I've carried these past few days over how I handled things with Evan.

Theo hops up from the dining chair and walks across the open-concept space into the living room, phone in hand.

"Sweetie, Jason and Gina just texted me and asked if six bottles of wine was enough for everyone coming tonight."

"Oh. Um . . ." Keely glances at me, her eyes nervous before looking back at Theo. "Yeah, that should be enough."

"Brian from work won't be able to come, so I think it'll just be about a dozen or so people. You think ordering pizza and salads would be enough to feed everyone?"

"Yup. That's fine," Keely says with a slight sharpness in her tone.

Theo looks over at me. "You're not coming tonight, are you?"

"Oh, um. No."

When he blinks, he almost looks relieved. "Cool."

I don't miss the frown Keely shoots him. Her cheeks turn pink as Theo clears his throat and disappears down the hallway.

"Sorry about that," she says, her voice quiet.

"About what?"

"It's pretty rude to plan a party in front of a person who's not going to it."

"Keely, it's fine. You don't have to feel bad about that."

"It's just . . . Well, I noticed you don't really like doing things with groups of people anymore. You seem to just like hanging out one-on-one. And I mean, I know that you used to be okay with group stuff before . . . um, well . . . I mean, the three of us—you, me, and Chantel, we would always . . . er, um, I mean . . . sorry, I guess I shouldn't have . . ."

Her eyes go wide as she bites her lip. She closes her eyes and shakes her head, like she's trying to erase what she's said.

All the muscles in my body tighten for the briefest moment, but the longer I watch Keely struggle through the obvious regret of what she's said, the more I soften.

I reach over and touch her arm. She stills instantly, the look in her doe eyes bewildered. "It's really okay, Keely. I get it. You're right. I'm not really into group stuff anymore."

I think back to all the parties, barbecues, holiday gatherings, and dinners Keely and I went to over the years, often with Chantel whenever she wasn't traveling for work. It was so easy back then . . . I was normal . . .

I swallow back the thought and focus on comforting Keely in this moment. Her expression shifts from shocked to relieved. "Theo and I are hosting a dinner for some friends tonight, and I thought about inviting you, but I knew you probably wouldn't come, since it would be a group thing. But we really shouldn't talk about it in front of you. I don't want to make you feel excluded."

I touch her arm with my hand. "You're not excluding me. It doesn't feel like that at all."

Relief washes across her face as she smiles. "You're always welcome. Anytime you want to come to anything, I'd love for you to."

I wonder if I'll feel up to hanging out with a big group of friends anytime soon. "I appreciate that."

"But hey, you're still up for going with me to the tasting for my baby shower at the Grey Plume, right?"

I tell her of course. She asked me weeks ago if I'd be up for it, and I said yes.

"Promise that will be just the two of us," Keely says. "Theo's mom wanted to come but no way." She makes an *ugh* noise that I laugh at. "She is the pickiest person on the planet, and I don't want her ruining my mood on a day when I get to enjoy a multicourse gourmet tasting menu. You're the only person I want to go with me."

I'm touched that she's making this a two-person event just so I'll go with her.

"I promise I'll be there, and I promise I will do everything to make it the best menu tasting ever."

I grab my purse and stand up to leave. Keely starts to say she'll walk me to the door but then winces. Her hand falls to her belly. "God, this baby. I love them so much already, but I don't love that they're using my bladder as a trampoline."

"I can see myself out. You go to the restroom."

We hug, and she scurries off to the hallway bathroom. I turn and head for the front door. When I'm slipping on my sandals, Theo appears.

He clears his throat. "You're taking off, then?"

"Yeah. I'll see you later."

The way he stands there, his hands in the pockets of his trousers, shuffling his feet slightly, he's clearly getting ready to say something. I wait for a moment, but he stays quiet.

"Well, have a good time tonight," I say.

I reach for the doorknob, but then he says my name.

"Isabel, can I talk to you for a quick second?"

The strain in his voice tells me this will likely be an uncomfortable conversation. And I think I know what he's about to say.

Tension finds my muscles once more. He's going to tell me off for what I put Keely through but in his own Theo way: measured, calm tone and polite wording but with an undercurrent of disappointment and subtle disgust. It's how he's always expressed himself whenever he's upset—and it's what I deserve after icing out Keely for the past two-plus years.

Still, though, I can't help the dread that consumes me. No one wants to stand there and be told what a horrible person they are—what a horrible friend they've been—even if it's the truth. It's like standing silently still as everyone around you points out your flaws to your face. It's as harsh and hurtful as it is true.

I spin around to face Theo. "Sure. What's up?"

His brow furrows, and he tugs a hand through his curly blond hair. Just looking at it triggers the memory of Keely gushing over him when they were dating.

"He has the most gorgeous curly blond hair," she said to me. "If we ever have babies, I hope they have his curls."

I start to smile at just how giddy Keely was over Theo and his hair, but I rein it in when I refocus on his serious expression.

"Keely's really happy to have you back in her life," he says. "I'm happy too. She hasn't been this excited to spend time with a friend in so long."

When he pauses, I sense the incoming "but" a mile away.

"But it really hurt her when you stopped communicating with her."

"I know. I'll feel bad about that forever." I almost wince. It sounds like I'm minimizing the hurt I caused. I'm not trying to . . . I just can't think of anything better to say.

He sighs and shakes his head, then looks off to the side. He doesn't believe me. I bite my tongue to keep from saying anything. Nothing I could ever say will convince him otherwise. I just need to let him say his piece.

"I'm sure you do feel bad," he mutters. "But I don't want Keely to go through the pain of losing you again. It hurt her so much. So if being her friend again isn't something you think you can do, don't give her false hope."

His stern tone hits me deep. The sensation is on par with a muscle pull or a stomach cramp. It's clear that he has zero faith in me. He thinks I'm going to ditch Keely again.

"I plan on being Keely's friend—being in her life—for as long as she wants me around."

The conviction in my tone is as strong as it's ever been. But Theo stands there, arms crossed over his chest, his expression stony as he looks at me. He's unmoved by my words.

"I hope you're right, Isabel."

When I leave their house and drive home, I quietly acknowledge that I hope I'm right too.

Chapter Eleven

"How many times have you gone to Red Rocks?" I ask Chantel.

"Four."

"Four? You've been in Denver barely three weeks."

"I like pretty rocks. Sue me."

I stroll around a path in Elmwood Park, holding my phone to my ear. I'm catching up with Chantel as I get my steps in for the day.

"What kind of souvenirs can I expect you to bring me?" I drag my forearm across my brow, wiping away a film of sweat. Just a few laps around the park has me drenched. I'm not even jogging today. Because of the high humidity, I'm sweating as much as I would had I done a round of sprints.

"Beer koozies. A shot glass. Some cool rocks I found. Rocky Mountain oysters."

I snort-laugh so loudly, the kids at the nearby playground turn to look at me as I walk by.

"Please no Rocky Mountain oysters."

"Oh, come on. When you fry them, they actually taste really good."

I make a gagging noise. "No way in hell."

"Fine. I'll get you chocolate or something, then."

"Chocolate Rocky Mountain oysters?"

We burst out laughing as I round the edge of the park and make my way down a grassy hill.

"Oh my god, you're so gross. I'm gonna vomit."

"I swear, Tel, if you—oof!"

Someone collides with me from the side, and I fall forward. My phone goes flying into the grass as I start to stumble, off balance, but then a massive hand grabs me and steadies me back on my feet.

When I turn around, there's Evan. His gray T-shirt is soaked in sweat, and his chest heaves as he catches his breath. His wide eyes and furrowed brow broadcast worry as he yanks out his earbuds.

"Crap, I'm so sorry. Are you okay?"

I mumble a yes, still stunned from the impact and the fact that I've run into Evan.

"Yeah, um . . . wait, my phone."

I spot a phone near my foot, but it's not mine. I scan the text on the screen.

How to make dementia patients happy.

Out of the corner of my eye, I see him point down to the grass near me. "I think that's mine."

I scoop it up and hand it to him. He twists his head around as he looks across the grass. I see my phone just a few feet from him. He bends down to pick it up, then hands it to me.

"Bel? Bel, are you okay?" Chantel's voice emanates from the speaker.

"Yeah, sorry, I'm good. I, uh, tripped and dropped my phone."

"Ouch. You okay?"

"Yeah, fine. Hey, listen. I have to go. Call you later?"

"Of course. Love you."

"Love you."

I hang up and glance up to see Evan gazing at me. He rests his hands on his hips as his chest continues to heave up and down. His cheeks are flushed red from running in the heat and probably the shock of colliding with me.

"I'm so sorry," he repeats. "I was changing my playlist on my phone and wasn't looking."

I tug at the hem of my tank top. "It's fine."

For a second, we linger and say nothing. I haven't seen Evan since we talked at his restaurant more than a week ago when I gave him his photo back. To have a collision be our next in-person encounter adds a new layer of awkwardness between us.

A loud "ahem!" pulls our attention off to the side. There's a golf cart parked to the side of us with two older men in it staring at us. That's when I realize we're standing in the way of the pathway that leads to the nearby golf course.

Evan mutters a sorry, and together we move out of the way so they can pass.

"How are you doing?" I blurt when I can't think of anything else to say.

"Fine," he says through a breath, like he's relieved I said something. "I'm really sorry I ran into you. And interrupted your phone call."

"Don't worry about it." I shove my phone in the side pocket of my yoga pants. "Funny seeing you here."

He shrugs, a slight smile on his face. "Figured I'd take a page out of your book and jog around Elmwood Park to sort out my thoughts."

His admission sets me at ease. It seems like he's choosing to try to process the stress and sadness from Opal's health and his breakup in a healthy way now.

"That's really great," I say. "Only you're doing it wrong. I said walk, not jog."

He laughs.

"So what are you sorting out?" he asks.

"Nothing today. I just wanted to get outside for a bit." I hesitate before asking the one question I've been wondering for these last few days. "Are you feeling any better since the last time I saw you?"

"A little." His gaze falls to his running shoes.

"Have you seen Opal?"

He nods. "Twice. Sober both times." He lets out a chuckle, but then he quiets, like he regrets what he said.

"That's good."

For a few seconds, we say nothing more. Instead, we stay standing in front of each other, me shuffling my feet slightly, Evan digging the tip of his sneaker into the grass. I take in just how different he looks since the last time I saw him. Those undereye circles have faded, as have the worry lines that were previously etched along his forehead and the outer corners of his eyes.

Clearly he's telling the truth—he's feeling better than the last time I saw him. Whatever changes he's making, whatever methods he's employing to cope with his stress and emotions, they're working.

Despite that, the urge to inquire further about his well-being persists. Maybe it's the chaplain part of me. I'm used to people insisting that they're fine during times of distress, then breaking down later on. I'd hate for that to happen to Evan. As much as we've butted heads, I still care about him and his family. I want him to be okay.

And even though he wasn't receptive the last time I asked him if he wanted to talk, maybe he'd be up for something more laid-back.

"You wanna get a drink?"

My out-of-the-blue question earns a surprised smile from Evan. "What?"

"Nothing alcoholic," I say quickly. "I'm not a big drinker. And I'm dying from this heat and humidity. I could use some hydration. Interested?"

He nods once. "Okay, sure."

We end up at a new smoothie bar in midtown, a few minutes away from Elmwood Park. As we sit at a two-person table in the frigid air-conditioning sipping our drinks, we make small talk about how refreshing our beverages are and the minimalist decor.

"I'm sorry about your breakup," I finally say, hoping he doesn't get upset that I've brought it up.

His eyebrows scrunch together slightly. "It's fine. We weren't going to go the distance anyway."

The grind of a blender behind the counter fills the silence that follows.

"Do you want to talk about it?"

He blinks rapidly at my question, like he's not quite sure what the right answer is.

"Look, I know you mentioned when we hashed things out at your restaurant the other day that you didn't want to get into what you were going through. And I totally get it. But maybe it would help you feel better to talk about it just a little. I'm happy to listen."

The look on his face turns focused as he gazes down at his drink. Then a small smile appears. "You'd be happy to listen to me whine about my breakup?"

I nod. "I listen to people for a living. Ever since I left the hospital, I've missed it, believe it or not."

"This is kind of weird, don't you think? Given that we haven't known each other long," he says.

"Sure, I'll give you that. But maybe that's a good thing. It means I haven't known you long enough to get tired of you yet."

He chuckles at my joke, then huffs a breath. "Okay. Let's give it a go." He leans back in his chair, assuming a more relaxed position. "Helen and I went out for almost two years. She was great. Pretty, smart, successful, hardworking, loving, all that. I just struggled a lot making time for her with running my restaurant and family stuff, especially when my grandma's health started to go downhill. Helen wanted to take things between us to the next level. Moving in together, marriage, all that. I wasn't ready. So she broke up with me."

I stay quiet for a few seconds after he finishes. "That really sucks. I'm sorry."

"It's funny in a way. I was fine when she broke up with me. When we had the conversation. I didn't even feel sad. More like relieved. But when she came to my house to get all of her stuff, it's like this moment of clarity hit. I was losing her forever. And even though I knew it was the right thing for both of us, it still felt shitty."

"Emotions are complicated. They don't always hit you when you think they will."

He nods, like he's thinking carefully about what I've said.

"It was more than that, though. I was sad about the breakup, but there was also the overarching sadness of Grandma Opal not remembering me. That's a feeling I'm dealing with constantly. And it all hit at once, in a depressing realization: both my girlfriend and my grandma don't want me."

Even though his voice is low when he speaks those words, their impact is brutal. Like metal crashing onto concrete.

"That's when I kind of lost it," he says. "Just started drinking my feelings that day."

"Evan." I say his name softly and wait for him to look at me. "That's not the case. At all. Remember how happy Opal was to talk to you on the phone the other day?"

He tugs at his hair, like he's frustrated but trying to keep it together. "Yeah, but as great as that was, it wasn't me, you know? She thought I was her dad. And don't get me wrong, I'm so thankful to you for making that conversation happen. That's the longest conversation I've been able to have with her in months. It's the happiest she's been while talking to me too. But it's not the same as when she remembered me, you know?"

I nod my understanding. I wait a beat, careful with how I word what I want to say next. "Even if your grandma doesn't remember you now the way she used to, that doesn't diminish all the happy times you had together. There are years—decades of wonderful times she's had with you. Nothing can erase that. Not even dementia."

He nods at what I've said, but the broken look on his face remains. "I know. But it's hard to remember that right now when she doesn't even know who I am, when she looks at me like I'm a stranger. When she tells me to get away from her." A hard swallow moves down his throat. "When that realization hits, it's rough. It feels like getting run over by a train."

A stretch of silence follows where I can't think of a single helpful thing to say. It shouldn't feel this uncomfortable. There were several times when I'd be with patients or families after they had received devastating news. In those moments, there was nothing helpful to say, and I knew that. All I could do was offer my presence, then tell them that if and when they wanted to talk, I'd be there for them.

But this is different. Offering that to Evan doesn't seem like it would be good enough. And it doesn't feel like the right thing to do either.

I will some magical comforting words to come to mind so I can make him feel even the tiniest bit comforted in this broken moment. But nothing comes.

So we just sip our drinks in silence.

"That was kind of a downer," Evan says after a bit, gaze fixed on his near-empty glass.

"It's not a downer to talk about how you're feeling."

He shrugs a shoulder. "You know, you were right. It's not that this feels good to talk about. But it feels better than just holding it in."

I'm heartened at what he's said, but I want to do more than just listen. I think back to the search I saw on his phone screen earlier.

How to make dementia patients happy.

And then I have an idea.

"When you dropped your phone, I saw what was on your screen," I say. "I saw what you searched."

He looks up at me.

"How to make dementia patients happy," I say.

"Oh. Right."

"I researched that, too, before I started working with Opal. That's why I went with the idea to pretend to be her mom on the phone that day. That's why I suggested that you pretend to be her dad on the phone. Because it seems like the best thing to do is gauge what makes her happy and just go along with that as long as reasonably possible. It's not perfect, but it's something. It's better than her being upset and confused. And it's a way for you to engage with her."

"Right," Evan says.

"Do you want to try something?"

His eyes turn curious and hopeful. "What do you have in mind?"

"Something off-the-wall. But if it works, it could be wonderful. Can you come to Opal's tomorrow afternoon?"

The corners of his mouth tug up the slightest bit, and he nods. "Okay, yeah. I'm in."

~

"My Sweetie Sparrow," Opal's favorite song, plays from my phone, which is lying on the coffee table.

The big-band melody echoes through the whole house. I found a high-quality audio version of the song on YouTube and have been playing it off and on this morning to put Opal in a happy mood.

She's sitting in her usual spot in the recliner, humming to the melody.

"It's almost lunchtime," I say as I sit down on the couch and look over at her.

"Good. I'm famished."

"Do you know who sings this song?" I ask her.

She stops, then stares off to the side, like she's trying to think hard about the answer to my question. "I feel like I should know this. I used to know this."

"His name is Evan Conklin. He wrote the song too."

She starts to nod, and that smile reappears. "Evan Conklin. Yes."

Hope ignites in my chest. I hope this works.

"Evan Conklin." I make it a point to say his name a bit slower this time. "He's a very talented songwriter and singer."

"Evan Conklin." She says his name twice more to herself before going back to humming.

There's a knock at the door. I hop up and answer it. When I let Evan in, he's dressed in his white chef's jacket and carrying a cloth bag of groceries. I stand next to him, and together we face Opal.

"This is my friend Evan," I say.

Opal gazes with a confused stare like she always does when she first sees him. But the lines in her forehead and between her eyebrows aren't as deep as they usually are. Maybe that means she's not as thrown off. Maybe hearing the name Evan in association with her favorite song so recently has softened the blow of confusion.

"Evan is going to cook us lunch today. Shepherd's pie. Your favorite, remember?"

Her expression eases at the mention of her favorite meal. "Okay," she says after a second.

"Evan is a chef. And he has the same name as the singer of your favorite song, 'My Sweetie Sparrow.'"

It's a few seconds before she starts to slowly nod. The song ends, but I lean down and replay it on my phone. When the big-band beat starts up again, the corners of her mouth curve up.

"Evan. My sweetie sparrow. Evan . . ."

I turn slightly and see the beginning of a smile on Evan's face.

"Evan. Sweetie sparrow. Evan. Sweetie . . ."

When she trails off, Evan moves like he's going to step toward Opal and give her a hug, but then he stops himself.

"Hi, Opal."

"Evan," she repeats while looking up at him. She starts to smile as she moves her hands and her head gently with the beat of the song.

He lingers for a second, staring down at her, the softest smile on his face. The he heads into the kitchen and starts unloading the grocery bag.

I walk over to him, about to ask if he needs help with the prep or cooking, but then he looks at me and flashes the widest grin I've ever seen him make.

"She said my name while smiling at me."

A breathy laugh falls from his mouth as he shakes his head, almost like he can't believe it.

I beam at him. "I know. Kind of awesome, huh?"

"More than awesome. That's the happiest I've seen my grandma look around me in almost a year."

I rest my palm against my chest, it's aching so hard.

Evan's eyes turn tender as he focuses on me. "Thank you for making this happen."

My grin fades to something smaller. It's a scrunch of a smile now because so many emotions course through me in this moment; I'm having a tough time keeping it together. Opal is genuinely happy to see her grandson. Finally.

I swallow back the lump in my throat and step to the counter. "It's my pleasure. Now, put me to work. I'm your sous chef, and we've got lunch to prep."

The emotion in Evan's face dials back to something more amused. Still so happy, though.

"You're on potato-peeling duty."

An hour later, the three of us sit at April's small dining table, a trio of clean plates in front of us.

"Well, my goodness. That was just delicious, Evan." Opal dabs her mouth with a cloth napkin.

I don't miss the way his eyes practically sparkle at how she says his name, the way she grins up at him.

"I'm so happy you liked it, Opal."

I notice he's careful not to call her Grandma. He almost slipped up a couple of times but quickly corrected himself to say "Opal" before she noticed. It's not that calling her Grandma would automatically set off her confusion. We're not really even sure at this point if there are certain triggers for her moods or if things are just random. But it's clear that Evan wants to make the joy of this moment last as long as possible. Calling her Opal while "My Sweetie Sparrow" plays in the background seems to be what keeps her mood up.

"You know, the first time I had shepherd's pie was when I went off to college. In Lincoln. There was this restaurant downtown called Gibson's. Best shepherd's pie I've ever had. And late at night on the weekends, it turned into a speakeasy. It was quite entertaining." A wistful look crosses her face. "Goodness, I wish I could go back there. They made a heck of a gin martini too. Do you know how long it's been since I've had a decent gin martini?"

"I thought you didn't drink much," Evan says, a slight tease to his tone.

She tilts her head at him, a mischievous glint to her smile. "Not anymore. But back then . . ." She makes a drinking gesture with her hand before letting out a cackle that has both Evan and me laughing too.

Then she claps her hands once, like she's just thought of an idea. She glances between me and Evan. "Oh, you know what would be so fun? If we could head to Gibson's one of these days. Wouldn't that be great? The three of us having some shepherd's pie and the best gin martini you've ever had in your life?"

"Maybe we could do that," I say, careful to keep my smile on my face. I'm certain that place doesn't exist anymore. I've been to downtown Lincoln more times than I can count, since I grew up there, and I've never once come across that place. I'm guessing that if it was around when Opal was young, it's now closed.

"We could make a road trip out of it! Oh, I haven't been on a road trip in ages."

Evan and I exchange a look as Opal continues.

"Where would you want to go?" Evan asks her. Something in his gaze turns thoughtful as he asks her. "If we were to take you on a road trip, what places would you want to see?"

"Well, Gibson's, obviously. And someplace pretty. Someplace away from the crowds. Somewhere in nature. And the beach. A beach would be so very fun. To step in the crystal-clear water and splash around a bit. Goodness, that sounds like heaven."

I can practically hear the gears turning in Evan's head. I want to ask what he's thinking, but not right now, when Opal is so immersed in the joy of this moment.

I clear the table and help her out of the chair. She walks back to the living room, and I turn to Evan, who's starting on the dishes.

"A road trip would be fun," he says as he scrubs a plate and sets it in the dishwasher.

"It would be. But do you think that's realistic?"

He peers over at Opal in the living room as she settles into her recliner. He shrugs. "Maybe not. But I didn't think it was possible for her to ever remember to call me Evan until today. So I guess anything's possible."

"Fair point."

"It's just, I keep thinking of that information I found online of how to make dementia patients happy."

I nod, recalling the general guidelines I came across, too, when I researched it myself.

Engage in exercise and physical activity. Reminisce about their life. Engage in activities that bring them joy. Explore nature. Listen to their favorite music. Encourage them to talk about happy memories.

Evan finishes loading the dishwasher, then shoves up the sleeves of his jacket. He rests his hands along the edge of the sink, then looks up to the kitchen window. The sunlight streaming in illuminates the golden stubble on his face. It makes his eyes shine brighter, too, like two gems. Now they look completely green.

"Maybe we can't do a traditional road trip where we're gone for a week and traveling all over the country exploring random places," he says. "That would be too hard on someone her age and with her medical condition. But we can modify it. Just go to a few places that she'd like a couple of hours away. Maybe just make a day trip out of it to start out and then go from there."

The longer I think about it, the more doable it seems.

"I can't do it this weekend, but the weekend after I have off from work. What do you think?" he asks when he looks at me. "Would you be up for trying to pull this off? Would you want to go on a road trip with my grandma and me?"

He laughs slightly at the end. I can't ignore the nerves swirling through me at the prospect. It's one thing to be in a house with Opal, where everything is familiar to her, where her loved ones can control the setting around her, where there's a clear and defined routine for her to follow. She might get restless sitting in the car for hours. And we'll have to keep an eye on her at all times, otherwise she might wander off or hurt herself.

I relay those concerns to Evan, who nods his understanding.

"Of course. We'll be as careful as possible. I won't let her out of my sight the whole time." His stare drifts back to the living room. "I just . . ." His chest rises and falls with the deep sigh he takes. "I just really want to make her happy. And it sounds like a road trip would make her really, really happy. Who knows how long she's going to be like this, in a generally happy state and in a good mood almost every day? Who knows how long before her dementia gets worse and she forgets . . ."

He swallows before finishing his sentence. He peers off to the side, his expression twisting slightly, like he's sad or in pain.

In that moment, I resolve to do everything I can to give Evan and Opal the best damn road trip possible.

"Okay. Let's go on a road trip."

Chapter Twelve

A week and a half later, Evan pulls his car into one of the parking areas at Indian Cave State Park. I twist to the back seat so I can see Opal's reaction. Behind her glasses, her green-hazel eyes bulge.

"Goodness. Look at all these trees. So green."

I smile at her. "Wait until you see the view from the lookout point."

I unbuckle my seat belt, hop out, then help her out of the car. Evan jogs around and shuts the door. I offer her my arm, which she accepts. Normally she can walk just fine by herself, but the pathway to the lookout point is a bit uneven, and I don't want her to lose her footing. Evan stays behind us, ready to help if she trips or wobbles.

There are multiple hikes and viewpoints at this state park, but because we want to keep things manageable for Opal, we're sticking to sightseeing at easily accessible viewpoints that we can park nearby.

When we make it to the wooden platform overlooking the Missouri River, Opal slips out of my hold and walks all the way to the edge. She grips the wooden railing and gazes out with wide eyes. The Missouri River snakes below along an endless mass of trees and greenery. Underneath today's clear blue sky, the water looks more white than blue. I quietly note how it's the exact same shade as the pond behind *Apong* Marie's house. The ache that surfaces every time I think about her throbs from my gut once more in tandem with the beat of my heart.

"Oh my. That's quite pretty."

It's a quiet minute after Opal speaks. She peers around, taking it all in. Evan and I stand on either side of her, quietly observing too.

"Was it worth the long drive?" he asks.

"One hundred percent," she says, her gaze following a flock of geese as they soar above.

We left April's house early this morning to make the ninety-minute drive. To my surprise, April didn't put up much of a fight when Evan and I approached her with the idea of taking Opal on a day trip to see some sights in the area. She was reluctant at first when Evan explained how we planned to sightsee at Indian Cave and then drive to Lincoln to find a place to eat before heading back home to Omaha in the evening. I don't blame her. Her mother has dementia, and that adds an element of worry to any travel situation.

But Evan explained that since it would be the two of us, we'd keep a careful eye on Opal and accompany her always. I told April I'd text her updates throughout the day on how Opal was feeling. And we promised that if at any point she started to feel or act a bit off, we'd come right home.

So far, Opal has been having a grand time. I found multiple versions of "My Sweetie Sparrow" online from various artists. I downloaded them and added them to a big-band playlist that we could listen to during the entire daylong trip. That's kept her mood up, and she's been alternating between humming along with the music and chatting since we left this morning.

But now, as she stands at the lookout point and takes in the view, she's quiet.

The sounds of birds chirping in the nearby trees seem to pull her out of her trance.

"What a magnificent sound. Nature in all its glory," she says.

"Beautifully said, Opal."

After a few minutes, I ask if she's up for a snack. She says yes, so we make our way back down to the car and drive to a picnic area. We find a shaded table, and I pull out the snacks and a thermos of tea I packed earlier.

"Goodness, this heat." Opal tugs lightly on the brim of her sun hat.

"You feeling okay?" Evan asks as he pours her a cup of tea.

"Oh, yes. Doing all right. This shade helps. Feels about twenty degrees cooler under this tree than if I were to take two steps back into the sun. Goodness, that smells amazing."

"It's raspberry hibiscus tea. From my friend Keely," I say.

I think back to how she made me take the tea, along with a bag of other snacks. Due to her pregnancy, she's been experiencing aversions to certain foods and drinks, tea being one of them.

"Keely. What a lovely name. Lovely name, lovely tea. Lovely, lovely . . ." Opal muses before sipping from her cup.

As I pull out the fruit bars Evan whipped up yesterday, Opal rubs her hands together. "That looks very yummy."

"They're strawberry and oat bars. I pulsed the oats extra fine so that they're easy for you to chew."

When Opal smiles a thanks to Evan, he beams. Ever since that day when he came over to cook lunch for us, Opal has been happy every time she's seen him. She can't remember his name, but she no longer greets him with a confused frown. There are always a few seconds when she looks at him while her brain figures out how to place him. Then I remind her that he's Evan, my friend who cooks her favorite shepherd's pie—the one with the same name as the singer of her favorite song. And then she smiles at him.

The three of us sit quietly and eat our snacks. I'm about to ask if she wants a refill on her tea, but I catch her gazing at Evan as he eats, a faraway expression on her face. Then she reaches over and pats his hand.

"You were such a cute baby."

He stops chewing as he looks at her. "I was?"

"You had chunky cheeks and so much hair." She stretches her hand up and touches his hair. "You've kept it long. I like it."

For a second, Evan doesn't move. He just looks at Opal, barely blinking. Like he's not quite sure he's heard her correctly.

I'm stunned as I observe Opal recognize her grandson. This kind of thing can happen—a person with dementia can randomly remember a loved one they've struggled to recognize as the disease progresses. I've seen it happen from time to time. The moment is sometimes fleeting— they'll eventually forget their loved one all over again. But it doesn't take away from how meaningful it is when they do remember.

Despite the stifling heat, goose bumps flash across my skin at the wonder of this moment, how special it is.

"You were so sweet," Opal says. "Even when you cried, it wasn't like other babies. The sound was softer. Gentler. Like a little birdie."

She pats Evan's hand before stretching her cup to me for more tea. I stammer for a second before I pour her more. Then I look up at Evan. Tears glisten in his eyes. It makes me tear up too.

"You okay?" she asks him.

He clears his throat, then blinks quickly. "Yes. I'm great. Just allergies."

Opal nods like she understands. When we finish, we walk back to the car to do more sightseeing. Evan walks by Opal's side, and after a few seconds, she reaches to hold his arm for support.

For a second, he freezes midstep and aims a shocked stare at her, like he can't believe this is actually happening. But then he relaxes, smiles down at her, and continues walking. As they make their way to the car together, he twists his head slightly to look at me.

"She remembers me." There's a quiver to his whispered words that makes my heart swell.

I smile at him. "Of course she does."

~

"Is this Gibson's?" Opal leans forward in the front seat of the car, peering up at the building Evan just parked in front of. The sign above boasts the word REMEDY in white cursive letters.

He shuts off the car. "Gibson's is closed today, sadly. We'll have to go some other time." He tosses a look at me as I sit in the back seat. "But this place has shepherd's pie and great gin martinis."

"It's just as good as Gibson's," I say as I lean over to Opal, gently patting her shoulder. "Just you wait and see."

Evan and I agreed to downplay the fact that Gibson's no longer exists and instead focused on finding a place with shepherd's pie and gin martinis on the menu. That's why we're at this offbeat dive bar–café hybrid on the edge of downtown Lincoln.

When we walk inside, we're hit with a blast of icy air from the AC. But that's nowhere near as arresting as the decor. Paintings of naked bodies adorn the walls. Each of the paintings has a string of multicolored Christmas lights wrapped around its frame. Mounted to the walls between the paintings are what look like random antique decor pieces. There's a crystal ashtray, a metal ashtray, brass candleholders, ceramic bookends, and a small mirror.

"Goodness." Opal gazes along the walls, and I feel my face heat.

I look at Evan. "I guess we should have looked up pictures of this place."

He lets out a chuckle as he glances at a nearby watercolor of two people in an acrobatic sexual position. His cheeks flare red as he rubs the back of his neck.

The hostess seats us at a table, and we order drinks while skimming the menu.

"How's the martini, Opal?" I ask.

"Pretty darn good. Not quite as good as Gibson's, but it'll do."

Evan and I laugh at her matter-of-fact tone. After we put in our order for dinner, an employee sets up a microphone and stool near the back wall several feet away from us. Then he turns the mic on.

"Hope you're all enjoying your meals. And I hope you're ready for a rousing night of poetry. Welcome to poetry night at Remedy."

Whistles and claps follow. He invites anyone who'd like to share their poems to sign up at the host stand.

"We start in five minutes. Thanks, everyone!"

I glance over at Opal, concerned. Will this be too overstimulating for her? I was expecting a relatively low-key evening of sharing a meal and chatting, but this poetry contest could get loud or distracting, which could upset her.

But then she smiles, her eyes bright. "Oh, a poetry reading! How fun!"

I'm relieved at how excited she is. We get our food just as the first poet starts. Opal is captivated as she listens while eating her shepherd's pie. She fixes her gaze on each performer, barely blinking the entire time they're onstage. When they finish, she claps and cheers.

"I didn't know you were so into poetry," I say to her.

"Oh, I love it. So much emotion conveyed in so few words."

The poems are a unique soundtrack to dinner. Some poets are soft-spoken, some animated, some bellow their prose, others gesture wildly. I don't pay much attention until a young woman with her long black hair in a braid walks up to the mic. She swipes her braid over her shoulder, smooths a hand over the front of her mustard-yellow sundress, then closes her eyes. The whole restaurant falls silent as we wait for her to start.

When she opens her eyes, her whole facial expression changes. There's a determined focus in her gaze, but it doesn't appear like she's looking at anything or anyone in particular. Almost like she's in a trance. And then she begins.

> Again and again we go and go.
> With the flow you say? Okay.
> Okay so then it's you and me and just us three
>   forever and ever.

But no. Wait. There's just us two.

Invisible, imaginable, tainted with tears and
blood and water.

Hold my hand, it'll be okay you say. But it's not.

It wasn't and it never will be.

But you love me. You love me.

You love me forever and ever.

Like Aphrodite's sparrow.

Like a song I can't ever forget.

Like a melody I hum forever and ever, even when
I can't remember the words.

Like a fish loves the sea.

Like an ant loves the earth.

Like I love you, forever and ever.

But you left anyway.

Three, then two, then one.

You went away.

I wasn't ready.

You say you're here even when you're not.

I don't believe you.

You say it again and again.

I wasn't ready.

But I am now.

I am ready, I am ready, I am ready.

Now.

When she finishes, applause erupts once more. It takes a second for me to join in, I'm still so focused on the words of her poem. *Hypnotized* is probably a better word. Like I was in a trance listening to the melodic register of her voice as she recited line after line.

I don't know why I'm so moved. Poetry was the unit in English class I slept through; I had zero interest in it. I can't think of a single poem—or story or book, for that matter—that has ever elicited this kind of response from me: pure awe.

The poet smiles shyly at the clapping patrons, then says a quiet thank-you before leaving the makeshift stage.

Evan starts to ask me a question, but I tell him to hold on a second. Before I realize what I'm doing, I dart up out of my seat and follow the young woman.

I catch up with her at the edge of the dining area. "Excuse me."

When she turns around to look at me, it finally registers just how weird this is going to sound. "I just wanted to say you were amazing. Your poem was so moving. You're incredibly talented."

She flashes a shy smile. "Oh. Thank you."

I stick out my hand. "I'm Isabel."

She glances at my hand, like she's thrown by the sight of it. "I'm Ruby." Her hand feels so cold and soft in mine.

For a few seconds after we release our hands, she looks at me like she's waiting for me to say something. But I can't think of anything. My mind is in a fog. Like I'm in a weird state of shock and can't manage to scrounge up enough words to even make small talk.

"Um, I was just wondering if you have a website or a book or somewhere you publish your poetry," I finally say. "I really love it and would like to read more."

"Oh. Of course." She smiles as she pulls up her phone and shows me her website.

I make note of it in my phone. "Thank you. So much."

"Well . . . I should probably get back to my friends," she says.

"Oh, sure. Um, thanks again."

She flashes a polite smile before walking off. I start to turn around, then freeze in place when I see my parents standing at the entrance of the restaurant, staring at me.

"Anak?"

"Isabel?"

145

They speak at the same time. Their mouths hang open when I don't answer them. It's like they're struggling to process the sight of me.

I'm doing the same with them. A funky diner isn't the kind of place my parents usually head to for dinner. They'd rather hit up a steak house or a cute bistro. Of all places I'd run into them, this is the last place I'd expect.

When my brain finally registers that I'm about to have a conversation with my parents—who I haven't seen in months—in public, I gesture toward the door.

"Do you want to go outside for a minute?"

They both nod at me, and the three of us walk out. The stagnant heat and humidity hit us like a slap to the face when we step outside. We shuffle off to the side to avoid blocking anyone coming in and out of the restaurant.

Mom studies me like she's looking at a science experiment. I don't blame her. My life for more than the past two years has consisted of going to work and then staying home. I never venture out.

I glance at Dad. His eyes are teary and bloodshot. He looks lost and broken. And then comes the recognition. Like he can't quite believe it's me standing in front of him. A lump in my throat forms instantly.

"Sweetie. Hi."

Despite the knot in my chest, I can't help but smile. My heart aches at seeing him after all these months.

He steps forward and pulls me into a hug.

"It's so good to see you, sweetie."

I savor the feel of his embrace, but after a beat, I notice that his once-strong arms feel thinner than they used to. When we finally pull away and I get a close-up look at him, I see more signs of aging and fatigue. The bags under his blue eyes that didn't used to be there. The lines in his forehead and around his mouth that look like they've been etched deeper into his skin. The gray stubble he clearly hasn't bothered to shave. That's the most jarring of all—he normally shaves every morning before work.

Mom pulls me into a hug. "What are you doing here?" she finally asks.

"I was about to ask you two the same question."

I try to chuckle, but it comes off so weak-sounding. Mom isn't amused. That look of shock remains on her face. Dad cracks a slight smile.

"The steak house we tried to go to had an hour-long-plus wait. So did every other restaurant we checked in the Haymarket," he says. "Figured we'd be spontaneous and give this place a shot."

"Oh. Yeah, I guess—"

"You never go out, let alone here in Lincoln."

I'm thrown off by Mom's blunt comment. "Well, um . . . I . . ."

Just then, the door swings open and out walks Evan.

"Hey." He sounds breathless, like he's been running around looking for me. "You okay?"

"Yeah. Fine." I dart my gaze back to my parents. "I ran into my parents."

"Oh." Evan flashes an easy smile at them, then moves to shake their hands. "I'm Evan."

Mom and Dad smile politely in return while shaking his hand. I catch Mom giving him an extra-long once-over. My insides harden. I know exactly what she's thinking. *Who the hell is this guy, and what is he doing with my daughter?*

"We were just out to dinner. With Evan's grandmother," I say quickly.

"Oh?" Mom's tone edges on accusatory more than curious. Every muscle in my neck and shoulders tenses.

"Isabel has been a wonderful caretaker for my grandmother," Evan says. "My family's so happy to have found her."

Both of my parents adopt a confused frown.

"Caretaker?" Mom chokes.

I press my eyes shut and take a breath in preparation for what I'm about to tell them. I turn to Evan quickly.

"I'll meet you back inside, okay?"

It doesn't take more than a second for him to catch my drift. He does a quick look between my parents and me, seeming to pick up the tension in the air.

"Sure thing. It was nice to meet you both."

They murmur niceties just before he scurries away.

"You take care of his grandma?" Mom asks.

I nod.

"For how long?"

"Um, about two months."

Mom's eyes bulge.

"But how?" Dad asks. "Doesn't that interfere with your job at the hospital?"

"Not really. I'm, uh, not working there anymore." I quickly explain that I've taken a break for the summer and started working as a caretaker to fill my open hours.

"Oh, well. That's great, sweetie." Dad sounds more bewildered than anything. But Mom? I can feel the steam rising from her like smoke billowing from a wildfire.

"Mom—"

She scoffs, then starts to walk away. Dad follows her, and I trail after them both.

"Mom, wait."

She ignores me for a half a block but then stops all of a sudden to turn around. "No, Isabel. You wait."

Her shoulder-length black hair swishes with the movement. Like a reflex, I hold up my hand at her. If this moment wasn't riddled with tension, I'd laugh. As if holding my palm in the air is going to stop her from going off on me.

"I know what you're going to say."

"Do you, Isabel? I bet you don't. I bet you didn't know I was going to say that I'm so damn hurt and mad right now."

I lose all the words in my mouth as I stare at her, the pain evident in her glistening eyes and her trembling lips.

Dad reaches for her hand, but she yanks her arm away. It's the perfect illustration of their dynamic. Mom's always been the fiery one, and he's always been the even-keeled one to stand by and attempt to calm her down.

"I gave you space, *anak*. Just like you told us to. We both did. Do you know how many times I—we wanted to come and see you? Do you know how many times we wanted to call you and hear your voice? Do you know how hard it is not to drive to your house and check on you every day? You shut us out for years. And now you're all of a sudden out and about. Honestly, I'm relieved to see that you're not holed up in your house day after day. But you took the summer off from your job? Why didn't you tell us? We could have seen you. We could have spent time together. We could have taken a trip. We would have dropped everything to . . ." She pauses to sniffle before wiping her nose on the back of her wrist. "We could have gone to the Philippines to see family. We haven't done that since you were in college. But no, you've been hiding out—hiding from us. You're here in Lincoln, and you didn't even think to come see us. Why? We're your parents. We love you. We're dying to see you."

Her voice breaks on her very last word, which sends a flood of tears pooling in my eyes.

"Mom, I—"

"You changed jobs? You take care of someone else's family now? You spend time with other people now instead of us? You didn't even think to tell us. You treat us like strangers. It's so hurtful, *anak*. I wish you knew just how much it kills us to feel you cut us out of your life like this. All we ever wanted was to be part of it."

She digs through her purse for a tissue and wipes her nose. Dad moves to rest his hand on her back. When she doesn't jerk away from his touch this time, he looks relieved.

He starts to speak to her, but she stops him.

"Maybe you can talk some sense into our daughter," she bites. "I'll wait in the car."

Mom stomps off, leaving Dad and me standing there on the sidewalk. We watch her walk to their car, which is parked a block way, and climb into the passenger seat.

I wipe my eyes and hazard a glance at Dad. The pained look on his face socks me straight in the gut.

"I honestly didn't mean to hurt you guys like this."

"I know that, honey."

He slides his hands into the pockets of his trousers, his gaze lingering on me. Like he's trying to commit my appearance to memory.

Traffic zooms by along the street next to us. We both stand and watch the cars whizz past for a few moments.

"We just want to see you—that's all this boils down to," he finally says.

"I want to see you guys too. It's just that, the last time you two tried to see me, you ambushed me with that intervention or whatever that was. That really hurt me. And it turned me off of seeing you guys."

I know he knows this. But I need to say it again. I need him to understand how it made me feel.

"I understand, honey. And I'm so sorry. Your mom is too."

"I just wish she would stop pushing me to go to church or get help or whatever. I'm not interested in doing that."

"Isabel, honey. She's trying. She really is. Can you just . . ." He rubs his temple with his fist. "We're sorry for what we did. We won't do it again, I promise we won't. Will you please consider seeing us again?"

The desperation in his voice, the pleading in his tone shatters me. I know right then and there I'm done distancing myself from them. I want to figure out a way to have them back in my life.

I walk the three steps into his arms and pull him into a hug. "I'm so sorry. Of course I want to see you."

He hugs me tight and sniffles into my hair. When we break apart, we walk arm in arm to their car.

Mom's tear-soaked face shines under the nearby streetlight. The way her tan skin glows, she looks like a sad angel.

I crouch to her side of the car and wait for her to roll down the window. "Let's plan a trip to the Philippines together," I say.

Her brown eyes bulge, and she stammers for a few seconds. "Really?"

"Yeah. Really. I want to go with you and Dad. Working this new job . . . taking care of Evan's grandma, being around their family showed me I can be around people again. I *want* to be around people again. I *want* to be around my family. You're right, it's been too long, and I miss *Apong* Marie, my cousins, aunties, uncles, everyone. I want to see them. Will you two go with me?"

For so long, I've been holding in this thought, not daring to speak it. It was like I was scared that saying it out loud would send me into a panic and would wipe away the urge. But it didn't. I feel the same as I did before—hopeful and eager.

Mom's trembling lips stretch into a smile. Then she opens the car door, hops out, and pulls me into a hug.

"Always hug," I whisper as I hold her tight against me.

"Always," she whispers back.

And then she dives straight into talking about flights and tickets and taking time off work. She speaks so fast, her voice practically a squeal, I can barely understand what she's saying. Something about how excited everyone will be when she calls them to tell them that I'm coming for a visit and how we'll need to bring extra suitcases for all the gifts she's planning to give everyone when we arrive.

Dad chuckles before reassuring her in a well-meaning tone that we'll have plenty of time to plan everything.

When we let each other go, I ask if I can come over for dinner next Sunday. They both let out excited yesses.

"We can start thinking about the exact dates we want to go, look at plane ticket prices, all the—"

Mom yanks me back against her in a hug before I even finish my sentence, just like before. I close my eyes and relish the embrace, the vanilla smell of her shampoo, the way she hums lightly as she exhales.

When she lets me go, I wipe my eyes. "I'd better go back inside."

They nod their understanding. I start to turn away, but Mom grabs my arm. "Thank you, *anak*."

"Thank you." I look up at Dad. "And thank you."

I hug them both one more time before they take off, and I head back into the restaurant.

Chapter Thirteen

"Sorry for leaving you guys at the table earlier," I say to Evan as he drives us back to Omaha.

"It's all right," he says before twisting around to look at Opal.

I turn to look, too, and notice a faint smile on her face. When she blinks, it takes her a second before she opens her eyes. She must be exhausted after today.

"Feeling okay, Opal?" I ask.

"Oh, yes. Just a bit tired. And my legs are a bit sore, too, from all the walking we did." She coughs. "But I suppose that's not a huge surprise. It was an eventful day. And wonderful too."

She leans back to rest her head against the headrest, then closes her eyes.

"Everything okay with your parents?" Evan asks.

"I think so."

"You wanna talk about it?"

I glance over at him.

"You listened when I talked about how crappy it felt to be forgotten by . . ." He nods at Opal. "And when I vented about my breakup. Over green smoothies, remember? Most people wouldn't do that without alcohol."

I laugh at the face he pulls.

"I want to be a listener for you, too, if you want it," he says.

The sincerity in his voice soothes me in a way I didn't expect it to. It's not that I haven't heard him sound like this before. If anything, Evan is one of the most sincere people I've met. He's been honest about everything in front of me, whether he's expressing frustration or regret or gratitude.

But there's something about talking to him about my own mess— about my family, our dysfunction, and my faults—that makes me the slightest bit skittish. I realize it's because I'm going to need to be vulnerable with him. And even though I allow myself to be vulnerable in front of my sister and more recently Keely, that's different. I have a past with them. Years and years of history. I've known Evan for only a couple of months. And there's something scary about letting someone in who I haven't known for long, especially when I've been so closed off from people in general for so long.

"If you don't want to or don't feel comfortable talking about it, it's okay," he says, almost like he's reading my mind. Then he takes his eyes off the road for a second to look at me. "Just, if you wanna talk about it, I'm here. We're friends, after all."

"Are we?"

I'm relieved that he chuckles. My tone was a tad bit hard now that I think about it.

"You don't think we are? Ouch." The corner of his mouth quirks up.

I let out a soft laugh. "I guess that was a weird thing for me to say."

"I want to be your friend, Isabel. Is that a weird thing to say?"

I smile at his honesty, at how he has no qualms whatsoever about putting his feelings out in the open—at how he admits that he wants to be my friend. I don't think I've ever heard anyone say that to me.

"It's not weird at all," I say. "Okay, yeah. We're friends."

He pumps a fist in the air, and I laugh, then cover my mouth at how loud I'm being. I turn around to check on Opal and am relieved when I see she's still snoozing in the back seat, unbothered.

"My parents and I have had kind of a strained relationship for the past few years," I say when I'm front facing in my seat again.

"Damn. Really?"

I nod. "I don't want to get into the nitty-gritty details. But the gist of it is that they wish that I would see them more. And go to church. And that I was more social. And some other stuff."

"Wait, you don't go to church?"

I almost laugh at the surprise in his tone. "No. I don't."

"Huh. I guess I just figured that, since you're a chaplain, you go to church. Is it bad that before I met you, I assumed all hospital chaplains were super religious people over the age of fifty?"

I laugh, then cover my mouth and quickly check behind me to make sure I haven't woken Opal. "My best friend, Keely, said something similar when I told her I wanted to become a chaplain. She said I was too young and too cute."

I shake my head at the memory. "So no, you're not the only one to have that thought. A lot of people assume what you do. But a lot of us chaplains, especially interfaith ones, are just people who want to be there for folks in their time of need."

"You're definitely that. You've been a pretty amazing support for my family and me."

His compliment echoes in my ears. I shift in my seat, uncomfortable, for several seconds until I realize why: Evan is sitting here, thinking I'm so selfless and dignified. I'm not. At all.

"I'm a fraud, Evan." Wow. I'm surprised I had the guts to say that out loud.

"What do you mean?"

"I'm a chaplain who believes in nothing," I murmur. "I'm not as amazing as you think I am."

He's quiet for a while, no doubt processing the bomb I just dropped. I brace myself for a bevy of questions, for him to be annoyed and disappointed—maybe even pissed—at what I've just told him.

But all he says is, "You wanna talk about it?"

I twist to look at him and laugh. Then he starts to chuckle.

"I wasn't expecting that."

"What were you expecting me to say?"

"I'm not sure, honestly. I thought maybe you'd be disappointed. Or angry. Or hell-bent on doing another background check on me."

That makes him laugh again.

"I'm not gonna do any of that," he says. "I'm the last person in the world to judge anyone on how they'd act. Especially not you, given the way I've let myself behave around you these past couple of months." He rolls his shoulders like he's stretching.

As we share another quiet moment, a weird type of calm engulfs me. I think it has something to do with Evan's nonreaction to what I've just confessed. And inside, I feel compelled to say more.

"I used to be pretty spiritual," I finally say. "But I'm not anymore. I guess you could say I'm having a crisis of faith."

I hold my breath. That's the first time I've admitted that to anyone out loud, other than Chantel. How is Evan going to react?

"How does that work with your job as a chaplain?" he asks.

"Fine so far. You'd be surprised just how little religion has to do with my job. People hardly ever want me to pray with them. Nine times out of ten, they just want me to be there as a supportive presence. They want me to listen as they talk through whatever emotional or traumatic stuff they're going through."

"I see." A soft smile tugs at his lips. "Kind of like me."

"Kind of."

"Can I ask you something else?"

"Sure."

"What do you do if someone asks you to pray with them? Does it feel . . . weird . . . or wrong, since you don't really believe in anything?"

"If they want a particular prayer of a specific religion, I don't perform that. Like, if they want a priest or a rabbi or an imam or any other religious clergy person, we have a list of contacts affiliated with the hospital I can call. We arrange for them to come and pray with or counsel the family. A couple of the part-time chaplains are clergy members, so they're able to do that too."

"What if they just want a regular, good old-fashioned prayer from an interfaith chaplain?"

"Then I pray for them. I stay general. Usually I start off by saying something like, 'I ask that you please give strength to so-and-so as they' whatever it is that we talked about they're going through."

He gazes at the darkened road ahead, his expression turning thoughtful. "I really admire that you're able to still pray even though you're unsure," Evan says.

"It's my job."

I'm startled by how strange it feels to speak those three words. It almost feels wrong. I haven't worked as a chaplain in two months, but I'm planning on going back at the end of the summer.

It's my job.

Then why doesn't it feel like that anymore?

I ignore the seed of doubt burrowing inside me and focus back on the conversation with Evan.

"Earlier tonight, my parents and I started to talk out some of the issues we've been dealing with," I say. "I'm going to be better about seeing them more often, and they're not going to push me to do things I don't want to do. We're not magically okay. But we're on our way to something better. I think."

That pressure in my chest eases as my words hang in the air.

"I'm so glad," Evan says, aiming a gentle smile at me. "And hey, feel free to ignore what I'm about to say. Or just tell me to shut up. But the things you say your parents disapprove of about you seem pretty minor. I'm sure you can work through them. You're an amazing person, and they'll love you no matter what. I think it'll all be okay."

Something about his words hits me where I need it most: in the center of my chest, where my heart is.

It'll all be okay.

When we pull into April's driveway, Opal is out cold. Evan climbs out of the driver's seat and steps to the back passenger seat, scoops her into his arms, and walks up the porch steps after me. She doesn't even stir, making that deep-breathing wheeze that emanates from her when she sleeps. I hold the door for him and unload the car as he gets her into bed.

When I finish, I go to leave, but he softly calls my name.

I turn around to him. The only light in the living room is from a nearby lamp. The rest of the house is pitch-black. Even in the dimness, I can spot the fatigue in the slight hunch of his posture and in his eyes from all the driving he did today. But when he smiles, it's like he's lit from within.

"Thanks for everything you did today, Isabel. This was amazing."

"Of course. I was happy to."

His mouth curls like he's about to say something more. But he stays quiet.

"Have a good night, then," I say.

"Good night."

I head out the door to my car parked along the street. On my drive home, I don't bother to turn the radio on or call Chantel to catch her up on what happened today. Instead I opt for silence. Until I open my mouth and speak.

"Friend."

It's been so long since I've said that word—since I've had someone new to call my friend.

"Friend." I smile.

Evan is my friend.

Chapter Fourteen

When I arrive at April's house in the morning and knock, there's no answer. I double-check the time and the date. I check my messages and texts to see if I've missed a call from April to let me know about a schedule change or a last-minute appointment or anything like that. But nothing.

I knock again but still no answer.

I think back to the last day I was here, two days ago. That was the day Evan and I took Opal on her mini road trip. We saw April that morning, but everything seemed fine. She didn't mention a schedule change for today or anything like that.

I pull out my phone again and call her but get her voice mail.

"Hi, April. It's Isabel. I'm here at the house today to look after Opal, but I don't see anyone here. Could you give me a call back and let me know if everything's okay? Maybe I got my days mixed up."

I hang up the phone, feeling the tiniest bit unsettled. Something is clearly off.

I sit on the porch and wait for a call back, but when twenty minutes pass and still nothing from April, I pull out my phone and call Evan. It rings for so long that I expect I'll get his voice mail too.

But then he answers. "Hello?" His voice is watery and rough. The sound rockets me back to the day we met in the elevator, when his eyes were red and teary and angry.

"Sorry to call you this early, but I'm at your mom's house to watch Opal for the day, and no one's here. Did they go somewhere? Is everything okay?"

He hesitates. "No. Not really."

Dread socks me in my stomach. He coughs, but it sounds like he's trying to cover up a crying sound.

"Evan, what's wrong?"

There's a shuffling noise that goes on for seconds before he answers me. When he finally speaks, I'm not prepared at all.

"Opal collapsed on Sunday. We took her to the hospital, and it's . . . it's bad, Isabel."

His voice breaks as he says my name. I open my mouth, but nothing comes out. I'm too shocked. I'm too numb. This isn't happening. It can't be.

"We're at the hospital. Immanuel in north Omaha. Can you come?"

"I'm on my way."

~

As I walk along the tenth floor of Immanuel Hospital, I'm in a daze. It's like I'm trapped in a sound cloud. I can barely hear what's going on around me. Machines beeping and elevators dinging and people talking, but the noises blur together like some distorted and muffled soundtrack.

When I make it to Opal's room, the door's closed. I knock softly. Behind it, I hear the soft shuffle of footsteps. Then the door opens, and I see April's flushed face. I zero in on her bloodshot eyes. Instantly, my stomach drops.

"I'm sorry."

I don't know why my first words to her are an apology. Evan said it was okay for me to come here. But as I stand and gaze at April, her swollen eyes, tears streaked along her cheeks, her expression agony, *I'm sorry* seems like the only appropriate thing to say.

She nods like she understands completely. Then she steps aside to let me in.

I explain that I tried to call her earlier when I saw there was no one at the house and then called Evan, and that's when he told me what happened.

As we huddle near the door, I look over to the middle of the room and see a nurse checking on Opal's IV. Opal's eyes look slightly swollen, like she hasn't slept enough. But otherwise she looks the same. Even the corners of her mouth are quirked up into a slight smile.

I notice that Evan's not in the room. Maybe he slipped out for a second.

"I didn't mean to intrude," I say. "Evan said it was okay if I came."

April pats my arm, smiling through her tears. "Of course it's okay. She'll be so happy to see you."

She peers over at Opal. Her lips wobble, but when she takes a breath, she steadies. She dabs a tissue at her nose.

"We got some bad news." April's tone is barely above a whisper. "Mom's been diagnosed with lung cancer. It's metastasized."

"Oh my god." My knees wobble so hard that I have to clutch the wall.

April's face twists in pain. As she lets out a soft cry, she covers her mouth with her hand. I hold her arm, willing myself to stay steady for her.

"I'm so sorry, April."

It takes a Herculean effort to keep my voice steady, but I manage. I can't fall apart when April has just been given the worst news of her life. First she has to watch as her mother slowly succumbs to dementia, and now she has to watch as cancer ravages her.

I bite the inside of my cheek until I'm certain I won't let out a cry.

I start to say that I can leave to give them some privacy, but she shakes her head.

"No. Please stay, will you? I'm honestly so happy you showed up. I should have called you this morning." She shakes her head while pressing her eyes shut, like she's powering through a headache. "I just didn't think to. My brain has been trapped in a fog since Mom collapsed. All I can focus on is Mom, all the tests she's been undergoing and all the updates from the doctor."

She tries to wipe her nose with a tiny crumpled tissue. I dig a fresh one from my purse and hand it to her. She garbles a thank-you before wiping her face and blowing her nose.

"She's never smoked a day in her life." April shoves the crumpled tissue in the pocket of the oatmeal-hued drapey sweater she's wearing. "How unfair is that?"

"It is. So unfair."

"I know that's not how life works. You don't have to smoke to get lung cancer. But still. It's absolutely gutting, knowing she has this to deal with now on top of her dementia."

"It's okay to be angry about it, April. Your mother is a wonderful person, and you have every right to feel upset for her. For you. For your family."

Her shoulders shake as she nods while taking a few deep breaths. "You know, when the doctor explained the diagnosis to her, Mom laughed. She said, *That's not possible. I'm not a smoker. Never have been, never will be.*"

My nose tingles as I fight the urge to cry. I manage a small smile instead. "I can just imagine her saying that."

"The doctor tried to explain that the particular type of lung cancer she has isn't necessarily connected to smoking, but she wouldn't listen. She just kept asking questions about her parents and if they were going to serve shepherd's pie for dinner and if she could have a gin martini." A weak laugh falls from April's shaky lips. "I shouldn't laugh. It's really not funny."

"It's okay to find moments of humor in things like this. It's a healthy way to cope. And it can be very comforting."

Her gaze falls to her shoes. "It's clear that her dementia is preventing her from fully understanding the gravity of the situation. In a way, that's devastating, but is it bad that I feel relieved, too, in some small way? Like, yes, it's unfortunate that she doesn't really know what's going on, but it's a blessing too. She's not consumed with fear or stress. She won't be stressing out about treatments or survival rates."

She hugs her arms around herself.

"I don't think that's bad at all," I say. "The good thing about this—if there is a good thing to take from it—is that she's operating in a state of mind that seems to be very joyful. That counts for a lot in a situation like this."

The smile April gives me nearly breaks me. Her lips are trembling as they hold that upturned shape. It's sad and happy all at once.

"I suppose you're right." She lets out a shaky sigh. "I hadn't thought of it that way."

She pats my hand, and I give her another tissue. The nurse finishes up and walks out of the room. Opal glances at the nearby window, that slight smile holding strong on her face. I almost lose it.

"I'm her medical power of attorney, so it's up to me what kind of treatment she'll receive," April says, pulling my focus back to her. "But I don't know what to do. I tried asking her what she wants, but it's no use. She doesn't understand this situation. She doesn't even know what's going on."

"I can't imagine how difficult it must be for you to have that decision weighing on you right now," I say. "But whatever you decide will be the right decision, I promise. Your mom loves you and trusts you. She'd be happy with whatever you decide to do."

She swallows as a few more tears cascade along her cheeks. I ask if the doctor who's treating Opal offered to discuss treatment options with her. She nods.

"We've been talking about the options as a family. Evan and my daughter say they'll support me no matter what, whatever I decide. But I don't know if I can."

She shakes her head, the weight of this situation evident in her pained expression, her hunched-over shoulders, the endless stream of tears running down her face.

"I just wasn't in the right headspace to even think about coming to a decision before," April says. "I needed some time to process everything. And to just be with her, you know?"

"Of course. That's more than understandable."

"I know time isn't on our side, though. I need to make a decision soon and tell her doctor."

I squeeze her hand. "Taking a day or two is perfectly fine. It's helpful, in fact. You don't want to rush into a decision like this. The fact that you're taking some time to carefully figure out what's best for your mom is a good thing. It'll help her doctor come up with the best possible treatment plan for her."

"I don't know how this is going to affect her daily life as of yet, but if she's able to come home with me again, you'll still come stay with her for the rest of the summer, won't you? She really loves seeing you, and I want to keep her spirits as high as possible right now."

"Absolutely I will. I'll be there as often as you want me to be."

She glances at the clock on the wall. "I'm supposed to call her doctor now. Do you want to go in and see her?"

"You sure you feel up to doing that? Would you want to wait until Evan can be here for support? Or maybe when your daughter comes back?"

She shakes her head. "Gwen had to leave and take care of Jonah today. I don't want to bother her with this. And Evan's here, he's just down at the cafeteria."

She closes her eyes and shakes her head. The sigh that shoots out of her is so heavy, so burdened.

"He's taking this so hard. I sent him down to get some food. He hasn't slept or eaten since Mom collapsed, he's been so distraught."

My chest cracks in half at the thought of how much this is destroying him.

April pulls her phone from her pocket, then pats my arm. "Go ahead and see her."

She steps out of the room, shutting the door behind her. And then I take a second to breathe before I walk over to Opal. She's sitting up in the hospital bed, smiling down at a pile of colorful drawings, probably from her great-grandson.

There's a tightness in my throat that threatens the little composure I possess in this moment. When I blink, my eyes water. Opal hasn't seen me yet, but she will soon, and I can't cry. Not now, not when she's received a devastating medical diagnosis. Sure, she may not fully understand what's happening to her, but I don't want to confuse her or upset her by crying.

I force a smile. "Hi, Opal."

She looks up, and a long second passes as she looks at me. "Oh! Hello, dear! You're finally here! Boy, am I glad to see you. Do you know that they don't have shepherd's pie here? Or even cottage pie? Or gin martinis?"

I start to chuckle, but my throat aches so much from trying to hold it together that it sounds vaguely like a cry. I cough to cover the sound and clear my throat.

"Well, that's a shame."

"Isn't it? Here, sit."

She gestures to the chair next to her, and I settle in, heartened the slightest bit by the cheery lilt of her voice.

"Those are some lovely drawings," I say.

"Bunny brought them in." She shakes her head, squinting down at them. "I can't remember who made them, though."

Again, I fight the throb in my chest and throat. She's so confused. She doesn't even know her own great-grandson drew those for her. Just like she doesn't even know what's happening to her . . . she doesn't know about the cancer inside her.

I shake my head slightly and order those thoughts away.

"They're from Jonah. Your great-grandson."

A blank look is her response.

"You look so nice today. Did you do something different with your hair? It's styled so chicly," I say to change the subject. I want to do everything I can to keep from confusing or upsetting her right now.

"You're so sweet to say that." Smiling, she runs a hand through her hair. "Why yes, in fact, I did try something a bit different today. I didn't bother washing it."

The chuckle I let loose is a godsend. It almost feels as if we're laughing and chatting like normal.

"Well, it's working for you. You look lovely."

She waves a hand, as if to brush off the compliment. "At my age, you gotta work with what you have."

Her shapely gray eyebrows crinkle as she studies me, like she's trying to figure out a puzzle.

"There's something bothering you, dear, isn't there?"

A lie sits ready to go on my tongue. "I'm fine. Just a little tired."

Judging by her narrow gaze, she doesn't believe me.

"You look like you're upset about something. It's in your eyes, dear."

I ready another lie, but it dies in my mouth before I can speak it. What's the use of holding back the truth if she can already tell?

"Actually, Opal, you're right. I'm very sad."

"Oh, you poor thing. Here, give me your hand."

I reach my hand to her, and she clasps both of her hands around mine. I look down, mesmerized at how small and delicate she feels. Her crinkled, crepe-paper skin is silky to the touch.

"Tell Opal what's on your mind."

"It's . . . a friend of mine. She's very ill. And I'm sad because I don't know how much time she has left."

"My goodness. Oh, I'm so sorry."

Her hands squeeze around mine so gently, I could cry. And then a second later, I do.

I try everything to stay composed. I bite the inside of my cheek, I take a deep breath, I close my eyes. I think of puppies and kittens and funny YouTube videos and ridiculous jokes, but nothing works. Tears tumble down my cheeks like someone has flipped a switch, unleashing every tear pooling inside me.

"Here. You come sit next to me."

I scoot next to her on the edge of her bed. She wraps a tiny arm around me, pulling me close to her.

"That's it, you just cry it out."

For a long minute, that's exactly what I do. When I catch my breath, I turn to her. "I'm so sorry."

She flashes a bewildered look at me. "Don't you dare apologize. Honey, you're sad. It's okay to cry when you're sad."

She grabs a box of tissues from the table next to her bed and hands it to me. I quickly wipe at my face.

"I just wish there was something I could do," I mumble as I clump the wet tissue in my hands. "But I can't. There's nothing. There's nothing anyone can do."

Opal's tiny, powerful hands find mine once more. She gives me a squeeze that feels so sure, so doubtless, so confident.

"Honey, you're doing plenty by being a good friend and spending time with her. I promise."

The look in her eyes is the surest I've ever seen. It's beyond strange, the way things have played out. I'm supposed to be the strong one, the one who can keep my shit together and stay focused on positive things. But I've never felt weaker, more fragile, more on the verge of disintegrating into a million pieces.

And there's Opal, suffering from dementia and metastatic lung cancer. She is a pillar. She is strength and comfort at once. And she has no idea.

I look at her for a long second, that soft smile and her steady gaze unwavering. She's so sure, so certain.

"Thank you, Opal."

She pulls me into a hug. "You're welcome, dear."

I go back to my chair. "How are you feeling?"

"Pretty good. I went for a walk along the halls earlier with a nice young man. He had long hair pulled back and was quite tall and strong."

"Evan?"

"Yes! Evan. Oh, and Bunny promised me that we'll go for another walk again before dinner. Which is good because I'm feeling so cooped up and restless. I really need to get my steps in."

I smile slightly until my lips start to shake too much. I pull them into my mouth and wait a beat before telling Opal that sounds like fun.

She frowns slightly at me. "You know what I wish, though? That I could listen to some music. TV is great, but I think I'd rather listen to music most days."

I think back on how ever since I discovered that "My Sweetie Sparrow" was her favorite song, I've played it every day I'm with her.

"Let's see what we can do about that." I grab my phone and pull up the song. This time when I smile at her, my lips don't quiver at all.

When the opening bars of the song play, Opal grins wide and bops her head along to the beat, like she always does. Then she snaps her fingers and sings along to the lyrics. And I sit back and watch, enamored with the joy of this moment, with how happy she is.

The songs ends just as there's a soft knock at the door. I get up to answer it, but it opens before I can.

In walks Evan, looking disheveled as hell in a rumpled T-shirt and gym shorts, his hair matted in its bun.

He looks at me with bloodshot eyes. "Hey."

"Hey," I say quietly.

When I turn back to Opal, I notice she's squinting again as she looks at him.

"It's my friend Evan, remember? Evan like the Evan who sings 'My Sweetie Sparrow,' remember?"

Her frown eases as her lips curl into a smile. "Of course. Evan."

She goes back to looking at the drawings. I offer him the chair, but he gestures for me to stay seated.

"I've been sitting all night. I need to stand."

He leans against the wall near the foot of Opal's bed and scrubs a hand over his face. It seems to take him an extra second to open his eyes when he blinks. I think back on what April said, how he hasn't eaten or slept since Opal's diagnosis.

"Did you eat something?"

He nods but doesn't look at me. "A little."

"Have you slept?"

He closes his eyes and leans his head against the wall. "Not really."

"Well, then maybe you . . ."

April walks in, her expression relieved when she spots Evan. "You're back."

He nods and pulls her into a side hug.

"I just got off the phone with the doctor, to go over Mom's treatment plan."

I take that as my cue to leave so they can chat in private as a family. When I stand up and grab my purse, Opal stops me. "You're leaving, dear?"

"Oh, um . . ." I glance over at April and Evan. "Yes, but only for a bit. I'm going to pop out while all of you chat. But I'll be back later, okay?"

"Actually, Isabel." I turn to April. "Would you be able to give Evan a ride to his place once we're done talking?"

"Mom, come on." There's a slight groan to his tone.

She holds up a hand at him. "Honey, listen to me. You haven't slept this whole time. You've barely eaten. You're not in any shape to drive yourself all the way home to your house in Midtown."

"It's no problem. I'm happy to do it," I say quickly, hoping that saves them the trouble of arguing about it.

"Fine," Evan mumbles. When he falls into the chair I was sitting on, I'm relieved. He looks like he was seconds from toppling over.

"I'll just be outside," I tell them. "When you're finished, come get me and we'll go."

April pulls me into a hug. "Thank you, dear."

I close my eyes and squeeze her back. "Anything I can do for you and your family, just say so."

I turn to Opal. "Is there anything I can do for you? To make you happier or help you feel better?"

When she blinks, the sunlight streaming in from the window catches from a different angle, making her eyes appear like they're sparkling.

She reaches up and takes my hand in hers. "Not a thing, dear. I'm happy as a lark."

I squeeze her back, hoping I don't look too sad. I walk out of the room and wait in a nearby sitting area. When Evan comes out minutes later, I stand up.

"You ready to go home?"

He offers a tired nod. "Yeah."

Chapter Fifteen

When I pull into Evan's driveway, he's quiet, just like he's been the entire ride to his place save for giving me directions on how to get here and telling me what he wanted when I stopped at a fast food place on the way.

He was just as quiet back at the hospital when he and his mom finished going over her meeting with the doctor. Even when April announced that Opal got the okay to head home in a couple of days and continue home care with me, Evan didn't react. Not that I expected him to say or do much—he's clearly in shock at Opal's diagnosis and still trying to process it all.

I follow him through his front door, paper bag of greasy breakfast burritos in hand.

"You should eat."

"Mm-hmm."

Instead of taking the bag from my hand, he heads straight for his kitchen to the coffee machine sitting on the island.

"Evan." I try not to groan as I watch him brew a pot of coffee. "What are you doing?"

"What does it look like I'm doing?" he mutters before tugging out his hair tie. His gold-blond hair cascades around his shoulders before he gathers it in his hands and ties it back into a low bun that's only slightly less messy than it was before.

"Why are you making coffee? You need to go to sleep."

"Can't. Gotta head to the restaurant in a few hours."

I roll my eyes. "Jesus, Evan."

I walk over to the kitchen island and chuck the fast food bag onto the counter. Then I grab his arm. He stills instantly but won't look at me.

"Hey," I say gently. "Will you just stop for a minute?"

A sigh rockets through him. It's a second before he looks at me.

"I don't think it's a good idea for you to go to work after this many days of no sleep. You need to rest."

He pulls out of my hold, then grabs a mug from a nearby cupboard. "You've been spending too much time around my mom. You're starting to sound like her."

The dismissiveness in his tone unleashes a tiny ball of fury inside me. "What is that supposed to mean?"

His shoulders fall forward as he pivots slightly to face me. "I didn't mean it like . . . I just meant that I'm fine, and I don't need you to tell me what to do."

"Apparently, you do need me to, Evan. Because you think it's a good idea to work a full day in a busy restaurant when you haven't slept or eaten. That's dangerous. You could hurt yourself or someone else. You know better than to do something so careless."

What I've said seems to set him off, because he jerks the coffeepot from the burner before it's even done brewing and fills the mug he's holding. A steady stream of hot liquid dribbles onto the burner. The singeing sound echoes in his kitchen as a small cloud of steam forms over the burner.

"Evan, be careful—"

"Isabel, would you stop!"

The boom of his voice shouting the same phrase I spoke to him a minute ago jerks me back, and I bump my ass into the edge of his slate countertop. All I can do is stand there, my heart racing, my mouth open in shock, staring at him.

He blinks as he looks at me, like he can't believe what he just did.

"I'm sorry," he says through an exhale, rubbing a hand over his face.

He drops his hand to his side. When he looks at me this time, I see every emotion he's harboring on the inside as it plays out on his face. The agony, the disbelief, the pain, the anger, the confusion. He looks like a scared kid, not the handsome and confident guy I'm used to seeing.

His stare falls to the floor, and he shakes his head. "I just . . . this is so fucked up." After a moment, he looks up at me. "It's so goddamn unfair. All of this. First she has dementia and now this? Fucking lung cancer? How does that even make sense? How is any of this okay?"

I don't say anything. I just stand there and let him vent every thought circulating in his mind.

"And I know . . . look, I know that life's not fucking fair, good people get sick all the damn time. And there are times when I tell myself that I shouldn't be mad because my grandma is pushing ninety, so of course some health problems were bound to get her. There are people who die when they're young. There are people who would give anything to make it to her age."

He stops when his voice begins to shake. I stay quiet but nod at what he's saying.

"But no matter how much I remind myself of that, no matter how many times I tell myself to just be thankful that I've had this much time with her, it doesn't make me feel better. She deserves so much better than this. I'm still so sad and angry, and I can't . . . I can't . . ."

His eyes fill with tears. When his lips start trembling, he purses them before covering his face with his hands. A soft, muffled sob escapes. And that's when I go to him.

I step into him and wrap my arms around his torso. Because I'm so much smaller than he is, my face comes up to his chest, just under his collarbone. I can't see his face or gauge his reaction because of that. So I hold my breath as I absorb the sobs that rattle his body and hope that this is giving him some sort of comfort. It's not long before I feel his arms wrap slowly around me. I let out a quiet sigh of relief.

This means I didn't cross a line by hugging him. This means what I'm doing is okay.

We've never hugged before. In fact, I can't think of a time where we shared any sort of bodily contact except for a few touches on the arm while talking to each other.

But right now, this hug feels so right, so comfortable. Like we've done it a million times before.

I don't know how long we stand there, but it feels like a while. When his cries begin to ease, when he starts to catch his breath, I lean my head away to look at him.

"It's okay," I whisper up at him.

Still crying, he nods at me.

"Let's go sit down."

He lets me lead him by the hand to the plush gray sectional on the other side of the open-concept space, what I assume is the living room.

I sit him down and ease him to lie on his side. I grab the blanket that's draped along the back of the couch and cover him with it.

He's not crying anymore. He's still now, a faraway gaze in his bloodshot eyes, like he's in a trance. When I'm finished tucking the blanket around him, I move to walk away, but he catches my wrist.

"Wait." His voice is soft and scratchy and every bit as pleading as his stare. "Stay. Please."

I start to sit down next to him, but he stops me.

"No, I . . ." He hesitates, his eyes scanning my face, like he's too scared to say what he wants to say.

And then he scoots back against the couch. He's making room. For me.

I look him square in the eye, just to make sure this is what he wants.

"I, um, I know I don't have the right to ask or to even . . ."

I press my hand gently over his mouth, quieting him. Then I slide under the blanket with him. I shift so that I'm facing him and tuck a pillow under my head. I rest my arm and my cheek against his chest; he drapes his arm over me.

Soon his breathing turns deep and rhythmic. It's a while before I can fall asleep, too, though. That word from the other day, when Evan and I were driving back with Opal, echoes in my mind.

Friend.

That's not what this feels like, though.

～

I'm lying on Evan's couch watching him sleep. I woke maybe twenty minutes ago, but I haven't moved. I don't want to wake him.

My hand still rests against his chest; his arm is still resting on top of me.

I shifted slightly so I can look up at him, though. Yeah, it's a little creepy. But I can't help it. He looks so peaceful bundled under this blanket, his head propped against a pillow, his chest rising and falling with each soft breath he takes.

This moment where I'm awake while he's asleep is also buying me time. I need to gather my thoughts. I have no idea where to go from here, what to do. It's been ages since I've crashed at a friend's place but never, ever like this.

I've never comforted a friend after they received devastating news by cuddling them to sleep. Sure, I've consoled them, hugged them, and cried with them. That's pretty standard friend stuff. But not this. This thing with Evan is different. And I'm not quite sure why.

Maybe it's because I'm just coming off a two-year-plus hiatus from associating with friends in general, and that's why this feels so foreign. Maybe it's because we're new at this whole friend thing, and jumping into doing something as physically intimate as falling asleep while cuddled together is throwing things off completely.

Or it could be that I haven't done something like this—fall asleep tucked into the chest of a guy—in years. Not since my last relationship, which was a handful of years ago.

As even more muddled thoughts swirl through my brain, I close my eyes in an attempt to silence them all. It's no use, though. Because no matter what I do or don't think about, one thing remains true: Evan and I crossed some sort of line. This isn't the kind of thing you do with a friend, at least not for me. And I'm guessing based on how hesitant and pleading he was when he initiated this, this isn't something he does either.

I shift slightly when my leg starts to fall asleep, careful not to move too quickly. When he starts to stir, I hold my breath. But then he opens his eyes. He blinks a handful of times before his gaze starts to focus. I catch myself wondering if that's how he wakes up in the morning . . . or just mornings when he's next to someone. The thought sends blood rushing to my face.

He clears his throat and starts to smile. "Hey."

"Hey. How are you feeling?"

"Better," he says, his voice groggy with sleep. "You were right. I definitely need to rest."

He leans his head back and lets out a soft grunting noise as he stretches. I'm instantly hypnotized by the slow movement along his stubbled throat as he swallows. When he peers back down at me, his eyes turn shy. Then his gaze moves lower, to my hip, where his massive palm rests.

When he starts to slide it off me, I stop him.

"You don't have to pull away."

He pauses, resting his fingertips along the curve of my hip. "I feel like a creep for asking you to sleep on the couch with me."

"You're not a creep, Evan. I'm your friend. I was happy to do it. I wanted to."

Even as I say the word *friend*, it feels off. Like it doesn't belong in that sentence.

The look on his face tells me he doesn't buy it either. When he lightly taps his fingers against my hip, I shiver.

"I'm such a mess right now, Isabel."

"You're not. You're human. And you're going through a lot of pain right now. Give yourself a break."

When he shakes his head slightly, the movement of his skin against the fabric of the pillow makes a soft rubbing noise. For a minute, all we do is lie there quietly and look into each other's eyes. Every few seconds, he taps his fingers on my skin. My heartbeat quickens. So does my breath.

When my eyelids start to flutter, I force myself to refocus.

"You should eat something," I say.

"I'm not hungry."

"You need to drink water."

"I'm not thirsty."

"What do you want, Evan?"

"You."

The word falls from his lips in a gravelly rasp. My eyes search his face for any indication that he's having second thoughts about this, that he isn't okay with where this is obviously headed. But all I see is his dilated stare fixed on me and his chest heaving with each breath he takes.

I don't know who makes the first move. But I blink, and my lips are on his. I cup his stubbly cheek with my hand, he grips my hip, and I move my mouth slowly against his. We stay that way for what feels like minutes. Until my phone alarm blares.

I'm so jolted by the sound that I jerk back and fall off the couch, landing on my back.

"Ouch!"

Evan shoots up. "Are you okay?"

"Um, yeah. Fine . . . just . . ."

I hop up and scurry over to my purse, which is sitting on top of the kitchen island. I'm wondering why the hell it's going off in the middle of the day. But then the reminder on my phone pops up.

Baby shower menu tasting with Keely at 4 p.m.!

"Shit." I check the time. It's three thirty.

"Is everything okay?" Evan calls from the couch.

I dart past him to the hallway bathroom and slam the door. Then I grab the mini makeup kit I keep in my purse and start swiping stuff on.

"Yup, all good!" I holler, hoping he can hear me beyond the closed door. "I just . . . I'm late meeting a friend."

I roll my eyes at my reflection in the mirror. That sounded so made up. But I don't have time to explain myself. I promised Keely I would be at the Grey Plume for her tasting. No way in hell I'm missing it.

The Grey Plume.

Thank god Evan isn't going in to the restaurant today. I remember Keely said that Miguel was the one putting together the menu for her baby shower. I don't think I could handle seeing Evan at the restaurant after that kiss and whatever else is currently unfolding between us.

I grab the mini hairbrush from my kit and smooth out my bob, then give myself a quick once-over in the mirror. I'm wearing cut-off jeans, a blue flannel button-up, and flip-flops. I'm not even close to appropriately dressed for a menu tasting at a high-end restaurant. But I don't have time to drive home and change. At least my makeup and hair are decent.

I duck out of the bathroom and to the front door. Before I leave, I turn to Evan. He's gazing at me, his groggy face bewildered.

"I'll call you later, okay?"

I leave before he can utter anything in response.

On my drive to the Grey Plume, I dial Chantel. When I get her voice mail, I swallow back a groan.

"Hey, Tel. It's me. I know you're probably busy on shift or exploring whatever new town you're at, but can you call me back, please? As soon as you can? Some weird and wild stuff went down, and I just—"

Her voice mail cuts me off, and I groan as I weave in and out of traffic like I'm driving a getaway car. I call her again and wait for her voice mail.

"Hey. Me again. I know you hate when I leave multiple rambling voice mails, but I've gotta talk this out because my head is a mess and . . . okay, I'll just say it: I kissed Evan. I kissed Evan, and I feel like such a bastard because he just found out his grandma has cancer in addition to having dementia, and he was crying, and I tried to comfort him, and I didn't intend to kiss him at all when I cuddled with him on the couch, but he seemed into it and—"

It cuts me off again right as I stop at a traffic light. I notice the person next to me is staring at me wide-eyed, clearly able to hear me talking through my open window.

I quickly roll it up and call Chantel again. "Just call me, please? As soon as you get this."

I hang up and speed the rest of the way to the restaurant. I walk in and see Keely sitting at an empty table in the back of the restaurant. She waves at me with a giant smile plastered on her face.

I scurry over and lean down to give her a hug. "I'm sorry I'm late."

"No worries! I just got here." She pats her adorably round belly. "This massive baby makes it hard even just to walk now."

I laugh along with her, grateful she doesn't seem to notice how flustered I am. Just then, the hostess I recognize from that time I met Evan here walks over to us, two bottles in her hand.

Keely introduces me to Moira, and I say hello.

"We're still thinking of serving champagne for the nonpregnant attendees and sparkling grape juice for any mommies-to-be in attendance, right?"

Keely nods yes, and Moira pours her a flute of the nonalcoholic wine. When she pours me a glass of champagne, I down it so fast, I cough on the bubbles.

"More, please, if I may," I say, holding up my empty flute. I try to laugh off how insane I must look in this moment, guzzling champagne like the world is ending, but I can't help it. I need something to calm my haywire nerves after that kiss with Evan.

Moira pours me another glass while Keely looks on with an amused stare. Moira says Miguel will be out with the first tastings in a few minutes before disappearing into the kitchen.

"Rough day?" Keely says with a chuckle.

"Um, kind of."

"You're not much of a drinker, so I just figured—"

"I kissed Evan, the head chef and owner of the Grey Plume."

Keely's mouth plummets to the floor. "What? How? When?"

I'm about to fill her in when Miguel arrives with the first round, an array of appetizers.

After he gives a quick explanation of each one, he leaves us to try it all; then Keely turns back to me. "Okay, back to the story."

I tell her about how we took a mini road trip together for his grandma and how that marked a change in our dynamic—it started to feel like we were becoming friends.

When I get to what happened this morning with Opal's diagnosis, I set my glass down and explain it as carefully as I can.

Keely's eyes water. "Oh my gosh. Oh, his poor family."

"He was so distraught. He hadn't slept in days, he was by her side at the hospital the whole time."

Between bites of food, I tell her how his mom insisted he go home and rest, how I drove him to his house, how we argued about him resting until he broke down in tears, venting all of his frustration and anger about the situation to me. How I coaxed him to lie down and rest—how he asked me to stay with him . . . to lie down with him. How we fell asleep together. How we woke up cuddled together.

Her eyes go wide as she stares at me, sipping her drink.

As frazzled as I feel, I admit to myself that it feels good to talk to Keely about this. For almost two and a half years, the only person I confided in was Chantel. But now I'm talking to my best friend again, I'm spilling my guts to her, and she's listening without judging or preaching, like she always has. Because she's always been the most supportive friend.

"And then when we woke up, something was just different, you know?" I say after swallowing a bite of prawn canapé. "Like our whole dynamic had shifted. He was looking at me, and I was looking at him, and I don't know who made the first move because it happened so fast and we had just woken up, but the next thing I knew, we were kissing and—oh my god, what is this?" I savor the tender meat falling apart in my mouth. "This is amazing . . ."

"It's a braised duck spring roll with a red wine reduction."

My head jerks up to see Evan walking out from the kitchen, clad in a white chef's coat. My eyes bulge; then I stammer.

"What are you doing here?"

My sharp tone causes him to flinch and Keely to whip her head at me.

"Working," he snaps. "We're short-staffed in the kitchen today so I'm helping Miguel with the tasting."

I bite back the comment I'm aching to make about how he should have stayed home and rested. "Well this tasting menu is . . . yum. Very, very yummy. Excellent job to Miguel on that one."

"I'll be sure to tell him." He turns to Keely and aims a polite smile at her. "How's everything? Is it to your liking?"

I internally applaud her for the game face she's put on, because she has a perfectly pleasant expression on her face and not the look of shock she's been sporting since I told her what went down with Evan and me less than an hour ago.

"It's all so delicious," she says.

"Glad to hear it. Next course should be out soon."

I'm frozen as I watch him walk away without giving me a second look. When the kitchen door swings shut behind him, she turns to me. "Oh my god! Did you know he was gonna be here?"

I slump forward, cradling my face in my hands. "No," I groan.

Soon I feel the warmth of her hand on my shoulder. I pull my hands from my face and look over at her.

"You should probably go talk to him."

Her brown eyes read kind as she gazes at me. Before I can say anything, Miguel is back with another round of finger foods.

"Dessert is next after this," he says, then tells us to make note of which dishes we like best.

When he leaves, I pick at a sesame-and-sriracha-glazed chicken skewer with my fork. "I'm sorry, Keely."

"For what?" When I peer over at her, she looks genuinely shocked.

"For ruining your menu tasting with my personal-life drama. God, I feel like I'm in high school all over again. Freaking out over a kiss with a guy."

I'm shocked when she giggles. "Isabel, first of all, I want you to know that I'm sorry this is stressing you out. And I'm sorry for what Evan is going through with his grandma. That's so horrible and sad. But honestly, I'm really happy you're talking to me about this. I love that you're here with me, venting about your guy problems. I don't mean to minimize the serious parts of this. I just mean that it feels really good to be back to this point. We're two friends gossiping about the drama in our lives. It feels like old times."

My heart aches at what she's said. I pull her into a hug. "That means everything. Thank you for listening to me ramble."

"Always."

We eat a bit more before dessert comes out. She makes a groaning noise.

"That good, huh?"

When she doesn't answer, I turn to her. She's wincing, like she's in pain. "Are you okay?"

She waves a hand. "Yeah, I'm good. Just stomach cramps. I've been getting them a lot lately at this stage in my pregnancy, especially when I'm eating. I'm feeling them a bit more today for some reason. Maybe it's the sriracha."

"Oh."

I notice a faint ring of sweat beads along her chestnut hairline. After a second, she smiles at me and holds up her flute. "All good. Promise. Now, why don't you go talk to Evan?"

I stand up, then slowly walk up to Moira as she strolls from the direction of the kitchen and ask if I can speak to Evan. When she leads me back and pushes open the door, I see Evan standing next to Miguel at the stove top stirring something in a metal saucepan.

"Chef Sanderson, you have a guest."

Moira walks off, and Evan looks up at me, his expression surprised. A second later, it hardens. He focuses back on the saucepan. "Is there a problem with the tasting?"

I'm taken aback at how clinical he sounds. Hurt, almost. But do I really have a right to be surprised? I kissed him barely an hour ago, when he was emotionally distraught and vulnerable, then ditched him.

"No, the tasting's delicious. But can I talk to you?"

"Okay," he mutters. He tells Miguel to take over. He walks over to another guy in a white chef's jacket, points at the oven, then comes over to me.

"Not here." I lead him to the hallway by the bathrooms, our go-to spot to have impromptu conversations, it seems.

"I'm sorry," I say before he can even open his mouth. "What I did when we were on your couch together was wrong. I crossed the line with you, and I shouldn't have ever—"

"Whoa, wait." He holds his hand up at me. "What?"

I cross my arms over my chest, shame heating me from the inside out. "I should have never kissed you, Evan. You were vulnerable. You were emotionally distraught. And I feel horrible that I let it happen."

He looks at me like I've grown a third eyeball. He closes his eyes and shakes his head, as if he's trying to make sense of all my babbling. "Isabel. What are you talking about? I kissed you too. I *wanted* to kiss you. Didn't I make that obvious?"

I hesitate. "I mean, yeah. I guess so."

"Are you telling me you didn't want to kiss me?"

"That's not the point."

He lifts an eyebrow. "It's not?"

"The point is that this is a really difficult time for you. You're going through so much right now with your grandma. I should just be your friend. Nothing more."

He stands there, hands on his hips, his expression on the edge of amused. "What happened on my couch felt like a lot more than just friends."

I open my mouth but can't think of a single thing to say in response.

"Okay, fine, you're right. But it can't happen again."

"It can't?" he says pointedly.

I shake my head. "No. Because I'm your grandma's caretaker. My priority is looking after her the best that I can. Nothing else can happen to jeopardize that. It's too important to me."

Resignation crosses Evan's face. Like he understands what I've said even though he doesn't agree with it.

"Okay. We can forget that it ever happened if you want," he says.

"I think that would be best."

We stand quietly in the aftermath of what we've agreed. It's the right thing to do, I know it is. But why does my stomach feel like it's in knots?

"I'd better get back to—"

A shriek from the dining room interrupts me. Evan and I whip our heads in the direction of the noise. Another loud screech echoes through the restaurant, and we take off for the dining room. Miguel and another kitchen staffer in a white coat dart out of the kitchen and follow us toward the noise.

When I see Keely doubled over on the floor near the host stand, I gasp. Then I run over to her. Moira is crouched next to her, rubbing her back with the barest touch of her right hand, almost like Keely's made of lava and she doesn't want to get burned.

"Moira, what's going on?" Evan asks from behind me.

She gazes up, her eyes alight with terror. "I—I don't know. She said she wasn't feeling well and wanted to get some air, so I was helping her walk over to the door, and then she just dropped to the floor, and then I saw . . . I saw . . ."

Keely's groans intensify. And then I see what Moira is talking about, the pool of reddish-clear liquid on the pearlescent marble floor.

"Shit."

"What?" Evan asks.

Keely screams.

"Her water broke. She's in labor."

Chapter Sixteen

Miguel and the nameless sous chef curse behind me. I maneuver so that I'm eye level with Keely and cup her face in my hands.

"Keely." I say her name as gently and as firmly as I can. "Keely, just breathe for me, okay?" I look up, ready to bark at someone to call 911, but Evan already has his phone out. "Call 911 and tell them she's in labor. Now."

He nods, his stare mimicking Moira's panicked one, both of them wide and unblinking.

For a second, I contemplate shouting if anyone in the restaurant is a doctor, but I glance around. There's no one here other than the six of us. And judging by how every single one of us froze in fear when we realized what was happening, I doubt anyone moonlights as a doula.

Something inside me ignites. Some dormant taskmaster part of me that I didn't know existed until now. It's strange, given I've never been in this kind of situation before. I've been present in the room while people have gone into labor and given birth at the hospital, but that's a totally different environment. There were doctors, nurses, and other medical professionals who were in control of the situation, who monitored everything closely, who knew exactly what to do in case anything started to go wrong. I was always just there to visit with the patient if they requested support or words of encouragement—it was never up to me to take control of things.

But right now, that's exactly what I'm doing. I claw through my memories to recall everything I can ever remember Chantel mentioning while she worked as a labor-and-delivery nurse. Maybe this is what happens when my best friend is having an emergency right in front of me. The urge to take control, to do whatever I can to help her consumes me, and nothing else matters.

I tell Miguel and the other sous chef to huddle down on the floor behind Keely to brace her body for support.

When she presses her eyes shut, I focus on the metallic-gold eye shadow swept across both her lids. Her chest rises as she takes a long, steady breath in through her nose, exhaling through her mouth.

"That's good. Really good, Keely. Keep breathing, just like that."

She grabs my hand in hers and squeezes so tight, I lose feeling. But for the next minute, I grit through it, coaching her along in her breathing. Then she stops and lets out another ear-piercing scream.

I whip my head up at Evan. "What the hell is taking so long? The hospital isn't even two miles from here."

I strain my throat to keep from shouting. Keely is the only person allowed to scream right now.

He relays my inquiry in more polite wording to the 911 operator.

"I'm only thirty-five weeks," she says between ragged breaths. "I . . . this can't be happening."

With the sleeve of my shirt, I dab at her sweat-soaked brow. Moira, who scooted away as soon as I crouched on the floor and began delegating orders, pops up and swipes a napkin from one of the tables, then hands it to me so I can dry Keely's forehead.

"I can't . . . Isabel, I can't have my baby here, I just can't," she wails.

"It's okay. It's gonna be okay."

It's the only thing I can think to say, even though my brain is swirling in my skull like an out-of-control carousel. I'm not even convinced as the words stammer from my mouth. I press my eyes shut and once more force myself to block out the chaos of this moment so I can remember as many of the random labor-and-delivery facts Chantel has rattled off to me over the years as possible.

Forty weeks is considered full-term, but babies born at thirty-five weeks are in great shape. Many may not even require NICU time after being born because most of their vital organs are fully developed at that point, which means they're equipped to survive outside the womb.

All of that is true . . . but I'm certain that relaying it to Keely won't be the least bit comforting. She's gone into early labor on the floor of a restaurant. The best thing I can do is reassure her and keep her calm until the paramedics arrive.

Her eyes shine with tears as she looks up at me. "You're sure this is okay? You promise?"

My heart cracks at how terrified she sounds. I smile at her, proud of myself at how that seems to ease her pained expression the slightest bit. "Absolutely. I promise."

She asks me to call Theo and tell him what's happening. I fish her phone out of her purse and dial him. When he picks up, I don't even wait for him to say hello.

"Theo. It's Isabel. Keely is in labor."

He starts to stammer, but I cut him off, telling him we're at the Grey Plume, paramedics are on their way, and he needs to come right now.

He thanks me and says he's driving here now. I look up at Evan, who's saying "uh-huh" over and over to the dispatcher while pacing back and forth just a couple of feet away from me.

"What's the holdup?" I say through gritted teeth. I glance at the massive gold clock over the host stand. It's been four minutes since he called.

He swallows and shoots his terrified gaze at me, like he's scared to tell me the truth. My stomach sinks to my feet.

"Some drunk-driving crash near the hospital just happened minutes ago," he says. "Emergency services are on the way, but with the traffic jam that accident caused, it's gonna be a few more minutes probably."

"Probably?" I snap, then silently scold myself when I see how my response has caused Keely's eyes to light up with sheer terror.

Through a breath, I give her hand another gentle squeeze. I'm about to parrot that totally worthless phrase, *It's gonna be okay*, but then her head falls back as she howls in pain.

"Oh, I can feel it. The baby . . . it's coming. Shit, I'm gonna have to push. But I don't . . . I can't . . ."

Keely wails once more.

The sous chef whose name I don't know makes a choking noise. Miguel whips his head to him. "Jax, you okay?"

Jax shakes his head no, then nods yes, then blurts, "Um, I don't know." Above me, Evan curses. Moira sniffles before muttering, "Oh my god." For a split second, I internally lose my shit along with them. But take-control mode hits once more.

I order Moira to run and grab my phone out of my purse. She darts back seconds later and thrusts my phone into my palm.

I dial Chantel, pin the phone between my face and shoulder, and whisper-chant to myself as I count the rings.

"Pick up, pick up, please pick u—Christ! Thank god you picked up. I need your help."

She laughs. "I just heard your voice-mail messages." She lets out a whistle. "My big sister is having some serious man drama. It's about time. It's been a while."

"Shut up, forget about that."

"Whoa, what's your deal?"

"I need your help to deliver a baby."

"What?"

As Keely lets out another earsplitting wail, I pause. Then with speed that rivals an auctioneer, I quickly explain the situation.

"Keely says it feels like the baby is coming," I practically scream. I swallow, silently ordering myself to keep my voice down. I need to stay calm for Keely.

"Shit. Shit, shit, shit," Chantel mutters.

"Would you please stop swearing and help me?" This time I say it through gritted teeth. Better than screaming.

"Okay, okay," Chantel says through a breath. "Okay, first I need you to look between her legs. Can you see the baby's head?"

When Keely finishes breathing through another contraction, I gently squeeze both of her hands and tell her to look at me once more.

"I have to check on the baby, okay?"

She nods, and I tell Jax to hold her hand as I shift over to her legs. Evan drops down to the floor to help brace her. When I push up her dress and peer between her thighs, I bite my tongue to keep from gasping. All I see is the top of a baby's head, covered in thick, curly dark hair. She's definitely crowning.

"Okay. Okay. Okay." I sound like a panicked broken record.

Keely and Chantel shout at once.

"What?"

"What is it?"

I straighten up and square my shoulders. "Keely. You're crowning."

Her eyebrows crash together as she groans. "No . . ."

"She's gonna have to push," Chantel says in my ear.

I relay the info to Keely, who wails once more. "I can't push yet. Not here. Not without Theo when I'm all alone."

I pat her thigh as gently as I can, hoping the softness is somewhat of a calming counter to the absolute chaos unfolding right now.

"Keely, I know. Sweetie, I know this isn't what you planned, but your baby is ready. And you're gonna have to push. You're gonna have to be strong. For your baby. Can you do that for me?"

"That was good, Bel. Really, really good," Chantel says.

I don't know if my actual words help calm her or it's just because of the even tone I managed to keep while talking to her just now, but there's a flash behind Keely's saucerlike brown eyes.

She nods once. "Yes, I can be strong. I can do it."

"You *are* strong, Keely. You're a goddamn queen. You are a fertility goddess. You got this."

The three men bracing her echo what an amazingly strong queen and goddess she is.

"Y-you got this, Keely," Moira repeats in a weak voice. She's crawled to her other side and is holding her other hand.

I crouch lower and touch my hands to Keely's thighs.

With the phone still pinned between my ear and my shoulder, I ask Chantel for instructions on what to do next. Moira hops up and grabs it, holding it to my ear to free up my upper body. I thank her, but she doesn't seem to hear me. Her gaze is fixed on Keely, just like everyone's gazes are, as Keely lets out another groan. The pitchy yell ricochets off every surface in the dining area. Moira flinches—she covers an ear with her other hand and leans her head into her shoulder as she holds the phone. I catch Miguel and Evan wincing slightly. It's like everybody's attention is trained on Keely and her reactions; every other sound and sight in the room fades to the background.

I refocus on the sound of Chantel's voice in my ear.

"Have her take a big breath and then push as hard as she can," she says. "Like she's going to the bathroom."

I look at Keely. "Take a big breath and push, okay?"

She does exactly that, her guttural yell bouncing against the walls.

My heartbeat thunders in my ears as I focus on the baby's head.

"Your little one has a ton of hair, Keely. Wow. And it's so curly. Just like Theo's. Just like you always wanted, remember?"

She lets out a cry-laugh as sirens wail in the distance. My chest thuds with the hope that in seconds, a team of paramedics will burst in and take over. But as she groans through another push, the doors to the restaurant entrance remain closed. It's just us still.

Soon, baby's head eases slowly out of the birth canal. I hold my breath until I see that the baby is facedown.

Ideally, babies will come out headfirst, facing Mom's back.

I don't even know when Chantel spouted off this random fact, but I'm grateful it's the one thing I can recall in the chaos and adrenaline. I tell her the positioning of the baby.

"Yes! That's good!"

I breathe out a sigh of relief and say a silent thanks that this baby is doing everything by the book during their surprise arrival.

"Bel, can you see the head? Is it coming out?"

"Yes, it's right there."

"Good, now cradle it with your hands, but don't tug, okay?"

"Okay."

I stretch out my neck before focusing back on Keely and the baby. I do exactly what Chantel orders and cup the baby's head in my hands, careful not to tug.

"Is the baby okay?" Keely's voice is a groan-whine. Her eyes are half open as her head lolls to the side. Evan scoots closer against her back to give her neck more support.

Through watery eyes, I smile up at her. "Baby is perfect. You're doing great."

"Tell me the positioning of the baby. How far out are they?"

I tell Chantel that the baby's head and the top part of the shoulders are out.

"Oh, damn, wow," she says. "Okay, one more big push should do it. Two at most."

I relay the info to Keely, who flashes an exhausted smile at the news that she only has one more push before meeting her baby. Evan gives her shoulders an encouraging squeeze. Jax and Miguel both say, "You're amazing, Keely! You got this!"

"Okay. Let's do this, Mama. One more good push."

Even though this is all unfolding in a matter of seconds, the visual is somehow slow-motion. A pair of tiny shoulders appears, then two chunky arms, then a torso, then a chubby bottom, then legs, then two of the tiniest feet I've ever seen.

The baby spills into my hands, red and swollen and covered in fluid. And so slippery. I tighten my grip so I don't drop them. For a long second, there's silence. Chantel starts to say something about clearing the baby's mouth and nose, but then a shrill, pitchy cry hits my ears.

I flip the baby over.

"It's a boy!" I shout.

A chorus of gasps and cheers follows. Head lolling and eyes droopy, Keely grins as she tears up. It's then that I realize I'm crying too.

The baby boy's screams are deafening. I don't think I've ever heard a creature that small make such a thunderous noise. I lay him on Keely's stomach, and she lets out a sob of joy as she cradles her little guy with her hands. I pull on the umbilical cord to give Keely more slack so she can scoot the baby up to her chest.

Miguel and Jax carefully lay her on the ground as Moira drops my phone and tucks a stack of towels under her head. Evan whips a table-cloth from a nearby table and drapes it over Keely's lower body before tucking another tablecloth around her to soak up the blood and other fluids on the floor. As I take in the scene, I'm breathing so hard, I'm certain my heart and lungs are going to burst out of my chest.

Evan slowly scoots over, arranging the towels in the most comfort-able and supportive position possible under Keely's head and neck. Then he grabs a nearby towel and starts wiping the baby's face and chest clean.

"He's got a healthy set of lungs. Just like his mommy," I say.

She lets out a laugh before kissing the top of her baby boy's head.

Just then, the doors burst open. A team of paramedics comes rush-ing over to tend to Keely and her little one. One clamps and cuts the umbilical cord, then swaddles the baby, while the other takes Keely's vitals and preps her to deliver the placenta.

I start to stand and turn away, but my legs are so wobbly, I nearly fall. Behind me, I hear muffled voices talking about pulse and rate of breathing and the way the baby's skin looks. My head feels heavy, like someone just filled it with wet cement.

"Whoa there," Evan says as he grabs me by the arm and steadies me.

He helps me stand upright, arm braced around me. Someone comes up from behind me and taps my back gently.

"Holy shit," Miguel says. He's looking at me, but his gaze is unfocused. "You were fucking dynamite."

Jax nods along. "What he said."

When Evan lets go of my shoulders, Jax immediately pulls me into a hug; then Miguel does too.

They step away, leaving me standing alone. I look over at Keely, who's being moved onto a gurney. She's the picture of exhaustion and bliss. She can barely keep her eyes open, but she's got the biggest smile on her face. She meets my gaze as they start to wheel her away.

Thank you, she mouths to me before they glide her out the doors. I smile at her. Just then a car screeches to a halt in a parking spot near the entrance of the restaurant. Theo jumps out and runs up to Keely. I watch as he climbs into the ambulance with her and their baby. Just before the doors shut, I glimpse him kissing Keely on the forehead and touching his palm to their baby boy's head.

Someone rests a hand on my shoulder. I turn and see Evan.

"That was . . ." He looks dazed, like someone just shined a floodlight in his eyes. "Who were you talking to on the phone?"

"My sister. She used to be a labor-and-delivery nurse."

"Oh." He blinks. "Awesome."

The ambulance pulls away. As the siren blares, I look up at Evan. The longer I stand there, the heavier my legs feel.

"Evan, I . . ."

He pulls me into a hug, like he knows I need the help to stand up. I burrow my face into his shoulder. Closing my eyes, I take a breath and softly sigh. My entire body feels like goo.

It's a while before he releases me. When he does, I know I'm not ready for this hug to be over. But it has to end.

He steps away, his gaze over me watchful. I love it.

"Are you okay?" he asks.

Not even close.

"Yeah. Thanks."

I can tell by the way he lingers around me that he doesn't believe me. But then he nods and leaves anyway.

And then I stumble to the restroom to wash up before driving home in a daze.

~

"Well, I am just in awe, dear," April says to me as she grabs her purse from the coffee table.

"It's really not that big of a deal," I say.

"Oh, it is most certainly a big deal. You delivered a baby, Isabel. On the floor of my son's restaurant. With no medical training whatsoever. If that's not the most impressive thing I've ever heard, then I don't know what is."

I fight the blush engulfing my cheeks.

My phone buzzes with a text. It's probably Mom. Ever since I told her about helping Keely give birth, she's been proudly telling anyone who will listen that I delivered a baby successfully with zero medical training. Every day she texts and calls me to tell me all the wonderful things people say about me.

Mom: Anak, guess what? I told Auntie Beth in the Philippines about how you delivered your friend's baby, and they're planning to throw a party for you when we visit in the winter!! Isn't that so nice?

Mom: They're asking what kind of cake you want. Uncle Bernie is going to bake you a big one. Four layers, he said! Any flavor you want!

Mom: Okay, so he said lemon cake is his specialty, is that okay?

Mom: I'm going to tell him to go ahead and make it.

Mom: Oh, and they want you to tell the story of how you delivered the baby during your party.

Mom: Aww Auntie Beth just told me that your little cousin Ada said she wants to grow up and deliver babies like her manang Isabel! Isn't that so sweet?

I let out an exasperated laugh.

"How's your friend and her baby doing?" April asks.

"Really good. He was a healthy one at almost seven pounds."

"Oh my goodness, that's so wonderful."

"Keely's good too. Just resting and spending time with her baby boy."

"What did she and her husband end up naming him?"

"Gabriel."

"Oh, I love that name. So precious."

I've visited Keely and baby Gabriel once since she gave birth and made plans to see her at the end of next week, but I don't want to come by too often. It's important for her and Theo to have plenty of alone time with their little guy.

For a moment, I dwell on the fact that I haven't yet seen Theo. He was at work the day I stopped over to their house. Part of me wonders what he thinks of everything . . . if he's mad that he didn't get to be there during the birth . . . if he wishes it were anyone else but me to deliver his baby given the way I treated Keely . . .

I tuck away the thought, annoyed with myself that I'd focus on such a thing. I shouldn't make this about me or how Theo may or may not feel about me. I should just focus on being a supportive friend to Keely.

I recall the day I told April how I delivered Keely's baby, how she was speechless for a solid ten seconds after I finished. Then she burst into tears and hugged me while saying she was so fortunate that some-one like me was looking after her mom.

It was my first day back caring for Opal after she had been dis-charged from the hospital. April's reaction probably had something to do with the fact that Opal's state of health has been good overall. April opted to do infusion treatments for her to mitigate the cancer. The plan is to do that for as long as Opal can physically handle it. She's only had one session so far, but she handled it well with no discernible side effects, and her mood has been happy as usual.

I glance over at Opal as she sits in her recliner and smiles at us both.

"You're a lucky lady, Mom," April says as she leans down to kiss the top of her head. "You've got this superhero watching over you."

We wave bye as April walks out the door.

"Oh, hi, honey," April says.

I look up and see Evan standing on the porch.

"Did you need something?" she asks him.

"I came to say hi to Grandma." He looks past his mom and locks eyes with me.

We haven't spoken to each other since that day I delivered Keely's baby. That's probably a good thing. Or a bad thing. Crap, I don't even know.

What I do know is this: I can't stop thinking about Evan, about our kiss, about how hurt he was when I told him we should just be friends and nothing more. I keep thinking about how he hugged me in the aftermath of the chaos the day that Keely gave birth. How he looked at me like he didn't want me to leave.

But I can't pursue anything with the grandson of the woman I'm meant to take care of. I don't want to be *that* person—the kind of person who overlooks what should be hard-line boundaries, who hooks up with a family member of the person I'm hired to look after. The kind of person who engages in something romantic with someone who's vulnerable and emotionally distraught.

I'm as flawed as a human being could possibly be. But I'm not a scumbag.

Evan walks up the stairs, gives his mom a kiss on the cheek, then walks inside after she leaves. This time when Opal sees him, she flashes a soft smile before turning back to the TV. She doesn't say his name, but the fact that she's not confused or outright rejecting him is a win. A relieved smile paints his face. When he looks at me, it fades the slightest bit, dialing back to something more restrained.

"I hope it's okay that I stopped by."

"You can stop by whenever. She's your grandma."

"Right." He glances at Opal once more before turning back to me. "I wanted to ask you for a favor."

"What is it?"

"I want to take her to visit a lake on my day off early next week. Would you come with me?"

When I don't answer right away, he turns to look at Opal once more. She's still enamored with the game show, not paying us one bit of attention.

"I don't know how much longer she's going to be like this. Happy. Able to move around." A hard swallow glides down his throat; his hazel-green eyes turn misty. "She goes to the new memory care facility at the end of next week. When that happens, it'll probably be a lot harder to take her places, and . . . remember how she mentioned visiting the ocean when she talked about going on a road trip?"

"I remember."

"I know we can't go to the ocean, that's too far and she's in no condition to travel that extensively. But what if we take her to a lake? Someplace pretty that's only a few hours away, where she can wade in the water and feel like she's somewhere far away."

Everything in me aches as I listen to him talk. My chest, my heart, my throat, my eyes.

"I want to do this for her," he says quietly, his voice watery. "I want to make this wish come true for her before it's too late."

"Of course I'll come with you."

Chapter Seventeen

Evan, Opal, and I stand along the shoreline of Wilson Lake in Kansas. It was almost a four-hour drive to get here, but Opal was a trouper. When we told her that we'd be coming here to fulfill the wish she told us about weeks ago, to wade in crystal-clear water on a hot day, she squealed.

Every time I glanced at her in the back seat during the drive, she had a smile on her face. But her smile now leaves all her prior ones in the dust. Right now, she's grinning wide, her eyes sparkling as she takes in the scenery. We're standing along the sandy shoreline, just a dozen feet from the water. Tall grass surrounds us. Sandstone rocks jut out of the ground sporadically, as if a giant came by with a handful of these rocks and sprinkled them randomly along the dirt and sand. In the distance, we see a cluster of massive sandstone pillars jutting out from the water, which are the distinct feature of this lake.

"Would you just look at that." Opal's gray waves sway as a gust of hot, dry air whips around us.

Evan stands to her left and peers over at her. "It's something, isn't it?"

When she looks up at him, the expression on her face is warm and content, like she's recognizing him as someone familiar.

I do my best to stay quiet and off to the side, to let grandmother and grandson have this moment to themselves.

"Should we dip our toes in the water?" He looks at Opal, then over at me.

I walk over, kick my sandals off, then help Opal take off her shoes. Then I offer my hand to her as we walk to the shoreline.

"Well, this is just the most wonderful day, you two."

I swallow back the surge of emotion that rushes through me. Evan's expression conveys that he's trying to do something similar.

His mouth quivers the tiniest bit, but when I blink, he's smiling down at her. "We're happy that you're happy, Opal."

The three of us step into the lake, which is as warm as bathwater thanks to today's heat. When she lets go of my hand, I start to reach for her arm, but I notice she's reaching for Evan, who's standing a few feet in front of her, looking out into the distance.

"Evan." He turns as soon as I call his name. When he sees Opal reaching for him, his lips part, but he reels in his expression quickly before stepping over to give her his arm. I can see it, though, the joy coursing through him at the feel of his grandma embracing him, of her actively reaching for him, wanting him and only him in this moment. It's the brightness of his eyes, the way he stands tall, the way the smile on his face lights his entire expression.

They stand there together, arm in arm, gazing around at the lake.

As I scan the water, I'm surprised at how there are just a handful of people here. On a hot day like this near the end of summer, I'd expect this place to be packed. But I'm so glad it's not. It feels like we have this patch of shoreline and water all to ourselves.

I close my eyes and take a deep breath, relishing the sunlight skimming my face, the hot wind ghosting across my skin.

In the distance, I hear the rumble of a boat engine. I open my eyes. It grows louder as the seconds pass. And then something happens.

The strangest sensation comes over me. A crushing feeling at the top of my chest.

As the noise of the boat engine roars in my ears, I press my eyes shut yet again and shake my head. But the crushing feeling persists. It's like I'm trapped between two massive walls as they crush me, squeezing the life out of me. It starts at the base my neck and moves down painstakingly slowly. Like molasses dripping down the side of a glass.

When I open my eyes, I can't see straight. Everything's blurry. The sky and water and grass and rocks are now blobs of blue, green, brown, and white.

The crushing sensation intensifies. I feel it everywhere now, in my bones, in my muscles, across my skin.

I close my eyes again because I can't endure not being able to see straight. It's terrifying.

Then I hear Evan's voice. I can't make out what he says, though. He sounds happy. He's laughing. There's splashing now. More laughter. More happy voices and sounds. I think that's Opal's voice, her laugh. Someone says my name, I think, but I can't be sure. It sounds like my name, but it's too fuzzy. Like I'm trapped underwater and someone is shouting for me above the surface.

Water.

My lungs contract with the breath I struggle to take. Those invisible walls flatten me; they're making it hard as hell to inhale. And exhale.

That Day.

The more I struggle to breathe, the worse I feel. My head is throbbing now. So hard that I'm scared my skull is about to blast open.

I'm soaked with sweat. My hands are clammy, and my tank top is drenched. No, wait, that's not sweat, is it? It's water . . . from the lake . . .

When I blink again, all I see is water. It's cold and murky and endless. My chest starts to fold into itself, smaller and smaller until there's no more room for my lungs to expand.

I try to inhale, but it's like my lungs are trapped in a tiny cage. There's not even an inch to let air in.

I blink again, and this time there's brown-green water all around me. The wetness coats my skin like slime, like I'm sinking fast, miles and miles from the surface, where I should be—where I belong.

I blink once more and see an arm. A small, slim, unmoving arm, floating right in front of my face.

That Day.

"Isabel, are you okay?"

That's Evan's voice. I can hear him now, actually make out the words he's saying.

My eyelids fly open. No more water. No more blurry masses of color. Just Evan's face twisted in concern. He's still standing next to Opal, except now there's a look of terror as he stares at me.

"Hang tight, okay?"

I'm numb, frozen, can't move. Can't speak or nod or acknowledge in any way that I understand what he's said to me. I just stand there.

He leads Opal out of the water to stand on the shoreline before rushing over to me. Leaning down so we're eye level, he grips my shoulders with his hands.

"What's wrong?"

When I say nothing, he glances over me, his gaze stopping at my hands. "Jesus, you're shaking."

I move my mouth, but no words come out. Just a weird stammering noise. That's how it goes for several seconds before I give up and clamp my mouth shut. Evan stares, his eyes wild with worry the whole time.

That Day.

I can't tell him.

A shiver works its way through me. Now my legs are shaking too. Evan must notice, because he pulls me into his chest and hugs me tight.

"It's okay. It's okay."

He whispers it over and over into my hair. When I feel the thud of his racing heart against my chest, my body starts to loosen. Something about his arms around me is so soothing, so grounding. Like feeling how his body works is a guide to show my body how it should work too.

My muscles unclench, my hands and arms and legs stop trembling. My heartbeat slows to a more normal speed.

The lake . . . the boat . . . the accident . . . all that water . . .

At this point, I muster enough mental strength to halt that thought in its tracks. I shove the memory of That Day back into the deepest recesses of my brain and lift my arms. Slowly, I rest my palms along Evan's upper arms. He loosens his hold around me, then leans away. His gaze never leaves me, though.

"Isabel . . ." His eyes are bright with worry. "What the hell . . . are you okay?" he asks through a huff of breath.

"I'm fine." I pull my lips into my teeth for a moment so he doesn't see them tremble. "Really, I'm good."

His mouth cracks open as he stares at me. He tilts his head and narrows his gaze, a clear sign that he doesn't buy one shred of what I'm saying.

"You weren't moving. You were just standing there, and . . . it looked like you were gonna pass out."

I step out of his hold and back away. I turn around to Opal, who's staring at us with a curious look on her face. I force a smile and flash a thumbs-up.

I turn back to Evan. "I just . . . I got a little queasy and felt like I was gonna be sick for a moment there. I think it's the heat, you know? Or maybe the humidity. But it's all good now. I feel fine now that I've had a second."

He stares at me like I've told him I want to hitch a ride on the next space shuttle to Mars.

"You're clearly not fine. Tell me what's wrong."

I clench down so hard, my jaw starts to throb.

No way. Not ever.

I loosen my jaw muscles, then reach for his hand, scooping it in mine.

"Evan. I'm fine."

I actually believe it when I say it this time.

I turn back to Opal. "Do you want to go check out more of the lake?"

There's a guarded smile on her face that destroys me. She can tell something happened . . . she can tell something is wrong with me. I ruined this beautiful moment, this perfect day at the lake just for her.

She says a soft okay, and I walk back over to her. I help her put on her shoes, slip my sandals back on, then look over at Evan, who's still standing in the water, looking completely mystified.

"You ready?"

He frowns slightly, then steps forward. "Yeah."

~

On the drive back to Omaha, the mood has flipped. Instead of the joy and excitement that powered our mood on the drive to Wilson Lake, the air is stilted now. Evan and I haven't said a word since Opal fell asleep in the back seat. If she had stayed awake, we would have kept up the halfway decent facade we managed at the beginning of our journey back home. Opal was so happy with the day trip and chatted about it nonstop until she exhausted herself.

But now there's just dead silence. Along the darkened highway, the city lights of Omaha sparkle on the horizon.

"What happened back there, Isabel?" Evan asks, his voice gentle and soft.

"What are you talking about?"

"You know what I'm talking about."

I knew he was going to say that, just like I knew he wasn't going to buy the feigned ignorance in my response. There's no way I'm going to tell him, though.

There's no way I'm going to tell him that being at Wilson Lake triggered the memory of That Day, a memory I've managed to bury deep for the longest time.

The sound of that boat engine . . .

I should have known. Sometimes all it takes is the littlest thing—a distant sound, a familiar smell, a strong flavor—to set off a painful memory you've spent ages burying.

When I turn to look at him, his chest rises slowly with the breath he takes before he twists his head to me. When we lock eyes, there's an intensity that floats between us.

He scrubs a hand over his face. "Something was happening to you back there at the lake. And it scared the hell out of me. It scared the hell out of Opal too."

I close my eyes, furious at myself for letting anything happen to disrupt her special day.

I shake my head and focus on the bright-red brake lights of the car in front of us.

"I told you what happened. I just felt a little sick. I'm fine now."

A huff of breath is his response as he continues driving.

And then out of the blue, he laughs. It sends a sheet of goose bumps across my skin. It's the same joyless and bitter laugh that he let out the day we met in the elevator.

"You've got to be kidding me," he mutters, his gaze glued to the road.

"I don't know what you're going on about."

I know what a massive jerk I'm being. But this is me. This is what I do. I can be so callous, so dismissive. I was like that for the past two-plus years when I cut everyone out. I was like that to my parents, to Keely, to the rest of my friends and family, and now I'm doing it to Evan.

Push away. Deflect. Then disappear.

I should have known this would happen again.

I'm a hopeless, unsalvageable, goddamn mess. Yeah, I can try to be normal. I can have friends and form connections and bonds, at least for a little while. But at some point, I hit a wall. Because I can't dive deeper than the surface. I'll never be able to open up fully, to talk about what scares me, what I'm truly about . . . what happened to me . . . what I've lost.

Something will trigger me at some point. I'll be reminded of That Day. I'll lose it all over again. People will want to know what happened, what's wrong with me.

But I can't ever tell them.

"Isabel. Why can't you tell me what happened to you?"

His low tone is pleading, begging. I stay quiet, though.

We're silent the rest of the way to April's house. When he pulls into her driveway, we go into quiet cooperation mode. He carries Opal to bed while I unload everything from the car and put it back in the house.

I'm about to leave when he walks out of the hallway.

"Isabel, wait."

I stand there, nerves crackling as I wait for him to speak.

"I like you, Isabel. You realize that, right?"

All I can do in the seconds following his admission is stammer.

"I really, really like you," he says.

My knees buckle. The way he says it, so soft and full of care . . . I wasn't expecting that.

"Why?"

He lets out a scoff-laugh noise. "Why? Because you're kind. And sweet. And beautiful. And you call me on my shit. I really, really like that. I like the sound of your laugh. I like how you openly roll your eyes when someone is trying to bullshit you. I like how you smile when you're flustered by a compliment. I like seeing you with my grandma. You're amazing with her."

I almost laugh. When the feeling subsides, the urge to cry hits me.

"You don't like me, Evan."

You wouldn't if you really knew me. And if you did—if you knew who I really was and the things I've done—you'd hate me.

The slight shake of his head, the way his expression doesn't fade, the way his eyes shine with emotion, they all show that what I've said hasn't fazed him.

"Yes, I do." His voice is calm and quiet because it has to be. His mom and grandma are sleeping just past the walls of the living room where we're standing. But that doesn't take away from the power, the certainty of his statement. And it absolutely floors me.

He steps closer to me and holds my hand. "I like you, Isabel. I wouldn't say it if I didn't mean it. And I want to be here for you. I wish you would tell me what's going on with you. I'm here for you. Always."

The gentleness of his hold translates to his tone. It's so soft, yet it shakes with the emotion that he so clearly feels.

With those green-hazel eyes, he pins me in place. "You can tell me anything. I promise, it won't change how I feel about you."

I swallow, my throat aching. And then I pull my hand out of his. He looks at me like I've slapped him.

"You don't know who I am, Evan."

"Christ, that's the whole point." He tugs a hand through his hair. "I know something was upsetting you earlier. I know you were going through some serious shit. You've been there for me, you've listened to me, you've supported me when I've broken down, when I've been absolutely fucking shattered. Why won't you let me do the same for you? Why won't you let me in?"

I shake my head as my eyes burn.

"I wish you would tell me. No matter what it is, I'll understand." His eyes glisten. "All I want is to be there for you. Please. Why won't you let me?"

I look everywhere but his face. "I can't."

"You can't?"

I shake my head. This time, when I blink, tears fall. I quickly wipe them away.

Evan moves toward me, but I hold up a hand. "I should go."

I run to my car and drive home. My phone blares the whole time, but I ignore it. When I get home, I collapse onto the couch, shut off my phone, then pass out.

Chapter Eighteen

A sharp pain shoots through the back of my head.

I don't open my eyes right away. Instead, I stay lying down, eyes pressed shut, waiting for my brain to crawl out of the sleep fog so I can process what has just happened.

After a few seconds, I open my eyes and blink over and over again until the fuzzy image comes into focus.

It's Chantel crouched in front of me.

"You're back."

She doesn't say anything. She just keeps scowling at me.

I rub the back of my head. "Did you . . . did you just hit me in the back of my head?" I slur. I can barely open my eyes. How long was I asleep for? It's like my brain and my body are trapped in wet cement.

"No, I didn't hit you," she says through a sigh. "I probably should have, though."

"Why does my head hurt like hell?"

Chantel shoves her long black braid over her shoulder with one hand, then holds up a pillow with the other. It takes a second before I realize it's one of the pillows I was sleeping on. Then she reaches over me and yanks the remaining pillow from under me. My unsupported head falls back, thudding against the wooden frame that rests underneath the thin cushioning of the sofa.

"Ouch!" I yelp, rubbing the back of my head. "What the hell? Why are you taking all the pillows away? I was sleeping."

"Isabel. Look at me."

I stay still on the couch, arms tucked around my head in an attempt to cradle myself. My eyes are pressed shut once more, like my life depends on keeping them closed forever.

"You've been lying on this couch in a stupor for the past two days. You didn't show up to take care of Opal. You haven't answered your phone. You've been existing as a worthless, lifeless extension of this sofa."

I shake my head, trying to make sense of what she's said. "No, that can't . . . I haven't been passed out for that long."

"Check your phone if you don't believe me."

I grab my phone from the coffee table and turn it on. When I look at the date and the number of voice mails and texts I have, I groan. "Shit."

"Shit is right," she snaps. "And just so you know, I'll yank away every last couch cushion from under you to get you to talk to me so we can fix this. You know I will."

I force myself up into a sitting position and look at her. My head throbs so hard, my vision goes fuzzy for a few seconds.

I catch her scowling at me, hands crossed over her chest, like she's disgusted at the sight of me.

"What?" I bark.

"What is the matter with you?"

I try to look away and off to the side, but she immediately plops down on the coffee table and moves into my line of vision.

"Don't try to look away. I've got you trapped, Bel. You can't go anywhere right now."

I pinch the bridge of my nose and lean my head back, silently asking the jackhammer in my brain to stop. "You know what's the matter with me, Tel."

"You're right, Isabel. I do know what's the matter with you." Chantel sighs. The frown twisting her angelic face eases. She looks so sad now. "But we're gonna fix it. We're finally gonna fix it."

There's something ominous in her tone. A long moment passes. All I can hear is my breath and hers.

She touches my knee. "Don't look away. This is going to be one of the last times you see me like this. You need to pay attention to what I have to say."

When the threat of her words soaks in, I'm shaking. My fingers and hands, my arms and legs. Everything is unsteady, unstable. I'm terrified.

She can't leave. I need her here. Always.

Still sitting on the coffee table, she leans forward. I take in all her features. Those expressive brown eyes that look so much like mine. That long black hair. That smile that always stretches her mouth from ear to ear. That face that looks like my face from three years ago on time delay.

My hands shake so hard, I have to twist them into the couch cushions to keep steady.

Her hand on my knee tingles. She squeezes it, this time a bit harder than before. "I'm not really here, Bel. You know that."

> You say you're here even when you're not.
> I don't believe you.
> You say it again and again.

The lines Ruby recited from her poem all those days ago echo in my head just before a ringing sound invades my ears. I'm gripping the couch so tightly that my fingers start to ache. Just then, Chantel reaches for both of my hands. In her hold, I calm.

> You say you're here even when you're not.
> I don't believe you.
> You say it again and again.

210

This time, it's Chantel's voice I hear echoing in my head, reciting the lines of Ruby's poem.

When I look at Chantel's face, it's through teary eyes. "If you're not here, then how come I can touch you? How come you feel so real? How come when I call you on the phone, it sounds like I'm talking to you?"

A sad smile turns bee-stung lips upward. "Because you want me to be here. Because you need me to be real in this moment."

When she leans back, she pulls her hands out of my hold. Then she stands up and backs a few feet away.

I watch it all with wide, unbelieving eyes. Her tan skin fades, turning the slightest bit lighter. She almost blends in with the eggshell-white hue of the wall. I try my hardest to focus on the freckles that dot across her chest, grateful that they haven't faded too much. After a few blinks, she comes back into focus. I can still see her.

"Talk about That Day, Bel." Her voice echoes around me. "You know you need to. It's the only way to make all of this feel real."

There's a shuffling noise. She walks off in the direction of the darkened hallway, and I lose sight of her. I whip my head around, searching the room for her, but she's nowhere to be found. "But I don't want to talk about what happened . . . I don't want it to be real."

A minute passes, and she says nothing. I still can't see her.

"Chantel! Please come back. Please, I—I need to see you."

Still nothing.

I open my mouth, but instead of words, a sob bursts from my throat. "I don't want to talk about That Day, okay?"

"I'm sorry, Bel." Her voice is a low echo that sounds like it's coming from across the room. "But it doesn't matter what you want. It's reality. What happened, happened. And I'm not really here because of it."

Her words settle like a kick to the skull. The pounding inside my head has morphed into thrashing. It's like vertigo multiplied by a migraine. I press my eyes shut, clutching my head with both hands as

I try to will away the pain. But it doesn't work. I just get dizzier and dizzier. Then my stomach curdles.

"I'm gonna be sick." I slump over, wrapping my arms around my stomach.

"Then throw up. You'll feel better," Chantel says just to the side of me. The heat of her body skims mine, and for the briefest moment, there's relief. She's next to me. I can feel her.

I try to lean up and turn so I can see her, but a tidal wave of bile rises in my stomach. I shoot up on shaky, unsteady legs that haven't functioned properly in two days, since I've just been lying on the couch; then I wobble all the way to the bathroom and collapse in front of the toilet, landing on my knees. Acid burns my throat and mouth as I spew into the bowl. It hits like lighter fluid, igniting me from the inside out. For a minute, all I can do is retch and gasp. Snot and tears drip down my face. Then I reach to the side, yank toilet paper from the roll, and wipe my cheeks, my heart thrashing inside my chest.

All the muscles in my body give out, and I fall back, my spine hitting the bathroom wall behind me. Hugging my knees to my chest, I struggle to catch my breath.

"Tel! Chantel!" I call her name over and over until she finally appears in the darkened doorway. The light from the living room hitting her from behind illuminates her as she stares down at me, pain twisting her expression. She looks like an angel.

I guess that makes sense.

"You . . . you're not really here," I say.

She shakes her head.

"You haven't been for a really long time," I say.

"Two years and five months."

My stomach settles, the urge to vomit long gone. But then my chest folds in half, then in half once more. And then I cry.

"Say it. I know you can." The softness in Chantel's face and tone breaks me.

"I can't."

"You can."

For a minute, all I can do is sob while I cradle my head in my hands. I almost don't say it. Maybe if I never say it, it won't be true.

"I need you to say it."

It's a gentle plea, like she's holding my hand without touching me.

"You're dead."

She was right. I *can* say it.

I look up and see her nodding slightly. "That's right. I'm dead."

My head bobs to the side, suddenly feeling as heavy as a cinderblock.

"Talk about what happened that day, Bel."

I shake my head and babble that I can't, but she stops me.

"It'll be good practice for when you start to tell everyone."

My mouth hangs open, but no words come out. I haven't spoken about this day for two years and five months.

She straightens up in the doorway before walking over and crouching down in front of me.

"It was a clear day at the lake, remember?" she whispers when I don't say anything. "We were the only boat on the water. Remember how weird we thought that was? On such a warm spring afternoon?"

I lock eyes with her and nod once, resigned to the fact that whether I want to or not, I'm going to have to talk about the day she died.

"You were wearing that ridiculous pink cover-up and that giant straw hat," I mumble.

Her mouth twitches just before the corners of her mouth turn up in a sad smile. "I took sun protection very seriously. I always joked that I didn't want to get skin cancer and die. The irony, right?"

Another sob rattles me. I wipe my face. "We thought we'd go for a swim. To that sandbar in the middle of the lake."

"We decided to make a race out of it," she says. "Because I ate the last of your beef jerky, and you were annoyed with me. So I suggested we race, and the loser had to buy the winner more. Just like when we were kids."

"Mom and Dad didn't feel like going in the water."

"We held hands as we jumped off the edge of the boat. We held our breath."

"And then we swam."

Chantel's voice is calm, steady—just like the water that day. All the words I speak are laced with sobs and gasps.

"I can't . . . I can't say any more, Tel. It's too hard."

"Yes, you can. You know you can. You have to."

Her measured tone is a delicate counter to my breakdown.

"I let go of your hand when we hit the water. I thought you were right next to me. I heard you splashing—I felt you splashing. I felt the water hit my arms and legs. You were right there. You even . . . you grabbed my leg when we were under the water, and . . ." I make a strangled noise as my chest caves in. "I swear I didn't know . . . I didn't know you were grabbing me because you needed help, Chantel . . . I thought you were just messing around . . . I thought . . ."

I grab more toilet paper and wipe away the snot and tears streaming down my face.

"I kicked you away when I felt your hand on my leg," I sob. "I thought you were joking . . . but you needed help . . ."

Again, I'm gasping. I'm crying so hard, I can't even see Chantel anymore.

"Bel. It's okay," she whispers. "How could you have known? There was no way."

For a few minutes, all I do is cry. And then I hear Chantel's soothing voice once more.

"Keep talking. You're doing so well."

"When I couldn't feel the splashing anymore, I thought that was because I was beating you. I thought I was ahead of you in the water, but . . ."

I close my eyes and let the memory of That Day wash over me.

The muscles in my arms were on fire as I cut through the water as fast as I could. My lungs burned, and my legs flailed. Minutes later, I hit sand. The sandbar. Crawling up the tiny strip of beach on my hands and knees, chest heaving, mouth hanging open, I was so exhausted. But happy. I was the first one to the sandbar. I won.

But when I stood up and looked around, Chantel wasn't there.

At first I thought she was swimming under the surface of the water. But as the seconds passed, the longer I gazed at the still water, the more dread set in.

The water shouldn't be still. Chantel is still swimming.

"I couldn't see you anywhere," I mumble.

Her eyes turn sad. She's observing me retell and relive the moment of her death, watching how it breaks me all over again.

"I waited too long to try and find you," I cry.

"You didn't, though."

"If I had gone back for you sooner—"

"It wouldn't have made a difference. I was gone by then."

She says it so casually, so matter-of-factly, it makes me want to scream.

"Isabel. I got tangled in that underwater brush not long after jumping in. There was no hope."

"But if I hadn't been so focused on that stupid race . . . If I hadn't kicked you away . . . If I had just stopped swimming when I felt the splashing stop . . . If I had just turned back to look at you once . . . If I had tried to dive under and look for you . . ."

"Then you would have drowned too. Or got caught in the brush. Then Mom and Dad would have lost both of us."

"But . . ."

She shakes her head. "Don't do that. It's not your fault. Nothing about what happened was your fault. It was a freak accident. Bad luck. Whatever you want to call it. It happens to people every day."

My body shudders as I relive the day we lost Chantel. How after I realized that her failing to surface meant that she was most likely drowning, I dove back in the water to try to find her. How between diving in and out of the murky green lake, I was screaming for my parents to bring the boat over. How I yelled that I couldn't find Chantel. How even though my vision was blurred from the water, I could see the look of terror on Mom's face when I told her Chantel never made it to the sandbar. How slow the game warden's boat was after Dad radioed in our emergency. How my lungs burned hotter and hotter every time I plunged underwater. How one of the rescue divers had to jump in the water and pull me out when I refused to give up searching for her. How that entire afternoon and evening felt like they both flew by and happened in slow motion.

How it took divers two days to find Chantel's body because she got pulled into an undercurrent that dragged her to the opposite side of the lake.

How I spent days, weeks, months reliving that day, replaying every moment in my head over and over. How if I had done just one thing differently, she'd still be alive.

When I look back up at her, she's sitting cross-legged on the floor just inches from me.

"Isabel, please don't do that."

"Do what?" I wipe my nose with the back of my hand. I blink. Everything from my eyelids to my legs feels heavy as cement.

"Don't second-guess yourself as you replay everything in your head," she says. "There's nothing you could have done differently. There's nothing anyone could have done."

The longer I look at Chantel, the more she starts to fade into the wall. I blink with panic and scold myself for all the crying I've been doing. It's screwing up my vision. I can't even see her clearly now because of it.

Even as I dry my eyes, her body continues to lose its shape. Her features blur and disappear like they did before, first along the tips of her fingers and toes, then the edges of her arms and legs. Her hair evaporates, its dark hue turning lighter and lighter until it's nothing.

I reach out to touch her upper arm, but it's gone. I grab at her knee, but it's not there anymore. And then I try to cup her face with both hands, but it's barely visible. Just the outline of her nose, the curve of her mouth, and the two deep-brown dots that are her eyes. She looks like an unfinished sketch.

"Please, Chantel. Don't go. I can't do this without you."

"Yes, you can." Her voice is a soft echo in my ear. I can't see her anymore. "You're gonna be okay, Bel."

I scan the room over and over but to no avail. She's gone.

I slump onto the cold tile floor, then force myself to crawl onto the couch and curl into the fetal position. Fatigue takes over, and I close my eyes. As I drift off to sleep, I hear the echo of her voice once more.

"You survived losing me. You'll survive this too."

$\sim$

I wake to someone gripping my upper arm.

"*Anak*, wake up. You have to wake up."

I moan, then groan, then press my eyes shut so hard, my eye sockets start to ache.

"Open your eyes, *anak*."

Her soft voice slingshots me all the way back to childhood, when she'd wake Chantel and me for school early in the mornings. Always that gentle tone.

Against every instinct that screams I should stay curled in the fetal position on my couch forever, I open my eyes. What I see breaks me, and I almost wish I had kept my eyes closed. Crouched next to me are

Mom and Dad, both of them teary, both of their faces twisted with worry.

Mom's lips wobble, which makes my chest ache. I take in the worried lines flanking her smoky topaz eyes, the countless frown lines etched in her brow. Then she cups my face with both of her hands, her chest rising as she inhales slowly.

"We were so worried about you." Her voice shakes as she cries.

Her hands fall from my face to wipe her cheeks, and Dad leans over and hugs me. It's awkward positioning, since he's sitting up and I'm lying down on my side, but it doesn't take away from just how comforting it feels.

With each second I'm in the warmth of his embrace, I loosen. I can feel it as it happens, my shoulders separating, my fists unclenching, the cramps in my arms and legs easing. My muscles feel loose and warm again.

And then it happens. Something inside me snaps. As I bury my face in his chest, I sob. There's a shuffling sound above me, and then I feel Mom's hands on me again, brushing my hair to the side. Then she kisses the top of my head.

"It's okay, sweetie," Dad says. "We're here now. We're gonna take care of you."

That invisible string that's been wrapped around my heart for the past more than two years, that's been digging into my flesh, cutting off all feeling and emotion . . . it breaks.

I can barely catch my breath. I'm wailing so hard, so loud, my gasps and exhales blend together. I can't tell when I'm blinking or when my eyes are open. It's all a blur. I don't know how long I cry. My parents stay by my side the entire time, though. Dad holds me tightly against him, his own soft cries quaking against my skin. At some point, Mom moves to sit next to me, resting my legs on her lap, stroking my calves and shins to soothe me.

When I finally catch my breath, I still. Dad leans back to rest on his knees. Mom dabs at my face with a tissue, then hands me a few so I can wipe up. It's impossible to breathe lying down with all the snot blocking my sinuses, so I sit up, blow my nose a handful of times, and then I look at them.

"How did you know that I wasn't okay?"

"Keely called us," Mom says. "You were supposed to meet with her yesterday, and when you didn't show or answer her calls and texts this time, she got worried. So she called us."

My heart plummets to my feet. Poor Keely, enduring yet another instance of me blowing her off. Things had been going well. I need to call her. I need to explain what happened.

I need to get ahold of Opal and April too. I spent the entire summer taking care of Opal, and I didn't even show up for my last day with her before she moved into the memory care facility. I didn't say a proper goodbye to her and April. Now, as my brain struggles to catch up, I realize just how badly I messed things up with them too. I clutch my hand to my chest as it squeezes so tight, it hurts to breathe. I need to talk to Evan too.

Just the thought of how I hurt him, how I rejected him when he tried to help me, sends a fresh cascade of tears down my face.

Mom pats my leg, as if she can tell that I'm struggling to process all of this.

I swallow past the painful boulder lodged in my throat. "I . . . I think I'm having a breakdown. It's bad. I'm really messed up."

Dad takes my hand gently in his while Mom pats my leg once more. They're like a team working in tandem to comfort me as much as possible.

"Does Keely know that you two are with me now? Does she know I'm okay?"

Mom nods. "We called her as soon as we walked in the door and saw you on the couch," Mom says. "She's happy and relieved. And she said she's here for you whenever you're ready to reach out."

I close my eyes and swallow. God, Keely. What an angel. I don't deserve her.

I let out a shaky breath and thank them for coming to me.

Dad clears his throat, his eyes shining with unshed tears as he speaks to me. "You said you had a breakdown . . ."

He and Mom exchange a look but don't say anything for a few seconds. They're hesitant, and I know why. They're afraid that if they say too much, if they ask me the wrong thing, I'll push them away or cut them out again.

But I won't. Not this time.

I get it now. I don't know why it took me so long.

As I sit here cradled in the arms of my parents, as I watch them cry over me, I can feel the worry and pain radiate from them. They love me. They love me so damn much. That's why they did what they did. That's why they pushed and pleaded so many times. That's why they never gave up on me. I'm their baby—their only baby now. And they want to help me. They want to see me happy and okay.

"Yes. I had a breakdown," I say quietly.

I tell them about going to Wilson Lake for my caretaker job. I tell them about the boat engine noise that sent me spiraling. I tell them how Evan tried to help me, but I pushed him away. I tell them about coming home and passing out, then waking up and seeing Chantel, speaking to her. Was it a dream? It felt so real, though . . .

Every single time I've seen or spoken to Chantel, it's felt real, as real as when she was alive and here with me.

The way I babble about her doesn't seem to faze my parents. They just look at me and nod, like they expected me to say all that.

I tell them that I cried and passed out again. I was shutting down. I was *breaking* down. Just like I did right after Chantel died.

Even now, as I rack my brain, I can't formulate a single clear memory in the months that followed her death. All I know is that I slept for hours on end, sometimes days at a time. When I woke, I'd barely be coherent enough to hold a conversation. Sometimes I'd wake with a splitting headache. I'd always end up crying. And then I'd sleep some more. Rinse. Repeat. For weeks.

I didn't know how to crawl out of the abyss. Mom and Dad suggested counseling, but I balked at that. I'd have to talk about everything I didn't want to. About how much it killed me to know that my baby sister was gone forever. About how the pain of losing her was all-consuming, how it felt like my entire body was being ripped to shreds, then carelessly stapled back together. Every step, every blink, every breath was agony. Losing my little sister eviscerated me.

I refused to speak about her death because then I'd have to talk about how every minute of every day I hated myself for being the reason why she was dead.

She grabbed my leg in the water, and I kicked her away.

It didn't matter how many people said over and over that it wasn't my fault. I knew better. If I had stopped swimming when she grabbed me, she'd still be here.

I didn't want to talk about it—any of it. I stopped talking to my old friends. I stopped talking to my parents. No, that wasn't a healthy coping mechanism. But they knew. They knew she was dead, and I couldn't think about life without Chantel.

And then, like an echo sounding in my brain, I hear Chantel's words.

You're gonna be okay, Bel. You survived losing me. You'll survive this too.

Okay.

I want to be okay again.

I squeeze my arms around my mom. "I want to be okay again."

The words fall broken and wobbly from my trembling lips. But there's a conviction in my tone—inside me—that I haven't felt in ages.

I'm a mess in every sense of the word. I've been crying nonstop for days, exhausting myself until I pass out. I haven't left this spot on my couch.

I have a problem. A serious one. And I can't solve it on my own.

I've tried ignoring it for more than two years. That hasn't worked.

"I need help." My voice cracks, but both of my parents practically light up at what I've said. There's a brightness in their eyes I haven't seen in years.

"I need to talk to someone. A professional. I can't do this on my own."

This time when they hug me and cry, I can tell it's not out of sadness and worry. It's in the way they hold me, so tightly, like they don't ever want to let go. It's in the way they kiss my cheeks and squeeze my hands, the way they tell me how proud they are of me, how happy they are, how they'll be here for me every step of the way.

It's relief. And hope.

Chapter Nineteen

I see Dr. Mortimer for therapy now, twice a week.

It's strange because I've only just started, but I think it's working. I'm starting to unpack a lot of the grief I've been repressing.

And there's a hell of a lot. Like why I think I've been able to see and communicate with my dead little sister for the past two-plus years. There's not a definitive answer. I don't think there ever will be . . . because I don't think one exists. But here's what Dr. Mortimer thinks.

I wasn't really seeing or talking to Chantel. I just thought I was.

Grief is a powerful emotion. It's all-consuming, even traumatizing at times. I was traumatized by the loss of my sister. I didn't want to let her go. In the weeks and months that followed her death, I existed in a grief stupor. I could barely remember to eat or drink. I alternated between sobbing and sleeping. I had no sense of time or place. I was just there, heartbroken, without Chantel.

As a way to cope with losing her—as a way to cope with the grief—I would imagine her. I would close my eyes and picture Chantel's face, her standing right in front of me, what it would feel like to hug her, to hold her, to laugh with her, to talk to her, to joke, to bicker, to gossip like we always did. When I was finally back to work at the hospital, I would imagine her coming by the chaplain office to visit me, like she did when she was alive and would pick up shifts there between travel nursing gigs. I would talk to her on the phone almost every day, like I did when she was alive and traveling for her job. I'd imagine our conversations about what city she was visiting, what work was like, what attractions she was exploring, what souvenirs she was planning to get me.

I was reenacting all the moments I had with Chantel when she was alive as a way to cope without her. If I pretended like she was still here, I wouldn't have to face the fact that she was actually gone.

And so that's the way I lived. I pretended. I imagined. I had a million conversations with my little sister who wasn't really there.

Mentally I orchestrated new moments and new conversations with Chantel. I was calling on previous conversations with her to craft entirely new ones to ease me through losing her. I imagined her coming to see me after I pushed Evan away when he tried to help me through the triggering moment at the lake. I imagined her yanking the couch cushions from under my head to wake me up. I imagined her arguing with me when I refused to tell Evan what happened That Day. I imagined her pressing me to talk about That Day, to finally acknowledge it after spending so much time repressing the memory of it.

Dr. Mortimer thinks that it was all me. She thinks that despite my efforts to hide the memory of Chantel's death, a small part of me knew it was wrong and unhealthy to do that. She thinks that small part of me is what led to my most recent breakdown and my imagined conversation with Chantel, which led to my reconciliation with my parents and me seeking out therapy.

Even now, as I mull all of this over, I have the hardest time accepting it. Logically, I know it's probably true. I accept the fact that I probably imagined my interactions with Chantel. Dr. Mortimer is an intelligent, educated, and respected therapist. This is what she thinks, and I believe her.

Still, though.

A part of me sits unsettled. Like there's something more to it than that, something more complicated. Even though I can't prove it or explain it, I can feel it.

Because all of those interactions with Chantel felt real to me. When I saw her at the hospital, when I spoke to her on the phone, when I hugged her, when I smelled her perfume, it was like she was still here.

But she's not. Not anymore. And no matter what I feel, I have to shove it aside and focus on getting better. It's the only way to move forward.

It's what Chantel would want.

When I walk into Dr. Mortimer's office, I sit in the plush leather armchair across from her office chair, and I say hello. There's a knot in my stomach. There always is. She asks me how I'm feeling, and I tell her that I'm okay—that's usually what I say.

This time, she asks how I'm handling my medication, which I take to prevent migraines. That's something else she and my physician agree on—that the stress of remembering how Chantel died triggered migraines. They think it's why during my most recent breakdown, I was vomiting and my head was throbbing. I say I'm handling the medicine fine. I haven't vomited or had a migraine ever since I started taking it, even when I talk to Dr. Mortimer about Chantel. She says that's a good sign. I tell her I agree.

She asks if there's anything in particular I want to talk about this session, and I usually tell her no. I just want to get better. I don't want to cry every morning when I wake up and realize Chantel isn't here anymore. I tell her that I want to have normal interactions with my parents that don't involve them worrying about me. I tell her that I should probably clean out Chantel's bedroom in my house—that's where she would stay when she was in between travel nursing gigs. I haven't moved a single thing in her room since she died. Everything in there is the way it was when she was still alive. I tell Dr. Mortimer I'm so, so scared. I'm terrified that if I move anything, if I pack any of it up, it'll be like I'm losing yet another part of my little sister.

The whole time, Dr. Mortimer listens, a neutral expression on her face, nodding slightly every once in a while to indicate that she understands what I'm saying.

She doesn't interrupt. When I stop talking, she pauses, a thoughtful expression on her face. And then she says, "It's okay. It's normal to feel that way."

It's a weird comfort. She's so neutral in her expressions and tone during sessions, but hearing her say that feels like she's patting her hand over mine, even though we're not touching. There's so much solace in what she's said. It helps to know that she doesn't think I'm being unreasonable. It helps to know that she understands.

I tell her that I still haven't visited Chantel's grave. It's too much, the thought of seeing my little sister's headstone jutting out of the ground, seeing her date of birth and date of death carved in stone, standing on the grass, on top of where she's buried.

She tells me that there's no handbook for grieving and that it's okay to feel this hesitation.

"It's okay if it's too much. It's okay if you can't do it just yet."

I tell her thank you, that I needed to hear that.

"It's okay if you can only do a few things at a time. It's okay if you want to hold on to some of her belongings as keepsakes. And it's okay if you want to get rid of them all. Whatever feels right to you, that's what you should do. But don't pressure yourself. Do it when you're ready. And be kind to yourself. Try not to feel bad about any of it."

That knot in my stomach is gone. I thank Dr. Mortimer for her time, we make an appointment for next week, and then I leave.

~

I'm on my way to the parking lot when I hear my name.

"Isabel."

I turn around and still instantly at the sight of Keely.

Her eyes are wide—disbelieving almost. We haven't seen each other in weeks. I haven't even called or texted her since she called my parents when I no-showed to our meetup.

I owe her a million apologies and then some for the horrible friend I've been. That's likely why she's just standing there, staring at me, instead of rushing up to me to give me a hug. That's why that warm, giddy smile I love so much is nowhere to be found on her face.

It takes a second before I spot the tears pooling in her eyes. When she blinks, two tears tumble down her face. And that's when I take the first steps toward her.

She doesn't hold a hand up to halt me. She doesn't shake her head. She doesn't push me away when I embrace her. She doesn't tell me to go away. Instead, she wraps her arms around me tight.

"Isabel." Her voice shakes as she says my name again, holding me in her tiny arms.

"Hey," I croak as I cry. "I'm sorry. I'm so, so sorry. I promised you I wouldn't drop off the face of the earth, but I did, and I should have called you to explain—"

"I was so worried about you." She stops as her voice breaks before she sniffles.

I deflate in her arms. "I know."

A million more *sorrys* linger on the tip of my tongue, but I bite them back. It wouldn't make a difference. It wouldn't undo the fact that I did the one thing she asked me not to do—I disappeared on her again.

"I know I don't deserve you," I say through a shaky breath. "I know you have every reason in the world to drop me out of your life completely—"

"Hey."

The abruptness in her tone jolts me. Then she pulls back slightly so I can see her face. "None of that." She sniffles, still holding me by the shoulders as her gaze bores into me. "I'll admit. When we made plans and you didn't show up, I was mad at first. I thought you were disappearing like before. But then I got worried. I guess I just . . . had a feeling. That something might be really wrong this time. You were doing so well. You were seeing me regularly, you were talking to me, you were acting like you wanted me to be in your life again, you were enjoying your new job, and I just . . . I think deep down, I knew something was off. You disappearing again felt so jarring—so unlike you now. And I knew that something bad had happened. And that's when I called your parents."

I stay quiet for a moment. "You know me so well. You always have."

My softly spoken words earn me a sad smile. "Yeah."

People walk around us in the busy commercial plaza, a few stopping to stare at the two sobbing women, but neither of us cares. All that exists in this moment is the two of us, a couple of friends trying to work things out while sharing a cry.

"You're going through loss, through trauma," Keely says. "Everyone copes differently, and you don't have any reason to apologize for that."

"But I should apologize for how I hurt you. Again."

"I accept your apology."

Her words are the comfort I've been aching for. I bite my lip to keep from completely losing it as she gives my arms a gentle squeeze.

"Chantel died more than two years ago, and it's still so hard," I say.

"I know. I miss her a lot too."

"I'll never be the same."

"That's okay."

Keely says it so resolutely, with zero doubt.

"Is it, though? Is it okay that I don't know if I'll ever be the person I once was? Is it okay that I'll never be as carefree or wholly joyful? I'll always carry a sadness underneath it all. I'll always miss her. I'll always think of her and the things I miss about her. Everything will always feel incomplete in a way because she's not here to share in it with me."

Instead of responding right away, Keely pulls me by the hand to a nearby empty bench so we can sit, then pivots to face me. "Yes. It's okay, Isabel. Because that's what happens when you lose someone you love so much. You're never the same without them. It shows just how much they mean to you, just how much of an impact they had on your life."

She hesitates for a second, her gaze falling to her lap before she looks at me. "I'm not the same either." Her lips quiver with her admission. "I know that what I lost isn't anywhere near what you did—she was your sister. But she was my friend. And when she died, a piece of me was lost forever. It always will be. I'm changed because of it."

I shake my head slightly. "You're still the same kind, sweet, and forgiving friend, Keely. That's what matters."

She smiles slightly, her eyes still teary. "Maybe I am. But I feel things more now. I cry harder. When I think of the times the three of us had together—going on weekend getaways, happy hours, dinners, lunches, movie nights at our houses, girls' night out, meeting my husband for Pete's sake—I almost always cry. None of that will ever feel the same without Chantel."

I nod, touched and pained at how Keely feels so much of what I'm feeling too.

"That fear I've always had about losing the people I love, it used to just linger in the background," she says. "But now it cuts deeper—I think about it a lot more. Sometimes I'm so scared of losing the people in my life, the fear paralyzes me. I just stand there, barely able to breathe."

I squeeze her hands tightly, my heart aching for what Keely is confessing to me. I never knew the pain she felt, how Chantel's death affected her . . . I should have asked her how she was doing, how she was handling the loss. I was so selfish.

"Maybe my change is more inward, but it's still there," she says. "So I get it. Not in the same way that you do—I never will. But please know that you're not alone. We can be here for each other. We can go through it together. We can support each other through the tough moments and try to figure out a way to move on and still have some sort of joy."

Her words leave me speechless. This is exactly what I want—what I *need*. I just could never verbalize it. I was always so internal with my pain, with my refusal to grieve openly.

But now that I know just how much Keely is going through and how similar it is to what I'm going through—and how willing she is to go through this together—something inside me eases. The muscles in my back and shoulders loosen.

"I want that too," I say. "More than anything."

Teary eyes frame Keely's smile. But I can see the hope in her expression clear as day.

"I'm seeing a therapist now," I say. "That's where I was coming from just now."

"That's really good."

"I should have seen her a long time ago."

Keely keeps hold of my hand in hers, like she can tell it's the exact kind of comfort I need in this moment. "We all process things on our own time. The important thing is that you're doing it." She pauses, hesitating for a moment before she speaks. "Chantel would be so proud."

I nod, my mouth trembling. I take a second to catch my breath and wipe my face with a fresh tissue.

"I want to start talking about Chantel again," I say. "I know that before, right after she died, I said I didn't want to bring her up because it was too painful. But I'm ready now. I miss her a lot, and I think talking about her, reminiscing about her would help. It would help her feel alive in a way."

"I'll always be happy to talk about her." Keely pats my hand in hers. "Anytime you want to talk about her, I'm here for you. I loved her so much."

I power through the tremble in my lips and manage a small smile. "I know you did," I rasp.

For a minute, we sit in silence, staring straight ahead as people walk around us. She holds my hand the whole time. I wipe my nose and take a breath as I turn to face her. "Thank you for being so patient with me. For still wanting to be my friend. I could apologize from now until the end of time, and it still wouldn't be enough to show just how much I regret messing all of this up, for hurting you so many times."

"Oh, Isabel."

I start to shake my head, but she continues.

"It's okay now. I love you. I always will."

Her words send a jolt to my chest. It's so strong, I have to force myself upright. That kind of love, that kind of friendship . . . I'm so not deserving. But I want it.

I pull her into a hug. "I love you too."

When we pull away, I ask her the question I'm dying to know. "How's baby Gabriel?"

Her smile is so wide, I expect her face to split in half. She tells me how sweet and chunky he is, how he sleeps more than any newborn baby in the world.

"He's like a housecat. All he does is eat and nap."

She whips out her phone and shows me a dozen pictures she took just that morning.

"Theo insisted I get out of the house for a few hours just to have a break, but I swear, I miss that little guy already. Must be the new-mom hormones."

"I can't wait to see him again."

"He can't wait either. He misses his auntie Isabel."

"Are you, um, still having your baby shower? Or, um, have you had it already? Sorry, my sense of time has been so screwed up lately."

"Not yet. It got postponed because of his early arrival. It's happening Sunday. And I want you to know that you're welcome to come. I know that crowds aren't your thing and you're going through a lot. I just want to make sure you know you're welcome. Always."

"Of course I'll be there."

And then I realize that it's going to be at the Grey Plume. I might see Evan when I go.

Just the thought sends a wild mix of emotions surging through me. Nervousness and excitement and dread. It's been weeks since I've seen him, and I have so much to explain and make right with him.

We stand up together, and I walk with Keely to her car. We hug goodbye, and as I watch her drive away, the pressure in my chest loosens the slightest bit.

Keely and I are going to be okay. Despite everything I did, I still have my friend. For that, I'm forever grateful.

When I make it to my car, an alert on my phone goes off. A reminder to complete the online training module before I head back to work at the hospital. That's when I remember I'm due back at my job next week.

I expect a wave of relief and excitement to hit me. But nothing comes. I just sit in my car and stare straight ahead. Nothing.

I stay that way for a minute, settling into the complete lack of reaction, waiting for my stress response to flare up, waiting to feel eagerness at the fact that I'll have the security of my job back in a matter of days, that I'll be back to offering support to people in their time of need.

Still nothing.

I finally put a name to what it is that I'm feeling: indifference.

It's then that I realize I don't feel the same about my job as I used to. It's not that I dislike it or dread it. It's that it doesn't hold the same significance it once did.

I could go back, but it won't be the same as before.

It's wild, given how much time I spent worrying about getting my job back just months ago. But it's been an eventful summer, to say the least. There's been a change within me. I'm not the person I was months ago. Months ago, I was actively repressing the trauma of losing my sister; now I'm facing it head-on. Months ago, I was hiding behind my work in order to distract myself from the pain of grief; I'm not doing that anymore. Desperation was my motivation then—I was desperate to keep that connection with Chantel, to stay at the hospital to be close to the memory of her, to surround myself with things that reminded me of her . . . but that desperation has faded. I still feel the ache of her absence; that won't ever go away. But that urge to immerse myself in everything that reminded me of her has faded.

Spending the summer working as Opal's caretaker felt different. It was a job where I was helping someone, like I was as a chaplain. But helping Opal felt honest and genuine in a way that being a chaplain hasn't felt for a long time.

That can't be a coincidence.

When I think of visiting patients and their families and hospital staff, I don't feel that yearning I once did. I could go back to work and resume my duties, but I wouldn't be wholeheartedly into it; I'd be going through the motions.

"I don't want that."

My whispered admission catches me off guard. I press my hand over my mouth as I think about what I've said to myself.

And then I let myself wonder what I'd rather do instead.

There's only one thought that comes to my mind. And when it does, it brings a satisfaction that I don't ever recall feeling.

My phone rings, jerking me out of my thoughts. When I see it's April, I answer it right away.

"Hi, April?"

"Hello there, dear."

I smile at the gentle tone of her voice. "How are you? Is Opal doing okay? I'm so sorry I haven't seen or spoken to you the past few weeks. I've been, um, working on some stuff and . . ."

"Oh, honey, don't you worry about it. Evan filled me in."

"He did?"

"He said you had some personal issues come up that you had to take care of."

"Oh. Right. I should have been in touch, though. I wanted to see Opal before she moved to the new memory care facility. I feel terrible."

"It's all right, dear. I just wanted to call and let you know that Mom is all settled in at the new place, and if you're feeling up to it, please feel free to stop by. She'd be thrilled to see you. She's been asking about you, actually."

"She has?"

April chuckles. "Almost every day. She misses you. No pressure, of course. I know you're busy. But if you ever wanted to, it would make her day."

"I'd love to," I say quickly. "Can I come this weekend?"

I can hear the smile in April's voice when she speaks. "Absolutely, dear."

Chapter Twenty

The door to Opal's room is cracked open when I arrive at the memory care facility. I knock and listen to the soft shuffle of footsteps behind the door.

April answers the door and beams when she sees me, then pulls me into a hug as she says hello. When she releases me, she leads me by the hand all the way inside the small room.

"Mom, look who came to visit you."

Opal's sitting up on her bed. A smile appears when she sees me. Her eyes look greener than before, maybe because of the blouse she's wearing, which is a similar shade.

"Oh, hi there, dear! You finally came!"

She holds her arms up at me, and I lean down and give her a hug. When I start to pull away, she stops me with a hand on my wrist. Her other hand cups my cheek.

"You're looking tired, dear."

April *tsk*s as she sits on the foot of the bed. "Mom, don't say that. It's rude."

"It's okay. She's just being honest." I pat Opal's hand before she lowers it down to her lap. "You're right. I'm tired. Trying to get more rest, though."

I settle in the armchair next to Opal's bed.

"How are you liking the new place?"

"It's pretty good. There's a nice garden in the back where Bunny takes me for walks every time she's here. The food's good too. But they don't have gin martinis. Can you believe it?"

April and I laugh. "That's a travesty," I say.

She chats about the new quilting book she just received, which is a gift from her granddaughter, Gwen, April explains. Opal tells me about the cute bunnies she saw near the rosebushes the other day, and how she wishes they would stop serving sugar-free Jell-O for dessert in the dining hall.

"It's not the same as the regular kind, not even close."

Opal starts to ask April about the stack of drawings on her night-stand. April grabs them and gives them to her to thumb through.

"From Jonah?" I ask her. April nods.

As Opal looks through them, April turns to me. "She's all about keeping up the schedule you got her on when you were looking after her earlier this summer. You were such a wonderful caretaker, Isabel. You were so sensitive to her needs. You made her days at home fun and meaningful. Without you, it would have been such a stressful time, and that definitely would have taken a toll on her. But instead, she had the best summer because of you. If I didn't know you, I'd think you'd been taking care of folks as a profession your whole life."

Her compliment has me soaring. Despite everything I've messed up lately, at least I got that right.

After a moment, I ask the question I've been thinking about ever since April called me. "How is she doing? With her treatment so far?"

Her eyes turn misty. She opens her mouth but hesitates, then glances at Opal once more before looking back at me. Opal studies the drawings with a furrowed brow, like she's trying to memorize the images.

"It's going okay so far. The infusion treatment her doctor recom-mended is administered every two to four weeks. Ideally it would be best if she could go every two weeks, but given her age and overall health . . ."

When April trails off, she shakes her head, then swallows. "So we're just doing every four weeks now. It's not as effective as it would be if it was more frequent, but it's better than nothing. I just . . . I have to remind myself that she's not young. She can't handle anything aggressive. I just need to be grateful that she's made it this far."

Opal holds up one of the drawings, pointing out how much she likes the colors. Through teary eyes, April smiles and nods at her. My heart aches for April, how hard it must be to have to put on a happy face when she's confronted with the mortality of her own mother.

Opal goes back to shuffling through the drawings.

"She's responded well to the treatments she's had so far," April says. "Even the doctor was shocked at how she's handled it. Both of us were afraid she'd have bad side effects at her age, but just a bit of abdominal pain is all that's happened so far."

There's a hope in her tone that sets off my urge to tear up. I blink rapidly, hoping no tears fall.

April rests her hands in her lap, then gives her mom another wistful look. "I know with her age and her dementia I'm probably being too optimistic . . ."

She trails off, her voice wobbly.

"Her oncologist said that even if we see good results at first, there's always a possibility that it will eventually stop being effective. Or the side effects could become too much for her and we'll have to stop treatment altogether to preserve her quality of life."

She turns away from Opal, cupping a hand over her mouth just as her voice breaks. I lean over to grab her hand, and she mouths, *Thank you.*

"But I just don't know how to feel anything other than optimistic," April says. "She's my mom. I have to have hope."

"Of course. Really, April, that's a great sign that she responded so well to the first treatment. That shows what a warrior she is."

April chuckles before wiping at her eye. "A warrior. A warm, tiny, chatty, gin-loving, eighty-eight-year-old warrior."

"Without a doubt."

She takes a second to breathe before rolling her shoulders. When she looks at me, I'm caught off guard at the slight amusement on her face. "Evan misses you, you know."

"Wh—he does?"

She nods, smiling slightly.

"Oh."

That's all I can say. I don't know how I feel about talking about Evan with his mom. I wonder if he told her about us . . . about what happened between us. My cheeks flare at the thought.

I turn to Opal, who is now thumbing through a quilting book, and try to think of a way to delicately word what I'm wondering, but then I think, *Screw it.*

"I miss him too," I say to April.

"I don't mean to pry. My son's a grown man, and I don't want to be one of those meddling moms." She chuckles as she rolls her eyes, like she's making fun of what she's just said. "I mean, I don't want to meddle *too* much."

I let out a laugh.

"He talks about you a lot," she says. "What a wonderful and caring person you are. How good you were with Mom. How happy you make her. How much he enjoyed spending time with you. How pretty you are."

When she winks at me, I laugh again.

"My son's not the kind of person to gush over a woman in front of me. He never has, now that I think about it. But he does with you. You're special to him, Isabel. Just thought you should know that."

She pats my hand.

"I think he's pretty amazing," I say. "I just . . . we had an argument the last time we saw each other. I think I hurt his feelings."

I cringe as I admit this. I don't want to get into the specifics with his mom, but I want to be honest and straightforward with her. She's always been that way to me.

When she shrugs in response to what I've said, I'm shocked. "We hurt the people we care about sometimes. All of us do, even when we try not to. It's just a matter of making it right."

I mull over her words. I hope they're true. I want to make things right with Evan—if he's willing to hear me out.

The hesitation I feel must be clear on my face because April grabs my hand in hers and says, "When you're ready to go to him, he'll be waiting."

She says it with such certainty, I'm heartened—hopeful, even.

Opal starts to cough, so I pour her a glass of water from the nearby pitcher on the nightstand. After she drinks, she pulls me into a hug. I start to laugh.

"She's been in a hugging mood this past week or so," April explains.

"That's perfect, because I'm in a hugging mood too."

As we embrace, I feel lighter than I have in days. Like always, her hug is surprisingly tight given how small she is. I give her a gentle squeeze back, and when she releases me, I sit back down in the chair next to her bed.

I do a quick once-over, taking note that she doesn't look different from the last time I saw her. Her eyes are still crystal bright, and her hair is neatly combed and styled in waves.

With all that she's going through with her dementia, cancer treatment, and moving into this new facility, joy radiates from her. She's bright and happy, and seeing that is the greatest comfort.

April stands up to go to the restroom, and I glance back at Opal, who's still paging through a quilting pattern book. "Are you working on a quilting project?" I ask.

"I'm thinking about it."

She says it so matter-of-factly, I laugh.

"You know what, though? I wish they played better music here. I really, really miss my song."

"'My Sweetie Sparrow.'"

"I wish they would play it here."

I reach into my purse, pull out my phone, then play it. Like every other time Opal hears it, she smiles wide, then closes her eyes and bops her head along to the beat.

"My brother hates this song. Says I play it too much."

I smile at Opal's remark, remembering how she said that same thing earlier in the summer when I started looking after her.

When April comes out of the bathroom, she's beaming. "It's your song, Mom."

"It sure is."

As they sit together and listen to the song, I sit back and watch as mother and daughter share in this moment together, so happy.

The song ends, and Opal immediately asks to hear it again. April plays it on her phone this time.

As Opal listens, April turns to me. "She's been asking to talk to her mom and dad again." Her eyes shine, and she blinks for a few seconds to hold back her tears. "I suppose I could do it, but every time I even think about it, I start to get so emotional. I know I wouldn't be able to last a minute on the phone with her before losing it. I . . . I know it's probably asking too much . . ."

She hesitates, but I know what she's going to say.

"I'd be happy to call her. Maybe the next time I visit, I can do it then?"

Relief and joy converge at once in April's expression. She gives my hand a squeeze. "Thank you, Isabel. You're an angel. I honestly don't know what we would have done if you hadn't come into our lives."

It's a long second before I can speak, the ache in my throat is too strong. "I feel the same way about you all too."

The song finishes, and I check the time. "I'd better get going."

They both hug me. April asks if I've got any fun plans for the day.

"I'm headed to my friend's baby shower."

"Oh! The friend whose baby you delivered!"

"Yes."

"How sweet."

"Will you be back tomorrow?" Opal asks.

I swallow down the emotion in my throat at the eager look in her eyes.

"Mom, Isabel will come when she can. She's busy, though, and she has to go back to work at the hospital too. She'll probably be busy and won't be able to come by every day."

A sad frown pulls at Opal's face as she nods her understanding.

"Maybe not every day, but I should be able to see you pretty often, Opal."

"Oh, that's wonderful," April says. "I just figured since you'll be back at work, it'll be hard for you to come around much."

"Truthfully, I don't know what I'll be doing job-wise just yet."

That's the first time I've said that out loud—it's the first time I've let that thought take hold in my brain for longer than two fleeting seconds before pushing it out.

But it's the truth. I see that now. I don't know if I'm meant to go back to being a hospital chaplain. I reflect on my time with Opal, how every day with her felt like it had purpose. How it felt like I was making a difference. How it felt like I was doing something truly good by looking after her.

Maybe I shouldn't give up on this sort of work just yet.

"Are you working someplace else?" April asks.

"Not sure. I'm just . . . trying to keep my options open. But no matter what I end up doing, I'll always be here for Opal and your family."

April's eyes turn misty once more. She pulls me into yet another hug. When I let go, I notice Opal reaches her hands up for another hug too.

After we embrace, I take another look at her.

"You're looking so good, Opal. So happy. And vibrant."

She takes a breath, her slight shoulders rising slowly, as if she's smelling flowers and trying to savor the fragrance.

"I feel it, dear. I really do." She cups my face with her hands. "It was so good to see you."

Delight dances in her green-hazel eyes, like she's looking at the most wondrous sight in the world. It sends a wave of joy through me.

"I'll see you again next week, okay?"

"I'd love that."

I tell her and April goodbye before heading home to get ready for Keely's baby shower.

Chapter
Twenty-One

When I walk into the Grey Plume, my legs are shaky.

I find Keely's face immediately in the crowd of attendees, pastel-blue balloons, and light-blue hydrangea floral arrangements. When she sees me, she stops midconversation. Her sleeping baby boy rests in her arms. Her mouth hangs open for a few seconds; then she hands Gabriel off to the person she was chatting with before rushing over to me.

"You're here!" she squeals as she pulls me into a hug.

When she sniffles, I bite the inside of my lip to keep from crying. She holds me tight, and for a few seconds, I just close my eyes and relish the feel of this hug.

Around us, people mill about, snacking and chatting, seemingly oblivious to the emotion in our embrace.

"Are you okay?" she asks, her voice shaky.

I sniffle. "Yeah. Getting there, at least."

She breaks our hug but keeps hold of my arms. "You have no idea how happy I am that you came." She sounds almost scared to admit it. Worry clouds her stare. "But if you're not comfortable being here, around all these people, I get it. I really do. If you want to leave, I understand completely—"

"I want to be here, Keely. I promise."

Yeah, it's a bit overwhelming being around all these people. But I'm here. I'm standing in this space. I'm doing it. And I'm okay.

With trembling lips, Keely smiles. Then she waves over the older lady she'd handed baby Gabriel to. She brushes her curly hair away from her face, then scoops him up in her arms.

"Remember your auntie Isabel, Gabriel? She delivered you on the floor, right over there." She pivots in the direction of the host podium where, weeks ago, he was born.

"Hi, baby boy," I whisper to his sleepy face. "It's so good to see you again."

"You want to hold him?"

I nod. Keely sets him in my arms, and I cuddle him against my chest. He's all cheek and chin. His nose is a delicate little button, and his mouth is a full rosebud. He's the chunkiest baby I've ever seen.

"He's the cutest, squishiest baby in the world," I say to Keely. "I can't believe he came from your tiny body."

Keely chuckles and smooths a hand over the floral maxi dress she's wearing. "I can't believe it either. He's growing bigger by the minute. And sucking the life out of me. I could nurse him all day and he'd still be hungry."

We laugh.

"Then you should eat something, Mama," I say, nodding to the impressive array of dishes that sit at every table in the dining area.

"Good idea." Keely turns and grabs a plate of stuffed mushrooms and smoked duck spring rolls from the table nearest us and wolfs half of them down in seconds.

"Damn." I chuckle.

Out of the corner of my eye, I spot a tall figure with a messy mop of blond hair decked out in a dress shirt and trousers. Theo.

We lock eyes, and I immediately go rigid. I can't tell what he's thinking by his expression. It's pretty much blank, save for the slight rise of his eyebrows. I'm guessing he's not thrilled to see me. I went radio silent on his wife. Again. After he asked me not to.

He walks over to me. "Hey."

"Hey." I glance down at snoozing baby Gabriel. "Your baby looks nothing like you."

When he laughs at my terrible joke, I'm grateful.

"Lucky kid looks just like his mom," he says.

"He's gonna be tall like you, though. Look at how long he already is."

A gentle curve appears along Theo's mouth as he looks down at his son. "Maybe." Then he looks at me after a few seconds of saying nothing. I can't take the silence, so I speak.

"I'm sorry for going dark on Keely again. I know I promised I wouldn't, and there's no excuse in the world for it, but I was in a really bad place."

His lips purse, and I brace myself for a scolding. But then he just nods.

"She's giving me another chance—a chance I don't deserve—but I just want you to know that I don't expect you to ever be good with me. You're one hundred percent within your right to be mad at me forever—"

When he holds up his hand and shakes his head, I go quiet.

"It's okay, Isabel."

His gentle words and tone are a shock to my system.

"Yeah, I was upset when you disappeared on her again . . . but then Keely told me she ran into you the other day, and she explained what happened, what you were going through. I get it. I'm sorry, Isabel."

I'm quiet as I process what he's said, the kindness and empathy he's giving me.

"But honestly? All I can think about is how grateful I am to you. I can't thank you enough for what you did when Keely went into labor."

His expression turns flustered as he stammers. "When she told me what happened, I was in shock. I couldn't believe it. How you took control. How you kept your cool. How you made sure she and our baby were safe. And for that . . . for that . . ."

It takes a bit before I realize he's choked up and that's why he keeps trailing off.

His blue eyes glisten as he looks at me. "For that, I'm forever grateful to you, Isabel. I take back every doubt I had about you. You're a truly good person. Thank you."

I smile up at him. "Thanks, Theo."

He wraps one of his arms around me, pulling me into a side hug. He's careful not to squeeze too hard, though, since I'm holding Gabriel. I catch Keely smiling as she looks between us, like she can tell we're making amends.

A woman who I recognize as Keely's mom walks over to tell her it's time to start opening gifts. Theo slips away to gather the presents. When Nancy catches eyes with me, she stills. Then she smiles. It's the same wide smile as Keely's.

Her brown eyes go glossy with tears.

"Isabel. It's been so long." She touches my arm while gently palming Gabriel's head.

"It has. It's so good to see you, Nancy."

"Likewise, honey. Thank you for what you did for my daughter and my grandson. We owe you forever. I mean it, anything you need ever, just ask us and we'll make it happen. A place to live? A loan? A kidney? You name it, it's yours."

"You don't owe me anything. It's the least I could do for what a wonderful friend Keely's been to me."

Nancy tears up and nods once. She waves over two elderly women and introduces me as the superhero who delivered Gabriel. They tell me how amazing I am. I blush as Nancy takes Gabriel from me and insists that I sit down at the same table where Keely is sitting.

Theo starts piling gifts next to Keely. I lean over to her. "The gift I got you is gonna be a little late. With all that was going on, I didn't think to order it in time. I'm sorry."

She frowns at me, like what I've said is the most ridiculous thing in the world. Then she grabs my hand. "You don't need to get me anything. You being here—you delivering my baby is gift enough."

As she rips into the first present, I notice the nerves from when I walked in are long gone. No one is gawking at me or whispering about me or wondering what I was up to in the more than two years that I went MIA after Chantel died. Everyone is gracious and kind and welcoming.

I had no reason to worry.

The rest of the baby shower passes smoothly. When people start leaving, I get up to head for the restroom.

Keely grabs my arm. "Evan asked me about you earlier. I told him you'd be here. He wants you to stop by the kitchen and see him."

My heart races. "I'll go see him now."

"Do you want to maybe meet up next weekend? I'd be saddled with a newborn, but I swear I'm still fun to hang out with."

There's a shy gleam in her eyes, like she's scared to ask.

I pull her into a hug. "I'd love that. Are you free Saturday?"

"Absolutely."

And then I head to the kitchen to see Evan.

He's the only one in there. He stands at the stove, whisking something in a metal saucepan. When I clear my throat, he looks up. And then he stills.

The first thing I see are his eyes. They're glistening. Not with tears but with surprise. Then he starts to smile. He turns off the burner, pushes up the sleeves of his white chef's coat, and takes a step toward me. "You're here."

He stands, shuffling his feet for a second. It's like he can't decide if he wants to walk over to me or not.

His eyes run along the length of me. "You look really pretty."

I run my fingertips along the mint-green shift dress I threw on this morning. "I wasn't sure what to wear to a baby shower."

"You chose well."

The smile that pulls at his mouth is so shy and gentle, I could cry.

The door swings open, and in walks Jax along with a server.

Jax turns to me and beams. "Well, hey! Dr. Isabel. How's it going?"

Despite the nerves whirring through me, I laugh.

"I'm good, Jax. Thanks."

Evan shuffles his feet as Jax asks him a question about the baby shower service. A trio of servers walks in to load up their empty trays with more finger food. I stand off to the side in this bustling kitchen and let them work. A minute later, Jax walks over to the walk-in, and Evan turns back to me.

"Can we go somewhere and talk?" I ask softly.

"Sure."

He asks Jax to take over the kitchen while he steps out. We walk to that darkened space down the hall to the back of the restaurant, near the restrooms.

"I feel like this is our unofficial meeting spot."

He lets out a weak chuckle. "I guess it is." Then his expression sobers. "Are you okay?"

I nod as I bear the weight of that question. He witnessed my breakdown at the lake. He tried to help, and I pushed him away. He admitted feelings for me, and I cut him off completely. I have so much to explain, so much to make right.

"I'm sorry, Evan. For how I treated you when we got back from Wilson Lake. You were reaching out, you were trying to support me, and I pushed you away. I shut you out. You didn't deserve that." I fumble with the fabric along the front of my dress. "I need to tell you something. I need to tell you why I acted the way I did at the lake."

It's strange. My heart is thudding like I thought it would, but as I gaze into his eyes, his expression tender as he looks at me, I can feel myself start to ease. My heartbeat slows, my muscles unclench, and my posture relaxes. I can feel his care and concern for me radiate off him, like heat skimming my skin.

"My little sister drowned in a lake two and a half years ago."

His mouth falls open slightly. And then he closes his eyes for a long second before looking at me. "I am so sorry."

"My family and I were out boating for the day. Chantel and I thought it would be fun to race to a nearby sandbar, but when we dove into the water, she got caught in the weeds underwater and . . . well . . ."

My throat starts to seize up. I can't say the rest of the words. It's too much. But I don't have to. What I've said is enough. Evan understands.

He reaches his hand to touch my forearm as I hug my arms around myself. "You don't have to talk about this if it's too hard."

I shake my head. "I want to. I'm ready to do it."

With a swallow, he nods, and his hand falls away. "Do you want to sit down someplace?"

"No. Standing is fine. I'll feel too restless otherwise."

He nods like he gets it. And then I tell him everything.

How I kicked Chantel away when I felt her grab my leg because I thought she was messing around.

How it took two whole days to find her body.

How I have no clear memories of the weeks that followed.

How I've been racked with guilt ever since.

How I pushed everyone close to me out of my life because all they ever did was tell me how sorry they were about Chantel, and I couldn't handle being reminded of her death constantly.

How I pushed my parents away because I couldn't handle how they doted on me—their last remaining child.

How I lost my faith when I lost Chantel.

I don't know when exactly I start crying, but the moment I do, he reaches out and pulls me into his chest. I tell him everything as I'm hugged against him. I don't hold back. I want him to know. Because he cares about me, and he said he wants me to open up to him. And I am. Finally I am.

As much as it wrecks me to relive the loss of Chantel, there's something cathartic about this, the way that I'm spilling everything to Evan and he's standing here, being my literal support.

I feel unburdened. I feel looked after.

And that is the push I need to say this next part.

"I acted like she was still here—like she was still alive."

He's quiet. All I can hear is the sound of him breathing above me and the gentle thud of his heart beating against my ear that's pressed to his chest.

"I would imagine her with me, standing next to me. I would imagine that I could talk to her on the phone still. It all felt so real . . . even though it wasn't."

I swallow, grateful that I don't have to look at him when I admit all this. He probably thinks I've lost it. He's probably thinking back to when I delivered Keely's baby and talked on the phone almost the whole time, and when he asked me who I was talking to, I told him that it was my sister . . . that she had helped coach me through the entire delivery.

Pressing my eyes shut, I stand there and endure the panicked embarrassment that hits me. It burns as it flashes across my skin. I wonder, since we're still hugging, if he can feel the heat of it, if he can feel just how much it pains me to admit all this—how ashamed I am.

But after a second, I feel something that makes me think all my worrying is for nothing. I feel the soft squeeze of his arms around me.

"It's all okay," he whispers. "I understand completely."

His voice is like a gentle protest calling out every doubt I harbor against myself. It makes me soften into his embrace even more.

"That's why I kept my job at the hospital, even though I didn't believe anymore. My sister used to work as a labor-and-delivery nurse there, then an ER nurse. We'd see each other almost every day whenever our shifts overlapped. It was my favorite part about working there, having her close by. And even though I knew I didn't belong there as a chaplain—because I no longer believed—I stayed. So I could be close to the place where she'd spent so much time. Where *we* spent so much time together for that handful of years."

His chest rises with a single slow breath. I can feel him nod above me.

"I still have her bedroom set up in my house the way she left it before she died. I haven't had the strength to pack up any of her things or give anything away."

"That's okay."

"Is it?" I lean up to look at him. I want to know—I *need* to know that this is how he really feels.

And then I see it. That shine in his eyes, the slight furrow in his brow, the way he's holding me in his arms like he doesn't want to ever let me go, it all convinces me that what he's saying is true.

"You lost your little sister, Isabel. You were consumed with grief and pain. This is your way of coping."

I nod and burrow back into his chest.

"I'm seeing a therapist now. It's helping a lot. I . . . I'm going to get better."

"There's no need for you to be better than you are, Isabel. You're already a wonderful person. But I'm glad you're seeing someone to help you with your grief."

I pull out of his embrace because I need to see him when I say this. "I'm sorry I pushed you away, Evan. You didn't deserve that. It's just that, it's been so long since I let anyone in."

"I get it. I promise I get it."

My heart thuds so hard, I can feel it all the way in my arms and legs.

"I know I need so much help to work through this. Losing Chantel is something I'm going to struggle with for the rest of my life, probably. And I completely get it if that's not something you want to deal with."

Evan opens his mouth, but I shake my head.

"I like you, Evan. And I want to keep seeing you, if that's something you want."

Brightness shines in his stare. And then he starts to smile.

"I want that too." His voice comes off soft, like a whisper, like a feather touching my skin.

Inside me, my blood pumps hot. My lungs swell with each breath, almost like they're aching. Almost like my entire body is struggling to process the joy and relief of this moment.

I nuzzle against his collarbone as he holds me tight. I close my eyes, suddenly aware of just how heavy my eyelids are. I could fall asleep right here, right now, propped upright in the cozy cradle of Evan's chest and arms.

"Maybe this is too much to say this right now . . ." Evan's throat pulses against my temple as he swallows. "But I'd love to hear more about your sister. She sounds like the most amazing person."

"I'd love to tell you all about her," I say through a shaky voice.

"Only if you're ready."

I wipe my face. He pulls out a fresh napkin from the pocket of his chef's jacket, then hands it to me. I dab away the wetness on my cheeks. Then Evan takes me by the hand and leads me through a back door to the alley behind the restaurant. In the distance, I hear traffic noise, but it's just us out here right now.

He lowers down to sit on the curb and reaches a hand up to help steady me as I sit down next to him. I lean my head against his shoulder and thread my arm through his. Together, we stare ahead at the brick wall of the building next to us. He doesn't push me to hurry and speak. He just sits there and waits patiently until I'm ready. It's exactly what I need.

Breathing in, I clear my throat, and then I tell him about Chantel.

"She was three years younger than me, but people always said we looked like twins."

I pull out my phone and show him a picture of the two of us.

"Wow. You really do look a lot alike."

I lean against him once more, and he rests his cheek on my temple. I tell him what we were like as kids, how we would fight over who got the front seat of the car, how our mom would dress us in the same frilly dresses for the holidays, how her favorite thing to do as a toddler was chase animals whenever she saw them.

"Even when our parents scolded her to stop, she would never listen. She loved dogs so much. And squirrels. And birds. Other little kids at the park would run away in tears whenever they'd see a big dog. Never Chantel."

Evan's lips stretch slowly against my forehead as he smiles.

As the minutes pass, the words pour faster from me. A million stories pop up in my brain, one after the other, like they're lined up on an imaginary conveyor belt. I can't tell them quickly enough. Evan listens the whole time, laughing when the story or memory warrants and asking questions when he's curious. He never lets go of me, not even for a second.

As I speak, there's a soft echo in my ears. I don't recognize it right away, but when I finally do, I start to shake. It sounds so much like Chantel's voice.

You did it, Bel.

Chapter
Twenty-Two

When I walk into the hospital, that sanitizer smell hits my nostrils. It's weird how much I like that scent, how comforting I find it. So many people hate it. So many find it nauseating. But I love the familiarity of it. It reminds me of all those days that I came to work and saw my little sister. I'm going to miss it.

As I make my way to the elevator and glide up to the tenth floor, I'm calm. It's surprising, considering what I'm about to do.

When I walk into the chaplain office, Martha is squinting at her computer screen. When she twists in her chair and sees it's me, she hops up.

"Isabel!" She pulls me into a hug, gushing about how good it is to see me.

Even as she leans away, she keeps hold of me with her hands on my arms. "It's so good to have you back! Everyone's been asking about you."

"Really?" I try to smile, but my mouth won't cooperate. I have to look away so that Martha doesn't see what I'm certain is a painfully awkward expression.

This is going to be so hard.

"They absolutely have. Arlene told me that she and the other nurses have been counting down the days. You're still their hero for standing up to Dr. Walder. They haven't missed him at all while he's been gone, unsurprisingly."

Martha gestures for me to take a seat in the chair across from her. She pivots in her chair to grab her notebook. "So! Did you have any trouble with the online workshop that HR sent you to complete? I know it was ridiculous that you had to do it in the first place, but hospital policy and all."

"Actually, I didn't do it."

She whips around to me. "Why not?"

"Because . . ." I hesitate for a second. "Martha, I need to tell you something."

"What is it?"

"I can't work here anymore."

Her expression turns puzzled. "What do you mean?"

"I'm giving my two weeks' notice. I'm quitting my job as a chaplain here at the hospital."

Her gray-blonde eyebrows arch slightly; then her mouth opens the slightest bit. She shakes her head, her shoulder-length hair swooshing with the movement, like she's struggling to process what I've said.

"You're quitting?"

"Yes."

She stammers for a second. "Wait, is it because of the suspension? I know that it was upsetting for you to have to go through, but I promise, it hasn't affected your standing here, Isabel. Everyone supports you one hundred percent. It won't affect your file or your salary or anything like—"

I reach over to rest my hand on her arm. She goes quiet.

"That's not it at all. I promise I'm not upset about any of that anymore. It's just . . . when I was away for the summer, I had a lot of time to think. And I tried a lot of different things to keep myself busy with the free time I had. I became a caretaker for an elderly woman with dementia. Opal. I don't know if you remember, but she was a patient here a few months ago. Her family gave you that card to give to me."

"Oh, that's right."

"I think I had a bit of a revelation while I was gone. I realized that as much as I enjoy being a chaplain, I enjoyed being a caretaker more. And I think I want to try something new. I'm going to nursing school. I want to be a geriatric nurse and look after elderly patients."

It's the first time I've said this out loud. When the idea to go to nursing school popped in my head, something happened. I felt excited. And I realized then that it'd been a long time since I felt this excited about anything.

I watch Martha in the seconds that follow my news. At first she blinks, her face blank. But then she shakes her head slightly and starts to stammer once more. Then she smiles.

"That sounds wonderful, kiddo. I'm so happy for you."

And then she leans over and pulls me into a hug. When I hear her sniffle, my eyes water.

"You've made working here an absolute joy, Martha. I'm sorry that I'm leaving like this. I'm going to miss you a lot."

She sniffles again before releasing me, then dabs her face with a tissue. "Oh, don't mind me, kiddo. You know I'm a big mush. I'm truly happy for you. If this is what you want, you go for it. I'll admit that it's not gonna be the same without you here. We'll miss the heck out of you. So much." She aims a shaky smile at me. "This would make your sister so proud, you know. She'd be so happy."

Her words land like an arrow to my heart. I flash a shaky smile of my own at her. "That means everything, Martha. Thank you."

She chats about how she's going to arrange a going-away party for me. I tell her that's not necessary, but she won't hear of it.

"You've been with us for five years. The least we can give you for all of your hard work and commitment is a proper send-off."

I start to protest, but I trail off and then go quiet. Because Martha's words bring to light the fact that for the past two years, I wasn't the person of faith I presented myself to be. I was being dishonest about that part of myself for so long in front of her. I don't deserve a send-off or Martha's kind words. I don't deserve anything, really.

"I need to confess—"

The phone rings, and she holds up a hand. "One sec."

As she chats with the person on the other line and scribbles notes on a pad, I do a slow scan of the office. I can feel my pulse beating in my throat as I take everything in. It's one of the last times I'll be able to do this. The dead flowers on the desk that have been there for months. The office workout sticker chart that we collectively gave up on sometime last year but never bothered to take down. The heart-shaped glass dish that Martha always keeps stocked with Rolos.

"Okay!" she says through an exhale after she hangs up the phone.

She flashes a tired smile at me. It never, ever fails. No matter the workload, no matter if she's had the most stressful day, no matter if she's emotionally drained from an especially tough meeting, Martha always has a smile to offer. I'll miss that too.

"What did you want to talk to me about, kiddo?"

"I've been hiding something from you. Lying to you, actually."

"About what?"

"About my position. My qualifications."

"What do you mean? You're qualified for this job. You have a degree; you have the proper training. You've got plenty of experience under your belt . . ."

She trails off as I shake my head and swipe a tear just as it falls from my eye.

"I . . . I don't believe. In anything anymore," I say. "I haven't for a long time."

"Believe in any of what? Isabel, what are you saying?"

There's an innocence in her tone that makes me want to hug her. Classic Martha. Always believing the absolute best in everyone, never thinking that anyone would ever purposely do anything wrong.

"I don't believe in God, Martha. I haven't since I lost my sister. I just didn't have the guts to say it until now, when I'm about to leave." Pressing my eyes shut, I shake my head slightly. "I know that sounds horrible. But I can't have you thinking I'm this honorable person when for the past two years, I haven't been."

The recognition that crosses her face comes slowly. First her eyes widen the slightest bit; then her lips part open. I half expect her to hold up both hands and say, *Excuse me?* But she blinks and presses her lips shut.

"I see."

"When Chantel died, something inside me snapped. I kind of lost it—I lost my faith. I lost my joy. I lost everything, really. I tried to hide it as best as I could. I didn't want to admit it, though, because working here with you has been the one stability in my life. It kept me grounded, coming here, seeing patients and their families, being a support for them. Being someone they looked to for guidance. When I was here, I didn't feel like such a disaster."

Martha nods along with the most sincere and focused expression, like always.

"The hospital was my connection to my sister, since she used to work here. I never wanted to leave, because then it would feel like I was losing her in this part of my life too. When I came to work, I was reminded of her. I pictured her everywhere around me. She used to drop by and see me almost every day."

I stop to swallow and press my eyes shut, wishing more than anything that Chantel would walk through that door and plop herself on the desk and take me to task for drinking too much coffee or letting her mug of tea get too cold. I even glance up and look at the door. But nothing happens. It stays closed.

"I'm sorry I hid my loss of faith from you," I say. "That was so dishonest of me. And I really don't think you should be having some going-away bash for me after what I've done. I don't deserve it."

I let out a breath when I finish. A beat later, the tips of my fingers start to ache. That's when I realize I've been digging my fingernails into the armrests of the chair. I pull them away and set my hands in my lap, mimicking Martha's position.

She glances down at her lap, then up at me. Her expression is as it always is: her lips in a neutral line, her eyes bright and kind. That's the single greatest poker face if I've ever seen one.

But then the corners of her mouth tug up into the smallest smile. "I don't think I ever told you what I did before I became a chaplain, did I?"

Her question catches me off guard. "Um, I don't think so."

"I was a nun."

Air lodges in my throat, and I stammer, shocked. "I had no idea. How long were you a nun?"

"Ten years. All throughout my twenties."

She twists to grab her purse from the floor, then digs through it. She pulls out a small photo and hands it to me.

My mouth makes a perfect O shape as I stare in awe at the image of a twentysomething Martha decked out in a habit.

"Whoa." I hand her back the photo as she laughs.

"It was a wonderful period in my life, but challenging too."

"What was challenging about it?"

"The fact that, while I was a nun, I fell in love with the man who would eventually become my husband."

"Oh."

It's all I can say for several seconds. I wasn't expecting that.

"It's an unconventional love story for sure." She chuckles, then explains how they met while volunteering at a local homeless shelter.

"The attraction was instant," she says with a wistful smile on her face. "And I knew the first time I met him that I was in trouble. There was this undeniable spark. I loved talking to him. He was so funny and charming and kind. It got to the point where I would get butterflies in my stomach before I'd head over for my volunteer shift. We got to know each other so well over the months that we volunteered together. And even though I was attracted to him, I pushed it aside. Told myself it was only because it had been so long since I had . . . you know."

I nod, my face hot. Never in a million years did I think I'd ever be chatting about sex with Martha.

"But after over a year of being such close friends with this undeniable attraction, my feelings never really went away. Sure, I buried them for a while. But they were always there. And then one day, he confessed that he was attracted to me."

"What did you do?"

"I told him that I couldn't leave the Church."

"And what did he say?" I sound like a captivated six-year-old being told a ghost story.

A small smile tugs at her lips. "His exact words were, 'I don't give a damn about the Church. How do *you* feel about me?'"

She pauses to sigh and glances at the picture of herself in her hand. Sadness radiates in her stare.

"I told him that it didn't matter how I felt. I'd taken a vow and I'd made my choice. I had no plans to leave my position as a nun, ever."

"Wow."

"Obviously that didn't end up happening. Even though I shut him down, he still kept showing up to volunteer alongside me. That was sweet torture, being around this amazing man who I held so much passion and feeling for but wouldn't allow myself to do anything about it. And then he pulled me aside one day and said that no matter what, he still wanted to be friends. I burst into tears. And then we kissed."

"Oh my gosh, Martha."

She shakes her head, smiling. "It wasn't my finest moment. There I was, a nun, making out with the guy I was in love with in the storeroom of a homeless shelter."

My mouth is open as I process everything she's said.

"Wow. That's, um . . ."

"Completely unexpected? Totally wild?"

I laugh. "Sure, that works."

She chuckles; then her expression shifts to regretful.

"I'm ashamed to say it took me almost a year before I officially left my post with the Church to be with Kirk. But that was the only time we did anything physical while I was a nun. One slipup was enough, I couldn't handle more. My conscience was already shot. I was so conflicted . . . I loved being part of the Church so much. I loved the sense of community and serving the parishioners. But then I finally realized I loved Kirk more. And I wanted a life with him more than I wanted to continue my work as a nun. And when that realization hit me, I left."

"That must have been so hard," I say. "But I bet that meant so much to him."

"It did." Her soft tone turns wistful. She tucks the photo back in her purse and looks at me. "I didn't go to church for a very, very long time after that. I thought I'd catch fire the minute I touched holy water. But I finally found peace with it all. I realized that being a nun was a wonderful part of my life, but it wasn't what I was meant to do. This is."

She gestures to the tiny office space.

"Wow. I'm speechless, Martha."

"It was the right thing to do. I felt it in my heart, in my soul. Now I feel a closeness to God I hadn't felt before, not even when I was a nun. It still astounds me to think about sometimes. And it was definitely a struggle getting to this point. In that year before I left, I was a mess. I felt like I wasn't serving the Church and its patrons properly because I didn't feel like my heart was fully committed to them in the same way I used to be. I was in love with Kirk and aching to be with him, and that made me feel like a fraud. And when I stopped being a nun, even though I was so happy to be with Kirk, I was so lost. I didn't know where I would end up in my faith. But I realized later on that it was all part of my spiritual journey. I started volunteering in the community again, which helped me fill that need to serve that had been so strong when I was a nun. But I still struggled. I still felt like I had committed a horrible sin. But eventually I learned to forgive myself. I learned that not every phase in life is meant to last. You can end your time in one place, move on to another, and still uphold your value system. It was tough for a while, but I made it. This place in my faith, it's where I'm meant to be. And everything I experienced—the good, the bad, the struggle, the doubt—was valid. Because it was all part of the journey. I'm still on the journey. I always will be."

Her words hit me square in the chest—in the heart.

"I'm so sorry that you've been struggling for so long by yourself. But I need you to understand that what you're going through is normal. To question a belief isn't inherently bad. It doesn't make you a bad chaplain. Or a bad person. Every single one of us struggles with what we believe in at some point in our lives. If someone says they've never once doubted a belief they've held, they're lying. Or they're delusional."

I let out a soft laugh.

"You're on your journey, Isabel. It's okay to doubt and to question things. It doesn't make you a bad person, at least not in my book."

I'm heartened by her words. I didn't know it until now, but I think I needed to hear someone say this to me. I think I needed to hear from someone I care about and respect that it's okay to be imperfect—and that they're imperfect too. And that whether or not I find my way back to some semblance of my faith, I'm still a worthy human being.

"I've seen the way you can get anyone to feel comfortable and talk to you, Isabel. You've counseled people from every religious background, from every walk of life, every age group. You listen to people. You don't judge or preach. No matter the background of the person you're working with, you set them at ease. You make them feel comfortable, and you do your best to help them. That's what made you a good chaplain. And that's what will make you a good nurse too."

I tear up once more. "Thank you, Martha."

When she leans over and pulls me into another hug, I sink into her embrace. All those remaining invisible weights hanging off me melt away.

When we pull apart, she hands me a tissue.

"Only you know what's right for you. If the right thing for you to do is to leave, then I fully support you. I'll be sad—everyone at the hospital will be. We love you to bits. But we'll be happy that you're making the right decision for yourself. And all of us know what a truly good person you are. Nothing will ever change that."

For the first time in more than two years, I actually believe that about myself.

"And nothing you can say will stop me from throwing you the best darn going-away party I can," Martha says.

I let out a laugh and tell her thanks. Then I settle in to work the rest of my shift. The office phone rings, and Martha turns around to answer it. I reach up and touch the crumbling, dried-out flower petals in the vase. I swipe a Rolo from the tray, unwrap it, and pop it into my mouth. The chocolate is so stale, it doesn't even melt on my tongue—it crumbles, the texture like dirt. The caramel is so hard, my jaw aches as I chew it.

I'm gonna miss this place.

When Martha hangs up, she turns to me. "Maybe you'll come back here when you're a nurse. Then we'd be able to see you again."

Her tone and her gaze are so hopeful. I catch myself thinking that might be pretty great.

"I think I'd like that."

Chapter
Twenty-Three

When I pull up to my driveway, I spot Mom sitting on the porch steps, a foil-wrapped tray of food next to her. She beams and waves at me, and a familiar warmth courses through my chest. She's been checking up on me daily with texts and phone calls the past few weeks, ever since I started venturing out on my own again. She listened patiently every time I reassured her that I was fine, that I was eating enough, that I was sleeping well. But I knew it was only a matter of time before she showed up with a tray of food, eager to feed me.

I walk up to her, and we hug.

"How are you, *anak*? Good?" she asks as she cups my cheeks in her hands.

Her eyes scan my face for any traces of fatigue or sadness. They're not completely gone, but I'm a million times better than I was when she and Dad found me passed out on my couch.

A small smile pulls at her lips. "Your skin looks good. Very healthy. Glowy, even. That means you're eating."

I tell her thanks, then unlock the door and hold it for her as she walks in. As she flits through the kitchen warming up the fried rice and chicken adobo she brought, emotion grabs hold of my throat. The last time she dropped by was the beginning of the summer, after we hadn't spoken to each other for months, and the air between us was riddled with tension. Our hug, our conversation, even the way we looked at each other was laced with reluctance. Not now, though.

I swallow back the feeling and sit at the table when she refuses my offer of help. As we sit and dig in, I ask her about Dad.

"Oh, he's fine. Working late as always. He wants you to come over this weekend so we can barbecue."

"I'll be there."

I start to ask how she's doing, but I stop when she suddenly sets down her fork and places her hand over my hand that's resting on the table.

"Mom, what's . . ."

Her eyes go teary. "I'm so sorry, *anak*. For the way I pushed you when you were hurting over your sister."

"It's okay. I understand now where you were coming from."

She shakes her head, squeezing my hand. "No. It's not okay. I need to make this right with you."

She tries to speak, but her lip is shaking so hard, she has to stop. It sends tears straight to my eyes.

"For the longest time, I wanted to help you, *anak*. I saw you hurting all alone, refusing to reach out, refusing to talk to anyone, and it destroyed me. I tried so many things, I tried to talk to you so many times about your sister and what you were going through, but nothing worked, and it killed me."

I lower my head, nodding, remembering just how much my pain hurt her and Dad.

"And then I got so frustrated. I let myself get angry at how stubborn you were when I should have been patient and loving. I'm ashamed to admit it. But it's true."

Her gaze falls to her plate just as her shoulders slump.

"Mom."

It takes a second before she looks up at me.

"Mom, listen to me. I appreciate you saying all that. But I hate how guilty you still feel about it. You shouldn't. It was such an awful situation that I contributed to too. Okay, yeah, you could have been more patient, but I don't blame you for how angry and frustrated you were. I would have been, too, if I were in your shoes. I practically cut you and Dad out of my life because I didn't want to deal with the pain of our loss. That didn't help things."

She nods like she understands. I pivot so I'm facing her and scoop her hand in both of mine.

"You're not the only one who needs to apologize," I say. "I do too. I'm so sorry."

Tears tumble down her full cheeks. "You were hurting, *anak*."

"So were you. We all were."

She stands up and pulls me into a hug. For a minute, that's how we stay—her standing, me sitting, hugging each other tighter than I can ever remember.

"You're my baby. I love you always."

Despite the softness of her tone, her words hit me like a lightning bolt to my heart. I'm her baby—her only baby now. It'll be that way forever.

"I love you, too, Mom. Always."

She kisses the top of my head before sitting back down. We continue eating in silence. When I turn to pour more water into her glass, I freeze and stare at her. With her hair pulled back, her delicate shoulders straight, and her face in profile, she looks so much like Chantel.

I almost don't say it. Other than the brief mention minutes ago and the teary conversation we had when she and Dad found me slumped on the couch, we haven't spoken about Chantel in ages. I know she'd talk about her all day every day if she could, but she's held back for so long because of me. Because I never wanted to talk or open up.

But I'm not like that anymore.

"You look so much like Chantel right now."

It takes a few seconds for her to process what I've said, judging by the way her hand stills. But then she slowly turns to look at me. Her eyes glisten with tears once more, but this time, she's smiling.

"You think so?"

I nod. "She was always your spitting image. More than me, even."

She dabs at her eyes with a napkin, then reaches over to squeeze my hand. "This was her favorite." She picks at a chunk of chicken with her fork.

"I remember." I help myself to another flavorful chunk of meat. "You know she tried to feed it to some of the squirrels in the bird feeder in my backyard one time?"

Mom lets out a watery chuckle as she wipes her nose. "That sounds like your sister. Always trying to feed the squirrels and whatever other animals she loved."

"I yelled at her not to. What a waste to give away such delicious food to squirrels."

Mom smiles down at her plate. "What did she say when you yelled at her?"

"Nothing. She ignored me and kept doing it. Like always."

We share a laugh and finish our meals. When we head to the sink to do the dishes, there's a lightness in the air. I feel it in how swiftly I move, how easily I smile and laugh. I see it in the brightness in Mom's eyes, in the way her whole body moves with an ease that's been missing for years.

When she heads for the door to leave, I follow behind her.

"What are you doing this week?" I ask. If she's free, I want to surprise her and Dad with dinner.

She mentions dinner with a friend and clearing the garage with Dad. She pauses for a second before speaking. "On Wednesday we'll go to Mass. Like we always do."

"Oh. Right."

I hate the way she winces when I speak. I know that right now, she's remembering every single time I've refused to go to church with her.

"Can I come with you?"

Her jaw almost unhinges as she looks at me. "You . . . you want to come to church with your dad and me?"

I nod, wondering if I should clarify, but I don't. It's not necessary. I don't need to reiterate for the millionth time how I don't abide by the church she follows. That's not the point. The point is to spend more time with her and Dad. The point is to show her I'm not the closed-off person I used to be.

"I'd really like to go with you. If that's okay."

This time, when her lips tremble, she's smiling. "It's always okay. Always."

She grabs my face and kisses both cheeks before hugging me and leaving. When I close the door, I take a second and lean against it.

I'm going to church on Wednesday.

~

I don't miss the looks of shock on my parents' faces when I show up on their doorstep. They smile through it and hug me the instant they see me, but I know deep down that they assumed I would never come.

It sends a jolt of emotion to my throat, but I swallow it back and focus on the moment.

I'm here now, with them. That's what matters.

They make me sit at the dinner table and give me a plate of fresh fruit and a small glass of orange juice. Dad practically beams at me from his seat.

"You look so pretty, sweetie."

"Thanks, Dad."

When I look at him, his eyes shine brighter than I remember seeing in a long time. He reaches over and squeezes my hand in his just as Mom hugs me from behind when she tops off my drink.

I let out a laugh. "Wow, you guys."

"We're just so happy you're here, *anak*."

The slight shake in Mom's voice and the way Dad squeezes my hand like he never wants to let go land heavy in my heart. It's then that I realize it.

This is so much more than the act of simply attending church with them—it always has been. It's the fact that I'm here. With them. That's all they ever wanted my whole life, but especially after losing Chantel. For me to be with them as often as possible.

We walk to the car, and Dad drives us to their local parish. Everyone greets them with smiles and hugs and handshakes. A few say, "Oh my gosh, is this Isabel?" and they both answer with pride in their eyes and voices.

"We're so happy she's here with us," Mom says.

I hug and shake hands with people whose names I'm not sure I'll remember, but that doesn't matter. I feel so welcomed by everyone I meet.

We sit in a middle pew. I fold my hands in my lap, but then nerves hit soon after Mass starts. I alternate between folding my hands and fiddling with the hem of the floral skirt I'm wearing to expend my nervous energy in this narrow space, in this solemn place. I don't plan on participating in any of the prayers or sacraments. It wouldn't be right— I'm not a believer, I'm just here to support my parents while also being as respectful as possible to the service. Maybe I should have explained that to them before we left.

I brace myself for hurt looks and confusion, but neither happens. Mom and Dad kneel for prayers without a second look at me while I stay seated and bow my head. When they're back up in their seats, they simply smile at me. No scolding look, no hurt feelings, no questions. I let out a silent sigh of relief, the muscles in my torso easing as I slowly realize that there's nothing to brace myself for. There's no pressure and no expectation. I'm here. To them, that's enough.

As I mumble my way through hymns and politely shake hands while wishing peace for everyone, calm sets in. It's not the homily or the music or the prayers that move me. It's the fact that I get to share it all with my family.

As I sit between them, I hold their hands. They both look over and flash smiles at me. Both of their gazes are teary but joyful.

I love you, I mouth to both of them.

I love you too, they mouth back.

I release their hands just as the priest recites another prayer. I close my eyes, bow my head, and then I see her. Behind the dark of my eyelids, there's Chantel. It starts as an image from when we were kids, sitting next to each other in church with our parents. She'd flash a mischievous smile before pulling a funny face, trying to get me to laugh during the quietest part of the service. And then her face morphs to adult Chantel, the face I remember best because it's her most recent one: grown-up, smiling, and so beautiful.

My eyes burn with tears as I take it in. I swallow to keep from breaking and focus as hard as I can on her face. In my mind, familiar words from the poetry reading at the restaurant Remedy echo.

> Hold my hand, it'll be okay you say. But it's not.
> It wasn't and it never will be.
> But you love me. You love me.
> You love me forever and ever . . .
>
> You went away.
> I wasn't ready.
> But I am now.
> I am ready, I am ready, I am ready.
> Now.

Chantel is gone, and that will never, ever be okay. But my little sister's love is forever. I'll feel her until my last breath. Maybe even beyond that. That's what these lines remind me of.

The feeling I'm left with is something so powerful, so all-consuming that I'm practically shaking.

It persists even after Mass ends, when I follow my parents through the church, waiting quietly as they say goodbye to everyone they know, focusing on those words.

Then there's calm. It leaves a sense of resolution I didn't think I was ever capable of feeling. But I feel it now.

On the drive back home, Mom and Dad are so cheery and insist I stay for a bit to visit, which I do. There's nowhere I'd rather be than with them right now.

As we dig into snacks and watch TV together, Dad glances over at me. He opens his mouth, like he's hesitating.

"I just want you to know, honey," he finally says, "it really means so much to me and your mom that you came with us today."

"We loved it, *anak*. And we know you probably won't want to come every time we go, but anytime you want to, you can. We always love to have you."

"I can't promise I'll be able to go every time you two go to church, but I can promise that I'll come again."

Mom's gaze turns misty as Dad beams.

"We'd love that, sweetheart."

There's that calm again, that ease. It hits like a warm cloud moving over me, steadying me, centering me.

You went away.
I wasn't ready.
But I am now.
I am ready, I am ready, I am ready.
Now.

"I'm quitting my job. I'm going back to school to be a nurse. Like Chantel."

I tell them I found a yearlong accelerated program that I'm in the middle of applying for. They both stare at me for a long moment. Then Dad smiles. Mom bursts into tears. They leap up and hug me. They tell me how happy they are, that I'd make a great nurse.

By the time they let me go, I'm teary and smiling too.

"Do you want to come live with us to save money while you go back to school?"

Mom chatters about how fun it would be to have me home again. I stammer, then say that I don't know. "I haven't figured that part out yet," I say. "I guess I should, though."

If I do end up going back to school, I'll have to figure out how to cover my bills, since I won't be able to work full-time. My job had paid for most of the mortgage, thankfully, since Chantel's paychecks were more irregular. I guess I could live with them . . . but that means I'd have to rent out my house. Or sell it.

That means I'd have to clear out Chantel's room.

The thought lands like a bucket of ice water dumped over my head.

They both tell me to think about it.

I catch Dad hesitating for a second before speaking again. "We, um, have the money from Chantel . . . when she passed . . ."

He clears his throat as soon as he drifts off, probably to cut off the break in his voice. Mom's smile fades as she nods her acknowledgment.

"We'd be happy to give you that money, sweetie, to help offset the cost of going back to school," Dad finally says.

I go quiet as I process what my parents have offered up. Chantel had life insurance and retirement benefits through her job, and she listed my parents as beneficiaries. They've held on to the money and haven't spoken about what they were planning to do with it. Until now.

The thought of using my sister's money to pay for my tuition or living expenses sits like a boulder in my stomach. It feels so wrong. It was meant for her and no one else.

My throat aches as I swallow. "I—I don't know. I mean, I appreciate you guys offering it to me. I just . . . something about taking that money doesn't sit right, you know?"

They both nod , their eyes sad, like they know exactly what I mean.

"Whatever you decide, we're here for you, sweetie," Dad says.

Mom smiles through teary eyes. "We support you all the way."

They send me home with enough leftovers for a weekend worth of meals and a million hugs and kisses. When I enter my house, I drop my purse on the kitchen island and walk over to Chantel's bedroom.

When I push open the door, I don't walk in. Not right away.

Instead, for a few seconds, I just stand there and stare at the space.

Right away, I'm hit with the stuffy smell. Like dust laden with floral body spray. Most people would find it off-putting. But when I inhale, my eyes water. Because through the stagnant air, I can still smell that light floral musk that was Chantel's favorite scent.

After all this time, it still smells like her, and I love it.

Her bedsheets are still a rumpled pile in the middle of the bed. I smile at the memory of how she could work seven twelve-hour overnight shifts in a row, sleep deprived and with a smile on her face, but she couldn't be bothered to take thirty seconds and make her bed.

I do a slow scan of the room, of the bedroom that's bigger than my own because she pestered me for the bigger room when I invited her to move in with me.

I smile at the memory of her wild hair tied up into a messy bun when she moved all of her furniture in, of how she yelled at me not to scuff her furniture on the doorframe as I helped her haul it all in.

And then I take a step forward. When both of my feet are in the room, I pause and look around again, taking it in for the last time.

My stomach curdles at just the thought. What the hell will I be like when everything is all gone?

I do another scan, but this time slower. Everything is in its place. All the photos on her bookcase against the far wall, the white chiffon curtains draped across the massive window by her bed, the pile of mail she stacked on her desk, the mound of clean laundry near the open door of her walk-in closet.

"You could never take the time to just fold it, could you?"

I stay standing there for another minute. When I walk out, I head for the kitchen island, pull my phone out of my purse, then text Evan.

Me: Would it be okay if you helped me with something?

Evan: Of course. Anything.

I take a breath and type what exactly I need him to do.

Evan: Absolutely. I'll be there as long as you need me.

Evan: Are you sure you're ready, though? It's a big step, and it's okay if you need more time.

Inside, my nerves go haywire at just the thought of what I'm about to do. But behind it, there's a calm, a certainty, a sense that I can do this. At least I can try.

I am ready, I am ready, I am ready.
Now.

I type out a reply to Evan.

Me: I think I'm ready.

Chapter Twenty-Four

I'm sitting at the foot of Chantel's bed. My chest aches as I try to breathe, but I press on. In and out, over and over, I let the stagnant, floral-musk air slide into my lungs, then back out again.

This is it. I'm going to start packing up her bedroom.

I run my hand over the pile of laundry on her bed. Instantly, my eyes fill with tears. I press them shut and let out a weak laugh.

"You were such a slob, Tel."

"I couldn't be bothered to make my bed. What makes you think I'd care about folding my clothes?"

My eyelids fly open, and I twist my head from side to side in search of her. But there's no one there. Of course there's not. I'm alone.

Adrenaline pumps through my body at hearing my sister's voice. Once more, I close my eyes, and I swear the air around me changes. I can feel the presence of someone here with me.

I scan the room again, but still nothing. There's no one. Just me.

Pressing my eyes shut, I shake my head at myself. I need to just get on with it. I should just open my eyes, stand up, and start packing her things.

But I don't. Something tells me to stay sitting with my eyes closed for just a little while longer.

So I do. And then, a dozen seconds later, I see her.

There's Chantel sitting next to me on the foot of her bed.

Before I can even say hello, I pull her into a hug. She feels just like she did before. *Real.* Her skin is soft and warm, and her body is firm underneath my hold.

"You're here." I'm crying. Of course I'm crying.

"I am. But I'm not." She squeezes me in her arms.

I don't know how long it is before I let go, but when I do, I have to wipe my cheeks and eyes with the sleeves of my shirt. I want to get a clear look at her.

Chantel flashes a sad smile. I take in her face, how young and pretty she appears, even now. I look at how the T-shirt she wears hangs over her delicate shoulders, almost like it's a cape. I glance down at her ripped jeans and those scuffed sneakers that she refused to throw away, even though I bought her a brand-new pair four Christmases ago.

She catches me staring and looks down at her feet before clicking her heels together. "I like them. They're comfy."

Wiping my nose with my wrist, I laugh. And then I grab her hand in mine.

"You're doing it today, aren't you?" she asks.

I open my mouth, but I can't say it. So I just nod.

"Bel." She grips my hand tight and shakes it gently, to get me to look at her. It feels like her skin on mine—it feels so real. "It's okay. I'm glad you're doing this. It's about damn time."

"I just . . . yesterday I was so sure I could. But now that it's time to actually do it . . . now that I'm in your room, preparing to pack it all up, I don't know if I can. Ridiculous, right? So back and forth."

A few moments later, my laughs turn to sobs. I pull my hand out of her hold and cover my face, my shoulders shaking.

It takes a few minutes before I stop crying. Then I lean my head against my little sister's shoulder. We both stare straight ahead at the photo collage above her desk. Most of the few dozen photos are of the two of us. There are a handful of postcards tucked between the photos of some of the places she's worked: Santa Fe. Phoenix. Maine. Denver.

On her desk, I spot a pine cone, a few red rocks, and a shot glass.

"What are you so scared of, Bel?" she asks.

"I'm scared of losing you. I'm scared that once I pack up your stuff and clean out your room, it'll be like you were never here."

"You worry too much, you know that?"

I start to protest, but she tightens her hold around me. "Bel. If there's one thing I know beyond a shadow of a doubt, it's that you won't ever forget me."

I lean away to look at her. A million questions collide in my brain. "Are you really here? Is this really you? Or is this just me . . . fooling myself?"

Her dark, earthen eyes sparkle. "Does it really matter? I'm here, Bel."

She's right.

"I miss you," I tell her.

"I miss you too."

We resume our mutual silent staring, but this time we look out the window at the massive oak tree that sits just outside her bedroom. She stands up to open the window before coming back to sit next to me. For minutes, all we do is listen. Birds chirping, leaves rustling in the breeze, a faraway siren, the sound of tires squealing. The sun melts along the horizon, the blood-orange hue turning the sky cotton-candy shades.

"It's weird not being able to see you all the time, like before," I say. My throat aches with everything I want to say. I shake my head. "No, not weird. More like awful. I miss you. I miss you so damn much all day, every day. It's not the same here without you. Yeah, I'm moving on. I'm coping. But I still ache for you. I'm managing now, but how am I supposed to do this forever? How am I supposed to live without you?" My voice breaks. "I don't know if I can do it."

She cradles me as I cry.

"When will I see you again?" It comes out in a shaky whisper from my lips.

She hesitates, like she doesn't want to tell me the truth. "I don't know," she finally says.

My body shudders as I breathe. The invisible hole in my chest throbs. I have to press my hand over my heart, it's so painful.

"I'll come back, Bel."

"Like before? Like you're here now?"

"I don't know. Probably not."

I cover my mouth as I sob, then wait until I steady enough to speak. "But . . . I love seeing you this way. It feels like you're here. Really here. Like you were when you were alive."

The word *alive* burns on the tip of my tongue. It's one of those words that feels wrong just to say . . . even though I want it to be true more than anything.

She squeezes my shoulders, as if to comfort me. As if this is the last time she's going to hug me, and she wants to take extra care in each action because she knows just how much I need it. As if she's savoring the contact because she needs it too.

"I loved being here with you, too, Bel," she says. "But I can't stay. You know I can't."

I sit up quietly, keeping her hand in mine. The silence between us stretches beyond the seconds, beyond the minutes. Soon the sound of birds chirping fades. It's overtaken by the buzz of cicadas as the sun slips below the horizon and the sky turns black-blue.

"I won't ever leave you," she says. "I'll still be here in a lot of ways."

"Like how?"

"Every time you see an unfolded pile of clean laundry."

I laugh, then hiccup.

"Every time you smell floral body spray. Every time you see someone wearing an old pair of sneakers that you wish they'd throw away."

I smile through a fresh stream of tears.

"Every time someone mentions Rocky Mountain oysters."

I let out a snotty chuckle.

"Every time I see a sparrow," I say.

She's quiet for a moment. "What is it about sparrows that makes you think of me?"

"You would chase birds when you were little, remember?"

I feel her nod against me.

"Sparrows, I think, symbolize love in some cultures. And I love you to the moon and back, so . . ."

When I slump forward as I cry, I can feel Chantel's hands cradling my shoulders.

"That's a bit cheesy." Despite the way she jokes, I can tell she's crying now. "But I'll take it. Sparrows it is."

I lean over and grab her hand. It feels real, even though it might not be. But I don't care. The softness of her hair, how smooth the pads of her fingers feel against mine, it all feels real to me in this moment. It all feels right. That's what counts.

I squeeze her harder. "Please don't go."

Despite every attempt to steady my voice, it shakes anyway. I've already cried so much. If this is the last time we see each other like this, I want her to see me strong and steady, not weepy.

But when I look at her, I can tell she understands why I'm breaking down. So I stop trying to be strong. I stop forcing myself to take those hard, long swallows and finally let myself break for the millionth time. A waterfall of tears crashes down my cheeks; snot runs down my nose. I wipe my face with the sleeve of my shirt. And then I squeeze her hand.

"I have to go, Bel," she says. "You'll be okay."

Wiping my face, I shake my head. When she starts to tear up, I hug her.

She sniffles and gestures to the window. "Hey, look. A sparrow."

I glance up and see a sparrow perched on the branch of the tree.

"I'm your sparrow, Bel."

Wetness hits my cheek, but it's not me who's crying this time. Out of the corner of my eye, I see Chantel wipe at her face. I start to twist to look at her, but she holds me in place. "Don't look at me when I cry. You know I hate that."

We stay holding each other until the sky turns pitch-black. And then she stands.

My heart shudders to a halt. Because I know what that means.

I press my lips together, trying not to fall apart. I stand up and pull her to me. And then I hug her so tight, like it's the last hug I'll ever give her.

"I love you, Tel. Forever."

"I love you, Bel. Forever and ever."

A dam inside me bursts wide open. When we pull apart, Chantel has to hold me up by the shoulders and steady me, I'm crying so hard.

"I'll see you later, okay?"

I can't speak, only nod. I grab her face and kiss her cheek. And then she releases me. She walks over to the doorway before turning around to me. Her face is as angelic as ever as she flashes a sad smile. Her cherub cheeks glow as if she wasn't just crying.

"Open your eyes, Bel."

When I do, she's gone. I twist my head around, but she's nowhere to be found. I press my eyes shut once more, but I don't see her. Over and over, I blink, but she's not there.

And then the doorbell rings.

I quickly wipe my face and hop up to answer it. When I open it, Evan's standing there, his hazel-green eyes shining with concern.

He pulls me into his chest immediately, without a question or a word. We stay standing in the open doorway of my house until I finally stop crying.

"It's okay if you're not ready to do this," he says into my hair.

I'm shaking my head before he even finishes speaking. "No. I need to. It's what Chantel would want me to do."

He nods his understanding, then picks up a stack of flattened cardboard boxes sitting at his feet on the porch. I grab a handful of plastic bags from under the kitchen sink, lead him into my sister's bedroom, and together we start to pack.

Chapter Twenty-Five

When I walk into Opal's room at the memory care facility, she greets me like she always does: with an unblinking, curious stare for a second, then a smile.

"Hello! You're back! Come in, come in."

She gestures for me to come hug her, which I do. I lean down and wrap my arms around her, collapsing into her embrace. I close my eyes and stay there as she squeezes me tight, and I resist the urge to tear up.

Yesterday Evan and I cleaned out Chantel's room, and I'm still reeling. I was a mess the entire time. I couldn't stop crying, alternating between tearing up and full-on sobbing. Evan was somehow unfazed. He cuddled me every time it got to be too much and I had to take a break. He was patient, staying with me until the late hours of the evening when I finally finished sorting through everything, even though he had work today. When I tried to apologize for keeping him so long, he wouldn't hear of it.

"You don't ever need to apologize. I'm here for you, Isabel. Always."

"You all right, dear?" Opal asks, pulling me back to the moment.

I sniffle and let out a shaky sigh before pulling back and looking at her. "I'm hanging in there."

"Me too," she says with a chuckle.

Her eyes are bright like always, and her smile is just as cheery as the last time I saw her. I take in the easy way she moves when she reaches for the glass of water on her nightstand. She's as spry as ever.

The muscles in my neck and shoulders loosen as I process that, despite her diagnosis and treatment, she's still okay.

I ask what she's been up to since the last time I saw her, and she tells me about the walks she's taken in the garden, the quality of the meals in the dining hall, how Bunny promised to curl her hair the next time she visited.

I listen, happy that she's in good spirits. When she pauses, I take that as my cue. I reach for the phone sitting on her nightstand and hand it to her.

"Your mom is going to call you."

Opal's eyes and smile go wide, just like I knew they would. "She is?"

I nod. "I'm going to slip into the bathroom to give you two some privacy, okay?"

When Opal nods excitedly, I have to swallow back a fresh wave of tears. Maybe it's the emotional hangover I'm nursing from last night. Or maybe it's the pure joy on Opal's face at the lie I'm feeding her. Whatever it is, I need to get ahold of myself. I want to give Opal as much joy as I can, and pretending to call her as her mom is one way I can do it.

When I slip into the small bathroom in her room, I pull out my phone and dial her. Beyond the thin wooden door, I hear the phone blare. She answers on the second ring.

"Mom! Hi!"

"Opal, honey. Hi." I force cheer into my voice.

"It's been so long! Oh, I've missed you so much, Mom. I've wanted to talk to you for ages."

"I know, honey. I'm so sorry I've made you wait this long. It's just been so busy."

I swallow hard on my last word to keep myself from outright crying. My eyes are burning, and the base of my throat is throbbing. I want to sound happy for Opal, to give her the memory of an upbeat conversation with her mom. But upbeat is the opposite of how I feel right now. I feel like I've gone nine rounds with a champion boxer, but all my wounds are emotional, not physical. My insides feel like they've been pummeled to a pulp.

All I can think about is Chantel, how much I miss her, how much I wish I could see her face, hear her voice, hear her laugh one more time.

I press my eyes shut as the hot tears pool against my eyelids.

This was probably a bad idea, to call and pretend to be Opal's mom today. But I promised her. She's going through so much, she deserves this—she deserves to feel happy.

It takes two more hard swallows before I can speak again. I ask Opal to tell me about her day. As she chats, I hum along and offer affirmations when they're needed in the conversation.

"What about you, Mom? What have you been doing?"

"Packing," I blurt when I can't think of anything else to say.

"Where are you going?"

"Um, I'm not sure yet," I mumble, my brain frantically trying to put together a convincing story to tell her.

"Well, where do you want to go?"

Opal's perfectly logical question has me drawing a blank. "Um, I don't know. I guess I hadn't thought about it."

Her laugh echoes both against my ear and behind the bathroom door. "Well, there's your first problem, Mom. You have to decide on a destination first."

A watery laugh falls from my lips before I sniffle. "I suppose you're right."

"If you could go anywhere, where would you go?"

The places flash quickly in my head.

"Santa Fe. Phoenix. Maine. Denver."

You name the place and I'll go, Chantel. If you were still here, I'd follow you anywhere.

A single blink unleashes a cascade of tears.

"Oh, what lovely places," Opal says. "Can I come with you?"

My lips tremble as I smile. "Of course you can."

I close my eyes and picture us—Opal, Chantel, Evan, and me in a car, making our way across the country, hitting up each spot. I can imagine the smiles and the laughter, the changing scenery, the road ahead, the hum of the car engine, the blare of the radio.

When Opal starts to chat about what she's going to pack and when we're leaving, that's when the guilt takes hold. This trip will never happen. I shouldn't have even brought it up in the first place.

"Actually, Opal," I say when she pauses, "I—I won't be able to do that. The trip, I mean. I won't be able to take you or visit you anytime soon. I'm so sorry, I just . . ."

I cover my mouth as I sob. Leaning back against the wall, I slide down until my ass hits the tile floor. Then I slump over and cry even harder.

"Oh, Mom. Please don't cry."

I sink my teeth into my bottom lip to stop myself, but it's no use. The sobs fall from me like boulders tumbling down a mountain, heavy and unstoppable.

When I finally get myself under control, there's silence on the line. For a moment, I'm scared Opal is so upset that she's about to cry. But when she speaks, her voice is clear and steady.

"Mom, do you remember what you told me when I was a kid about to start school and crying because I was going to be away from you?"

"What did I say?"

"You said that whenever I started to feel sad and miss you, I should look outside at the sky and think of you. You said that you'd be doing the exact same thing whenever you missed me—staring at the sky, thinking of me. And in our minds—in our hearts—we would be together, no matter where we were, because we'd be staring at the same sky. Remember?"

Something about the wistful tone of Opal's voice holds me steady. "Yes. I remember."

"It's okay if we can't see each other right now," she says. "I look at the sky and think of you all the time. And it's like we're together."

All those times I saw Opal staring out the window have a whole new meaning now. It sends fresh tears to my eyes. I rip off a few squares of toilet paper from the nearby roll and dab my face and nose.

I glance down at my ratty sneakers and think of Chantel.

Every time I see someone wearing an old pair of sneakers . . . Every time I see an unfolded pile of clean laundry . . . Every time I smell floral body spray . . . Every time someone mentions Rocky Mountain oysters . . . Every time I see a sparrow.

There's one place I can for sure see Chantel. It's the last place I ever wanted to see her. But she's there. And I need to go.

"I look at the sky and think of you, too, Opal," I say. "I love you, honey."

"I love you, too, Mom."

After ending the call, I clean myself up in front of the mirror and walk back out to see Opal smiling as she looks out the window.

"How was the chat with your mom?"

She turns to me. "It was wonderful. Like always."

When I sit down on the chair next to her bed, she tells me what they talked about. I listen and nod along, pretending like this is the first time I've heard this. A young man in green scrubs stops in the open doorway and tells Opal it's lunchtime.

"Are gin martinis on the menu for today?" she asks.

He chuckles. "Unfortunately not."

She shakes her head and laughs. I help her up and out of her bed. The staff member walks over and offers Opal his arm to take her to lunch. I follow behind them as they walk out the door and turn in the direction of the dining room.

Opal stops and pulls me into a hug. "Thank you for coming, dear."

"Thank you. For everything. I'll stop by and see you again soon, okay?"

She cups my face in her hands, her eyes shining bright with warmth, affection, and something else. Something subtle, but knowing.

She moves to take both of my hands in hers. And then her mouth curves up into the gentlest smile. "You'll be okay."

Her words echo in my mind the rest of the day. I hope with everything in me she's right.

Chapter Twenty-Six

Evan's fingers laced with mine are the only thing I can focus on. Not the grass crunching underneath my sneakers, or the sun beating against the back of my neck, or even the birds chirping around us.

All I can process is the warmth of his skin on mine, the gentle way he squeezes my hand every few seconds.

As I gaze down, all I see is gray. I'm staring at the edge of a headstone I was certain I'd never see in person.

But here I am, standing in front of it.

"I'm sorry we've been standing here for so long," I finally say.

"Isabel."

My name falling from his lips in a whisper compels me to look at him. There is so much in his eyes. Concern. Pain. Understanding. Affection.

"You don't have to keep saying that," he says. "Take as much time as you need."

I reply with a whisper of my own, a thank-you, and a squeeze of my hand against his.

And then I look away, back to the headstone, back to the name carved in granite in the ground.

CHANTEL ESTHER MYLES

I've been working up to this moment, ever since Evan helped me clean out her bedroom weeks ago.

Ever since I broke down and finally admitted after all this time that my little sister was, in fact, dead.

Ever since the last time I saw her.

Ever since I decided to stop pretending and start moving on with my life.

Ever since that conversation with Opal made me realize that I needed to do this—I needed to come see Chantel in the only way that's possible now.

"It's taken me so long to get here, Tel," I say to her headstone. "I'm so sorry."

Again, Evan gives my hand the squeeze he knows I need.

"This isn't the way I wanted to do this." My voice shakes so hard and my eyes ache as though they're on fire with a million tears. But I swallow. I pause, and I breathe. And I keep going.

"But I know that you wouldn't buy that excuse." I peer up at Evan, whose eyes are glistening now. He kisses my forehead.

"So. Here I am. Finally. And I have so much to tell you." I squeeze Evan's hand. "This is Evan, my boyfriend. He's amazing."

In one smooth motion, his hand slips from mine, and he wraps both of his arms around me. I stay pressed into his chest for a minute until I stop crying and can catch my breath.

And then I lean away, clasp his hand in mine, and keep going.

"You'd like him a lot."

Out of the corner of my eye, Evan turns to look at Chantel's headstone. "Hi, Chantel. Isabel has told me so much about you. I wish . . ." He stops to swallow, his eyes shining with tears. "I wish I could have met you."

He makes a clearing sound in his throat, like he's trying to keep it together. It's a strange sort of comfort hearing him cry for my little sister, for a person he's never met. But he knows so much about her after listening to me talk about her. He knows just how much she means to me. He knows there is forever a hole in my heart now that she's gone. And that's enough to make him tear up, to make him feel a smidgen of my pain. And that means everything.

With my free hand, I wipe at my cheeks. "He's a hottie, Tel. You'd think so for sure."

He lets out a watery laugh; then I do. And then he inhales, his broad shoulders lifting.

"Your sister is the most wonderful person I've ever met, Chantel. She's so kindhearted and supportive. She's also an epic ballbuster. And beautiful. And strong. And sweet."

My vision goes blurry once more as another wave of tears hits. Chantel's headstone is just a gray cloud in my line of sight. Evan fishes a tissue from his pocket and hands it to me. It takes a minute before I'm cleaned up enough that I can see her name etched in the stone once more.

I pull my hand out of his, then step away to scoop up the bouquet of white roses we picked up this morning. I kneel in front of the headstone and set them down.

"I love you, Tel."

I stay crouched, hugging my arms around my torso. I feel the warmth of Evan's body shrouded over mine as I sob until I can't feel my legs or feet, they're numb from being in the same position for so long. Then he helps me up.

"Could I have a few minutes to talk to her alone?" I ask.

He says of course. He kisses my forehead, then walks down the grassy hill toward his car, which is parked at the bottom.

I focus back on Chantel's headstone. "I quit my job. I'm going back to school to be a nurse like you. Not because I'm trying to keep you alive in some weird way. God, that sounds morbid. You'd think that for sure."

A sad chuckle falls from my lips.

"I spent this summer being the caretaker for Evan's grandma. It was by total chance. Never in a million years did I think I'd be cut out to do that kind of work. But I did it. And I loved it. And I want to keep doing it, I want to help people in this way. I think . . . I really think you'd be proud of me, Tel. Or you'd give me loads of crap and joke that I'd never be as good a nurse as you. And you'd be right."

I pause to swallow through the ache in my throat. "Mom and Dad are letting me use your money so I can pay for school and cover my expenses. I wasn't going to accept at first, but then . . ." I let out a snotty laugh. "But then I remembered all those times you gave me crap for only charging you a couple hundred bucks in rent when you lived with me. All those times you tried to pay me more. I figured you'd want me to have the money."

I take a second to dab at my face again. "I'm excited to do this. And I hope that if you're here in some way, if you can hear me, that you'd be happy and excited for me too."

I lower back down to the ground and sit cross-legged in the grass. I reach out and press my palm to her headstone. "I'm moving on, Tel. I'm living my life the way I should be now."

Eyes closed, I keep my palm pressed against the cold stone for what feels like minutes. When I open them, something catches my eye.

A sparrow, perched at the top right corner of her headstone.

For a moment, my heart stops. I hold my breath so I don't scare it away.

It lingers for a second before flitting over to the other side of the headstone, its tail facing me. I fixate on the black and brown feathers covering its backside. A second later, it turns its gray head to me, then the rest of its body.

"Hey, Tel," I whisper.

I count the seconds as it stays standing on the stone in front of me. And then, as if it senses me staring at it, it moves closer. Only for a second, though. Then it flies away.

I'm your sparrow, Bel.

The words she spoke to me sitting on her bed the last time I saw her, right before I packed up her room, echo in my head like a quiet song.

It's not long before I'm crying again. But this time, I'm not broken. I'm so, so happy.

Because she's still here with me.

I walk down the hillside to Evan's car. He's leaning against it, but when he sees me, he hops up and walks over to me. He hugs his arms around me.

"Are you all right?" he asks with care.

"Yes."

"We can stay here as long as you want to."

I tell him thank you, that his support and his presence mean everything. But I don't need to stay. Now that I've been here to see Chantel, I know I can do it again. I can come and visit my sister's grave and be okay. I can come back and see her always. And even when I'm not here, she'll find a way to see me, just like she promised she would. Like she did just now.

The smile I flash at him is weak, but it's also joy. It's a mix of every emotion inside me right now. It's a peek of the happiness I can feel myself crawling back to. It's a sliver of the hope coursing through me.

"It's okay. I'm ready to go now."

Acknowledgments

This book started as a wild idea, then became a terrible and messy first draft, then ended up as the book I'm most proud of writing. I owe that to my incredible editors, Chris Werner and Krista Stroever. Thank you for your insight, brilliance, support, and patience. I couldn't have written this without you. I'm so fortunate to be able to work with you both.

Thank you to Sarah Younger for being the best agent.

Big thanks to the interns at Nancy Yost Literary Agency for slogging through that early draft.

Thank you to Lake Union for supporting me and my work. Thank you to the copyeditors, proofreaders, and designers for everything you did to turn this into a beautiful book. And thanks to the marketing and publicity team for all the behind-the-scenes magic you work to get my books out in the world. I'm blown away by what you do.

A million thanks to Sandy Lim, Skye McDonald, Sonia Palermo, and Stefanie Simpson for being the most amazing friends I could ever ask for. Your friendship and our group texts get me through the tough moments of being an author. I love you all to absolute bits.

To Alex, thank you for loving me and supporting me. I couldn't do this without you.

Thank you to my friends and family for cheering me on.

And thank you so, so much to all the readers out there who have read my books and shown me so much love. You mean the world to me.

About the Author

Photo © 2015 Nick Zielinski and Jessi Reiss

Sarah Echavarre earned a journalism degree from Creighton University. The author of *Three More Months*, she has worked a bevy of odd jobs that inspire the stories she writes today. When Sarah's not penning tear-jerker women's fiction, she writes sweet and sexy rom-coms under the names Sarah Echavarre Smith and Sarah Smith. She lives in Bend, Oregon, with her husband. For more information visit www.sarahechavarre.com.